SEEKING JUSTICE

Courtroom Drama in a Medical Malpractice Setting

ROLAND J. BECKERMAN

NEWMAN SPRINGS PUBLISHING
320 Broad Street
Red Bank, NJ 07701

First originally published by Newman Springs Publishing 2021

ISBN 978-1-63692-554-7 (Paperback)
ISBN 978-1-63692-555-4 (Hardcover)
ISBN 978-1-63692-556-1 (Digital)

Printed in the United States of America

To my very good friend of decades, Mr. C. Mitchell Minges, who lived his life based on principle and merit. Aside from being a close friend, he was eccentric and a very generous and kind human being that loved life and all that it gave. He especially loved his wife and family, I am sure of it.

Foreword

I have known Roland Beckerman for many years. He is not only an honorable person, but he also had a wonderful family, successful and affluent position in business, and a really good guy. However, he has gone through some of the most difficult times of anyone I know.

How he has survived the series of events, which he details in his book, are beyond my ability to understand. To put this book, and especially his medical/legal events and attempts to obtain accountability into perspective, I must say, I am a seasoned medical negligence attorney who has practiced this area of law many years. Roland's recall of what occurred is totally in line with the realities of today in the medical legal arena. Roland called me after he was diagnosed with lower extremity/nerve problems, asking my firm to accept his case. Because of our relationship and knowing he was seeking immediate recourse, which I could not quickly guarantee as our firm had a massive trial schedule, I recommended him to a very good friend and lawyer, Atticus Wentworth.

The events, which he details, are actually similar to a massive roller-coaster ride of reality, except they involve someone's medical and legal journey with a very high level of need for resolution. I do not know or realize many of the intricacies of this case but realized them for the first time upon reading his novel. It is a very compelling story, not only about what occurred to him but also about our medical and judicial system. It is labeled as a book of fiction, but the medical and legal aspects are indeed facets of our present-day issues which are absolutely nonfiction.

I would, without equivocation, not only recommend this book to everyone but especially to someone wishing to be entertained on a level of intrigue who really enjoys feeling as if they were there. My only additional request is that no one read the last chapters at an early point and then allow the final verdict and its impact be a *surprise*.

Lastly, it was an honor to be asked to write this foreword, and I suspect you will say it was a genuine pleasure to read this account of what I genuinely perceive to be a very difficult and dark period of Roland's life yet also very interesting.

William H. Elam
Attorney, Charlotte, North Carolina

Author's Note

This is a story of the medical journey of Roland J. Beckerman that led to a life of pain and suffering for the remainder of his life, to date, after being harmed by a surgeon that made a huge mental mistake that could have easily been avoided. Although unintentional, the damage was done. Until something of this magnitude hits home and, in particular, hits you personally, it is very hard to explain and express just how it changes so many things we all take for granted every single minute of every day we are alive.

In this book, I will explain just how these changes occurred and the effect they had on my life and the lives of my family and the destruction thereof. During the course of this book, I will take you through all of who were involved during the illness ultimately leading up to having major surgery that went off the rails of normalcy that clearly didn't live up to the expected standard of care of the surgeon. And I will navigate through the legal system and, ultimately, the trial.

This mystery will be illustrated in chronological order that will reveal what can and does happen in the medical arena of medical malpractice. The contents are written to show just how difficult it is to even file a medical malpractice lawsuit, and it will demonstrate the steps necessary to get through the system to reach a courtroom.

This is a book of fiction; however, it is based on facts and actual events. All names have been changed to protect the innocent characters involved and the one that caused the harm. It will also demonstrate the difficulties of getting someone and, in this case, a general surgeon to get a lawsuit filed against, to obtain moral justice, admitting fault, accepting responsibility, and even something as simple and human as offering an apology.

Chapter 1

I was very much a family man with a wife, son and a daughter, a mortgage, and I was a hardworking husband and a good provider. Taking care of my family was of utmost importance to me. This is something I would like to think we all do as a father and husband. Going to soccer practices, games, dance recitals, and affording them to go on school-sponsored trips and just being a taxi service for them seemed to be what parents just do for their children. Supporting my wife in her ideas, especially in how she wanted to decorate the house and combining our mutual love for each other and our children was just something that was or seemed to be written in stone, the American way, right?

My career at this time was just before reaching a pinnacle success in sales, marketing, and business development. I had been with a company for seven years when the crunch of our economy came along, starting in 2001. It seemed the events in New York City, with the bombing of the Twin Towers, started a downward spiral that had a strong and crippling effect on our economy here in the United States.

At Southern Services, we continued to battle a strong downturn of loss of revenue, due mostly to uncertainty and lowered confidence in our overall economic climate. While being part of the top tier of management at Southern Services, I was privy to financial reports and could clearly see changes that needed to be made in our structure. Although this was a real problem, the owner, Conrad Winchester, wanted me to try to weather the storm with him and try to ride out this downturn.

So it was business as usual for a while. We made several changes in our daily operations, and unfortunately for some, we had to make some cuts in certain areas, but at the same time, we brought on and made a couple of new positions we thought would not only make up for the areas we had to eliminate but also increase those areas by less doing more. It was a simple economic move in our minds, and it seemed to work.

As time passed, and my children continued to grow and prosper, my son, John, was now in high school, and my daughter, Gretchen, was entering middle school. They were both normal, I guess, kids of that age doing what kids do but not exceeding any limits or boundaries I knew of anyway. John and Gretchen were both great students and were always in the top levels of their classes. So being a proud parent just came quite easy. Did they occasionally do something I felt I needed to step in and correct? Absolutely, they are kids, remember? All kids need some guidance of an interested parent, and I felt, at times, I had to advise—strongly advise—

them on various things about making decisions. That is just part of being a caring parent.

I learned so much from my own father, and he always was supportive, and he did give me a lot of advice along the way. The one thing that sticks with me to this day is he always told me, no matter what, just "do the right thing." And that is some very strong advice, and it comes from earned wisdom on his part. So since he was much older than me, and he was a very successful man in so many ways, for some reason, I listened to his words, and it has worked well for me.

Doing the right thing sometimes didn't seem to be the thing to do, but overall, in the long run, it always appeared to make things work out properly and for the best for all concerned. Now my days at Southern Services seemed, to me, to be getting shorter because the economic forecasts were not getting any better. As a matter of fact, things were really slowing down within our industry and seemed all other industries also were hitting and landing on hard times. It was a trickle effect because of so many companies work in support of each other. One supplies this for that one, and the others supply and depend on others for various goods and services, therefore, rendering a total slowdown. I knew it was time to perhaps leave a great company I helped build into the successful company it was and had become very close friends with Conrad Winchester, president and CEO. But as you know, the old saying is quite true: "business is business."

Chapter 2

Just before my departure from Southern Services, I was on a business trip in Greenville, South Carolina, and I wasn't feeling well. If the truth be known, I hadn't been feeling well for a few months. I seemed to tire more easily and felt lethargic at times. My thought paths didn't appear as sharp during certain times of the day, and there were dull pains in my abdomen. All of this was, I thought, attributed to stress because of my inside knowledge of knowing I needed to make some major changes at Southern Services that would mean me leaving the company.

The reason I needed to leave the company was mainly to free up revenue. I was a highly paid employee that I thought could continue to certainly stay in business without me. So many people in high positions feel they are irreplaceable in the positions they hold and couldn't go on without them. I know better; everyone is replaceable in some way or another. I am not that naive, and by me leaving, it would lighten the financial load and drop the payroll down quite a bit. That money then could be put in other areas.

I made an appointment with my doctor, and he checked me over and, of course, did the usual blood work. A couple of days later, his office called me and told me everything looked good except my cholesterol was up a little, and my white count was not out of range but was higher than perhaps it should be. But overall, there wasn't anything to be alarmed about. I felt a bit of relief, but I still didn't feel well. I went on about my normal schedule of spending time traveling, as I often did, and in the office with my daily routines.

I looked at a P and L statement during a meeting, and there it was, in black and white—I was one of the highest paid employees aside from Conrad. I wasn't part of the service side of things. In other words, I was the highest paid nonproducing employee. My job wasn't in the plant producing goods and services. My job was outside of all of that. I was responsible for a lot of employees, but in reality, due to the downturn of business, in general, Conrad could do my job, and I knew that, and again I knew my time there was limited.

I was in Richmond, Virginia, and had a three-o'clock appointment. I left early and drove to Richmond, but on the way up, I became ill. Upon arrival, I went ahead and checked into my hotel room early and just lay down thinking, *I will be all right if I just lay down for a while.* By then it was about two fifteen, and I was due at my customer's office for my appointment at three o'clock in the afternoon. I called him and apologized but told him I couldn't make it. There I was, in a hotel room in Richmond, with severe abdominal pain and going through and having some terrible experiences, all the while losing a lot of blood. I thought I needed to get to a hospital.

I don't know why, but the pain eased, and I was so exhausted I fell asleep. It was by then around five o'clock, and I slept until one o'clock in the morning. It was amazing, but I felt much better after dealing with severe abdominal pain and losing so much blood, and since I was wide awake, I knew only one thing I needed to do. I checked out of my hotel and headed for home.

After the long drive home, I went straight to my doctor's office. They all knew me there quite well, and they worked me right in. After telling Dr. Mowji the symptoms I was experiencing and going back over blood work from my recent visit with him, he asked me to wait as he needed to make a phone call. In just a short few minutes, he came back into the examining room and told me Dr. Stanton, gastroenterologist, was waiting to see me. It is really good to have a general practitioner and friend, Dr. Mowji, as he was able to get me right in with a gastroenterologist. And he knew I needed to see a specialist because everything I told him I had experienced in the last twenty-four hours needed to be looked into by Dr. Stanton.

It was just a short drive to Dr. Stanton's office from Dr. Mowji's office, and sure enough, I got right in. Dr. Stanton was very thorough in his examination, and he was full of questions. His mention of colon cancer was an attention-getter for sure. Although, he made it clear he wouldn't know until he further examined me but did mention it. Just the mention of it alone was enough to send my thoughts into orbit. I lost a brother, when he was quite young, to colon cancer and that thought really scared me, and old memories resurfaced. So he made some changes in his procedure schedule and worked me in for a colonoscopy. I was forty-eight years old and had never had anything like this before. And until this all came up, I really had never been sick other than having the normal common cold or a little viral infection, but nothing ever serious. Dr. Stanton explained it to me and told me how it worked and what he would be looking for during this procedure. The fact is, he would be looking for colon cancer.

The colonoscopy was successful and thankfully didn't find cancer, thank goodness, but did find some lesions that were not normal by any standards. Recovering from a colonoscopy was quite simple and very short. I felt quite well and pretty much went on to being my normal self in a few hours afterward. Dr. Stanton put me on a series of some timed medication and a light steroid to help with the inflamed lesions. His diagnosis was colitis but told me with proper medications, we could work through it.

I had a lot on my plate regarding business and stuck to the medications, and I seemed to be doing a lot better. Well enough to fly out to Iowa for a pheasant hunt. This hunt was sponsored by a manufacturer that we represented at Southern Services. Conrad and I were invited due to our previous success in becoming the number 1 distributor of their equipment in the United States. That trip had been on our calendar for several months, even though business wasn't great at the time, but we went anyway. So it seemed my health had gotten better, no more bouts with pain and no more loss of blood, and I am sure it was because of the medications that seemed to be working. I think because of the illness or potential of it, Conrad asked me to stay on as I had mentioned to him I was considering leaving his company. He knew the reasons, although I had gone over them with him a few times, but he wasn't ready to hear of it, not yet anyway.

We continued to move along the best we could at Southern Services, and there was a turn of events. One of our really good customers spoke to me at a trade show and asked me to take a walk with him, and I did. As we were walking the floor of the trade show, he stopped, looked at me, and said, "I will cut to the bone here, I want you to come work for me and expand my company."

I was both very flattered and taken by complete surprise, being offered this in a downturned economy. There I was, contemplating leaving Southern Services, and now another position was being offered to me, providing a place for me to land. After stopping in my tracks, I turned to him and said, "This is something we can talk about but not right now, not here."

He responded by saying, "I have said what I wanted to say to you, so just give me a call."

Now that I had a parachute and knowing I had a place to land if I did leave Southern Services, it would make it a lot easier for me to do the right thing and leave Southern Services that would free up some much-needed relief of my salary which had reached six figures. So I met with Richard Lancaster, CEO of Sanders Industries, almost to the day a month later. I felt badly about meeting him for this purpose, as I felt like I was betraying Southern Services and Conrad Winchester, who had become a very close friend. But on the other side of that coin, I felt I was really doing him a favor. So that eased my feelings quite a bit, and I went on with my meeting.

I actually molded the meeting into and made it a two-fold meeting: first it was a bit of a sales call, but Richard wasn't buying it and pressed me into discussing what we were actually there for and that was to discuss me joining his company. He laid it out nicely and quickly, as that is his personality—short, quick, and to the point. It is much like the way I approach business, so I related to it quickly and easily. He told me he would give me carte blanche to grow his company. Sanders Industries was a small distributor that had a great facility that could easily handle growth. It must have been built with that in mind because the facility was set up for growth. He offered me a company car, of course, expenses, and just the freedom to do as I see fit to make some serious growth occur.

All of this was what I already had with Southern Services, except my future there was very uncertain. So I obviously had to bring up the ever-present subject of salary. I always felt I was a good negotiator, and right now was when I need to shine. So let the games begin. We danced around with each other on the subject, and then I felt it was time to bring it to a head. I told him what I was making and started pushing and arguing my case. After all, money is pretty important when it comes to accepting a new position, as you don't want to ask for too much that might push things away, but I was bringing a lot of positive baggage to the table, and that was the strength my argument.

After a two-hour meeting, we seemed to have met and found some ground we both could stand on and feel good about it. Nothing, however, was settled, but we were very close to having the handshake to consummate the deal. I left feeling good about everything and feeling like now I could leave Southern Services, knowing I have a place to land. It seemed now things at Southern Services had tightened up even more, and I felt maybe time has now come for me to resign.

So I called Richard at Sanders Industries and told him I might be ready to make a move, so we scheduled an appointment. Upon arriving at his office, I was graciously met by his attorney, his vice president, and his assistant. We went over everything and put it all in writing. The only thing that wasn't exactly up to my expectations was my salary. But he made me a deal that was tied to my performance, and being the optimistic businessman I am in my ability, I took his offer. The salary alone was good but the potential was even better. So I think my skills as a negotiator paid off.

It seemed we all left the meeting happy with everything we accomplished. They accomplished getting someone that they are confident can grow Sanders Industries as they are well aware of my record of growing Southern Services from what it was when I came on board, and what I did regarding its overall growth in revenue until the crunch came. The only thing left for me to do was to let them know a start date. I now have a clear path to leave my current company and my very good friend Conrad Winchester and start a new chapter.

Chapter 3

I put a letter of resignation together for Conrad, although it was hard to do, but I felt it was absolutely necessary in more ways than just one. The content was right to the point, with a few very valid reasons but all-encompassing my sincere gratitude toward him to allow me to have been myself in how I helped him with many successes over the years. There were some very good years of very positive growth in revenue, and along with that, we were recognized with many prestigious awards given to us by many of the manufacturers we represented. But the time has now come for me to leave.

Conrad read the letter while I was sitting across his desk. He put the letter down after he read it, looked at me squarely in the eye for a few seconds, that seemed like ten minutes, and said, "I am going to read it again.

This time instead of looking at me, he just stared out of the window for a bit, then turned to me and said, "I just wish things weren't the way they are, but you truly understand our situation."

My comment was, "I think it is time for a change, don't you?"

We had a really good exchange of conversation about my reasons and how this could actually help him, and I offered to work an eight-week notice. We both agreed to cut it to four weeks, but he made me agree that he didn't want it announced until he wanted it known that I was leaving. That was reasonable enough for me to adhere to his request. It was about 3:00 p.m., and Conrad said, "Let's go downtown."

Why? I thought, but as we approached our favorite bar and steak house, and we had both aired our laundry, I knew well this was a celebration. *But wait,* I wondered, *are we celebrating our success together, or are we celebrating my departure?* Well, I guess it didn't really matter because I think it was a lot of both. After having drinks at the bar and reminiscing about the many things we did to take his company to another level and just being two old friends, it felt good. I really never knew if he was elated I was leaving or just the fact he now had over $100,000 he wasn't on the hook for anymore. Either way, I still had a feeling of a sense of accomplishment. I did what I thought needed to be done, and I had a parachute waiting for me when I was to jump. I was also asked not to speak to anyone about my joining Sanders Industries, and Conrad didn't ask me what was on my plate until two days before my four-week notice was up. I reminded him of his request for me to not let anyone know at Southern Services I was leaving nor speak about it to anyone. And I informed him the same request was made by the organization I was soon to join and said he would be the first to know. "But I need to keep my word as I kept it for you."

He fully understood and said, "I didn't think you would have any problem finding a place to land, and you likely had offers while you were here with me."

In fact I did, but the only one I took seriously was from Richard Lancaster, CEO of Sanders Industries, because I knew I could deliver strong growth there because of my knowledge of the industry and contacts. And all the while knowing we were in a downturned economy, the product line was different. Therefore, I had a strong feeling I could really make things happen, sort of like I did when I took the position of marketing director early on at Southern Services.

The transition was rather smooth regarding leaving Southern Services and entering into my position of director of business development at Sanders Industries. I spent my first week in the plant at Sanders because I wanted to get a feel for the infrastructure, including the administrative office staff. My reason was I wanted all of the employees to know who I was, and the fact that I spent time in the plant assisting and getting to know them and finding out about their families just gave them a sense of I am, not just someone coming in to make their life harder. On the contrary, I wanted them to understand I was there for them and to make their lives better in one way or another. I think it worked, as I made some friends there in the plant that week. The administrative staff members were super accommodating and appeared both happy and anxious of what I would be doing. I think they were more or less wondering if there would be changes in jobs or description of said jobs, but that was not anything I would even have considered. I was leaving that up to someone else inside because my plan was to be on the road, doing what I do, and that was expand the business.

Things were going quite well with Sanders Industries as we were already showing signs of growth. I was bringing on new accounts almost on a daily basis. It seemed easy and it was, but when you enjoy your work, it does appear easy; however, being good at it helps, a lot. Even in this depressed market I have referred to before, we were starting to grow rapidly. Richard told me he had to add to the staff in the plant to keep up with orders and noticed a lot more raw materials were being sourced to fulfill the orders. Seemed that was a great problem to have during these challenging times.

After two months of going to Sanders, I was able to bring on a distributor that really turned things up quite a bit. If you recall, I said my salary wasn't quite what I wanted, but my income would be tied to my performance. Well, it had already started to pay off. I was setting a good pace for myself financially. I was gaining quickly, and so was Sanders Industries, so Richard and I were both happy with our direction. My days were long, and my travel schedule was heavy, but I was on a mission, as I am always on some kind of mission when it comes to business. I have always been looked at and considered to be an aggressive businessman that was dependable and just seemed to know how to make things work. Doing the customer justice is something I feel is very important, and when you tell someone you're going to do something, you better damn well do it and get it done on time. You don't get many chances, so one must prove they are the right one to work with and not make promises you can't keep. Work ethic—hard work ethic—is a virtue and seems to only be held by a few at the top, and that is why they are at the top.

I was at the top of my game as business was good and continuing to grow, and surprisingly the slow market didn't seem to affect us and what we were doing at Sanders Industries. My good friend Conrad Winchester and I are still in contact. As I said, we became good friends, and leaving his company didn't have a bearing on our friendship; perhaps it strengthened it. But he has made more changes with Southern Services, and now he seems to be in better shape. He recently told me he was spending more time on the road in front of many of my old customers, and it has been different, but things are moving along, and I am sure they will continue.

Just when things were really moving upward, due to my efforts with Sanders, I was on a return flight from Cincinnati, Ohio, and I was so exhausted and just started feeling like I was coming down with the flu or something. But when I got home, luckily it was Friday, and I had the weekend to recover from what I thought was some kind of viral thing or just not feeling well. Monday came, and I started out on a day trip to visit a few customers and ended up cancelling my last two appointments and just drove home. My wife, Becky, was already home from her office job. She was an administrative assistant at a local branch of a capital management company. As I walked in the house, she looked up at me and came close and gave me a hug in a loving welcoming way, as usual. However, she stood back, looked me over, and said, "You look tired, sit down, and I will get you a drink."

I thought, *Yeah, that's what I need is to just sit down and have a nice scotch on the rocks and relax a bit.* After some soothing conversation, we decided to go out to dinner; however, Gretchen, our daughter, was home, but our son, John, wasn't home. John, of course, now was a senior in high school, and Gretchen was a freshman in high school. John was at a beta club meeting and was expected to be home soon. So we waited on him to arrive, and we went downtown as a family for dinner.

During dinner, I started feeling rather weak, and I felt faint, so I got up and went outside. Becky was soon to follow and asked me what was wrong. I just said I didn't feel well. But the truth is that the same kind of abdominal pain was back. I didn't finish my dinner and gave my card to Becky and told her to stay with the kids until they finished their dinner and pay the bill, and I would be in the car. I told her, "Just take your time, and you finish your dinner too."

She asked if I wanted her to box mine up so I could have it later. My answer was brief, but I said, "Don't bother, just pay the bill, and I will wait in the car."

It was a long night of severe abdominal pain, and I lost a lot of blood. I called my office and informed them I would not be on the road as I was going to my doctor, that I wasn't feeling well. I didn't bother to call Dr. Mowji, rather I just showed up and told Susan I really needed to see him badly. After Dr. Mowji and I spoke, he called Dr. Stanton, the gastroenterologist, again for me and got me right in. Dr. Stanton told me that it sounded like the lesions were back, and he wrote a prescription for, once again, a light dose of steroids and told me to take the rest of the week off and just rest, and I should be all right, but rest with no travel should be best for me.

So along with my medication, I went home and called Richard and told him I needed to take a few days off and why. I discussed my visits with Dr. Mowji and Dr. Stanton and told him about the intestinal lesions. Just getting some rest and taking the medication should take care of it, as it did before.

It turned out to be a very long week. I didn't get better; things seemed to be on a downward spiral, and on Thursday, I ended up right back in Dr. Stanton's office. While I was waiting on Dr. Stanton to come into the examining room, there was a soft knock on the door and in walked my wife, Becky. I said, "What are you doing here?"

I have always been a private person, and that isn't one of my good traits, I don't think. She told me she was really worried about me. I don't know why I said what I said to her, but I think perhaps it was the fact I felt so bad, and I was physically beaten down and was so concerned mentally about myself—I snapped. I sternly asked her to leave the room and told her I was worried about what might be wrong with me. She left but was quite upset when she walked out, and I realized what an ass I was to her. That was one time I probably needed her support. I guess it was bad timing, but I truly was an ass, and I am forever sorry for treating her that way. All she wanted to be was supportive and to show her concern of and to me, and I pushed it away. I still don't know why I acted in such a way but I did.

Dr. Stanton came into the examining room with a puzzled look and stated my wife was crying, and he asked her if he could do anything for her, and he said she just shrugged her shoulders and said, "Please do something for my husband," and continued to walk out.

He then asked me if he could do anything, and my answer was, "Yes, please fix whatever the hell it is that is wrong with me, I feel like I am dying." Dr. Stanton gave me his cell phone number and told me if I started losing any more blood, or anything of the sort, to call him. He sent me home and told me to stay in bed. I had a very hard and long weekend, literally in bed, and seemed to get weaker and weaker by the hour, and by Sunday afternoon, I started losing more blood, and this time, it was a lot, bright red in the toilet. After seeing two doctors and being seen by them more times than I would prefer in the last few weeks, I was at a loss of what I should try to do next.

Sunday night, about nine thirty, I got a call; it was Dr. Stanton. He said he had me on his mind and wanted to know how I was doing. I told him all about the experiences I have had since leaving his office, and he told me to go to the hospital first thing in the morning. He instructed me to go to the front desk and just tell the staff person there my name, and he would have everything lined up for me to be admitted. He said he had an early morning procedure to perform but would go talk to me as soon as he could. But he said, "Let's get you checked into a room, and we will figure out what our next steps will be."

My wife, Becky, drove me to the hospital on her way to her office. I insisted she just drop me off as I wanted her to go to work. There I went, being an ass again. I seemed to be getting better at being an ass, but I was just a lot sicker than perhaps I even thought, and maybe that is part of my verbal behavior toward her at the time. I am certainly not proud of the things I said to her during those times. She was just being a concerned wife, and I made her feel she was in my damn way. I have no excuse for this type of behavior, but it is the truth. I was dropped off, and I walked into the main entrance of the local hospital.

About halfway to the front desk, I had to stop and take a seat. It was a cold and wet day that seemed to fit my mood and the way I felt. Trying to walk into the hospital was more of a chore than I thought it would be. I was so exhausted from all of the pain and loss of blood over the weekend I could hardly walk. But I did finally make it in and to the desk. The lady behind the front desk greeted me, and I told her my name.

She immediately said, "Oh yes, Dr. Stanton has orders here for you to be admitted."

She asked me if I needed a wheelchair. I don't recall answering her because I fainted right there and hit the floor. Luckily I didn't injure myself by falling nor do I remember actually fainting, but I do recall just prior to doing so, and I think I was on my way down when it took over my ability to stand. I think I was only out for less than a minute, but I remember sitting upright when some staff members came to assist me. They got me into a wheelchair and swiftly rolled me to the elevators and up to my room that had been requested by Dr. Stanton. When I arrived to my room, the staff gave me a gown and told me to get my clothes off and put the gown on and get into bed, and they offered to assist me with that simple task. But me being me, I told them to just get out, and I would take care of it, no problem. But I just took a seat on the recliner by the window and caught myself staring out of the window, and I was engulfed in the darkness of the day that was cold, windy, dreary, and frightful in every way. All while wondering what is going on with me and thinking of my wife and my two children that were in school and my wife at her office, working.

Not being at work was something that didn't seem important to me, and for me, that was very strange because my job was a top priority to me. I really had it going in a very positive direction, coming off of a successful run with Southern Services, and now here at Sanders Industries. Calling Richard or anyone wasn't on my mind, but all of a sudden, I thought I needed to call Richard and let him know, to the best of my ability, what was going on with me. And I also remembered he had taken out a one-million-dollar insurance policy on me as a valued employee, so if something were to happen to me, well, my loss would be well taken care of, but I hoped that wouldn't be needed.

He was very concerned for me and told me several times not to worry about things at Sanders and that everything would be all right and to keep him abreast of how things went that day. We ended the call, and it hit me that perhaps I didn't give him enough information because I don't think he really got a grasp of the seriousness of the problems I was having. At that moment, it became a very dark time for me.

The door opened, and it was a nurse, and she looked in the bathroom and then looked at me and asked me where the patient was. I told her I was the patient, and there I was, fully dressed, looking like I was going to work; I even had on a necktie, as it was my normal attire at the time. She quickly got me up and helped me undress, and there I was, in one of those very stylish hospital gowns. But I was so damn sick I didn't care if my rear end was exposed because that was the least of my worries at the time. She informed me that Dr. Stanton told her about me and to make me comfortable and to start me on a couple of medications and to get IV fluids started and to have a lab technician to get some blood work done on me as soon as possible.

All of a sudden, things started happening at a very brisk pace. For the first time, I felt like something was going to be done to help me and hopefully get this turned around so I can get back to work and make things better with my wife. I created a void with her the last week or so, but I couldn't say anything except I was just scared of what all I was going through, and that was all I had to say about that, except again I am sorry.

Dr. Stanton came in shortly after I was in bed, all hooked up with IV fluids, and the lab technician had just left. After saying hello, I asked him for something for a headache. I had seemingly the worst headache I had ever had, and he told me he would take care of it. He said with a smile, "I heard you fainted on us at the front desk."

And I mustered up a smile too and said, "Yeah, went out like a damn light."

He proceeded to tell me what he was going to do for the rest of the day. The first thing was going to get another colonoscopy done because he wanted to see what was going on inside of my lower colon. He mentioned cancer again. I just wished he would stop saying that unless it was a fact, but it was a possibility. And there were a couple of other things he was going to have done regarding various tests but first to come was another colonoscopy. Since I hadn't eaten anything for a few of days, except just drink water, Dr. Stanton seemed to think he could do a full colonoscopy without any problem. So within a couple of hours, away I went into the procedure room, and out I went from the anesthesia for another full scoping and exploration of my colon.

Chapter 4

After the procedure was over, I was taken back to my room, and shortly thereafter, Dr. Stanton came to discuss the results. Dr. Stanton proceeded to tell me that my colon was full of lesions, top to bottom, and that was why I was losing so much blood. He told me I had an acute case of ulcerative colitis. During the procedure, he took some pictures of the interior, and it was horrifying for me to see what it actually looked like. He showed me what a normal interior of a colon should look like compared to what was going on inside of me, and it scared the daylights out of me to see it.

That was when reality hit, and it hit hard. The real problem that he found was the colon had started to perforate in various places. He told me unless we take drastic measures, my predicament could become quite grave.

"All right, please explain what drastic measures mean and clarify *grave*," I said.

Dr. Stanton paused for a few moments, I think trying to tactfully tell me how deadly this could be and truly was, and he said, "Roland, I don't know how else to say this, but you could die if we don't act now. Your colon is falling apart, your white cells are in overdrive but can't fight off the infection, and what is leaking out of your colon into your interior is poisonous, and we can't stop it from happening."

He then informed me what he thought we should do, and he went on to explain what a complete colectomy was and expressed how dire it was that this surgical procedure be performed. To me that sounded horrible.

"What are the options?" I asked.

And there didn't appear to be any other options because if things went along as they were, I wasn't expected to live but maybe a few days at the most. So without any more hesitation or discussion, I told Dr. Stanton to get it going, as I knew then it was time to make some drastic moves to save my life. About that time, my wife, Becky, walked into the room and was briefed on the current situation and plan. She absolutely lost it right then and there and wouldn't hear of such a thing, and there I was, so weak and sick, I couldn't deal with that at the moment. But thanks to Dr. Stanton, he was able to reason with her and get her on the same page.

At that moment, I felt a sudden turn in her behavior toward me; all of a sudden, I was becoming a liability. She seemed to have gone from a caring loving wife to becoming distant and not fully being onboard with what I was facing, as the truth was I had no other choice. Even though Dr. Stanton filled her in on what needed to be done, and she seemingly was on the same page, I felt like she removed herself mentally from the situation.

Dr. Stanton told me he needed to go make a few phone calls and would be back as soon as he could make some arrangements. Becky stayed, but I could easily tell she didn't want to be there. The room was full of dramatic stress, and it seemed to be full of negative energy, and my thoughts were bouncing around like a BB in a beer can. All she kept saying to me was, "How did this happen, what did you do," and, "I don't deserve this, how could you let yourself get in this shape?"

It was all hard to listen to, but I tried to realize this had hit her quite hard, and her reaction was not what I had hoped it would be, and it wasn't. It seemed like an hour went by before Dr. Stanton came back in, but it was only about twenty or thirty minutes. He proceeded to tell me he had spoken to Dr. Calabria, who happens to be head of GI surgery at one of the best teaching universities in the area that was about four hours away. Dr. Calabria understood the dire situation I was in, but he had a full schedule of surgeries for the next three days, and both doctors didn't think I had that much time to play with, so Dr. Stanton suggested he consult with Dr. Larson, general surgeon, who happened to be on staff in the hospital. He left the room and was back in a very short period of time. Becky had left to run a couple of errands, and I actually needed the time alone to try to get my thoughts together on what this all meant.

Dr. Stanton apologized for not being able to get me in with Dr. Calabria, as he was going to arrange for me to be airlifted to the university hospital as he felt very confident in Dr. Calabria's ability to perform a complete colectomy, as it was quite a serious operation. But in the same breath, he reminded me that time was crucial, that this got done as we were down to hours, and this was turning into somewhat of an emergency. I sensed some hesitation in Dr. Stanton's voice when he was telling me why he wanted Dr. Calabria to take my case, and I asked him how he felt about Dr. Larson's ability.

He said, "Oh, he can do it, but I would just feel better about Dr. Calabria because this is his specialty, but don't concern yourself, Roland, Dr. Larson is a great surgeon, and I am sure everything will be just fine."

I was anemic, dehydrated, and had lost a huge amount of blood, and I had a constant fever of 100–103 that couldn't be eliminated. I was very sick and felt life was being drained out of me, hour by agonizing hour. Then my two children, John and Gretchen, walked in; I guess school was out by then, and that seemed to perk me up a little, or perhaps I had a shot of Adrenalin, as I was so happy to see them. And Becky was soon to follow, so my family was all together, as if we were all bidding a farewell of sort. I don't know, it just seemed that way due to the circumstances.

Dr. Larson came in, along with Dr. Stanton, and was introduced, then immediately began talking about removing the cancer. I was startled and alarmed, so I interrupted him in midsentence and looked at Dr. Stanton and asked, "Why are we talking about cancer again? What is going on?"

Dr. Stanton apologized and corrected Dr. Larson, who then said, "Oh, I am sorry, I had you mixed up with another patient."

My immediate thought was, *This isn't getting off to a good start.* And after, the subject was dropped and reaffirmed of what and why a complete colectomy was to be performed and to do so as soon as possible. But knowing I didn't have any other choices, I listened and confirmed with Dr. Larson to move forward. So after signing all of the presurgery paperwork and getting all of that out of the way, I was told I would be prepped for surgery at seven o'clock in the morning.

Wow, a lot had happened in a day, and my life seemed it was being fast-forwarded at a very rapid pace. I do thank Dr. Stanton for everything he had done for me up to this point, but his part in this was about to come to a close. Except for his moral support, he was now pretty much out of the picture.

After all of the events during this day, and after my wife, Becky, Gretchen, and John all left for the night, I felt I needed to make a phone call. I felt I should call my boss, Richard, at Sanders Industries and give him a complete synopsis. So I called him about 9:30 p.m., and I talked and he listened, and then I think he fully understood the seriousness of what was about to happen to me. He again assured me that everything would be all right and for me to not worry about things there at Sanders. He told me I was very important to him and the company, and my position would be waiting on me upon my return. So the conversation went well, but at this moment, my job just wasn't my priority as I was concerned about living and watching my family grow and prosper. Little did I know, that would be the last time Richard and I would speak for quite some time.

Chapter 5

I don't think I really rested because of the uncharted waters I was about to experience, and the morning came rather quickly. By then I was actually getting so toxic I wasn't sure if I was coming or going and think I was in and out, not really knowing what was going on around me. But I would have moments of spurts of energy that seemed to go away rather quickly but just enough to keep me mostly aware of my surroundings. I recall two staff members came and transferred me onto a gurney, and I was whisked away. Becky wasn't there as I insisted she just get John and Gretchen up and off to school as if everything was normal. Disrupting my children's day wasn't something I wanted as I was trying very hard to shelter them as much as I could from the reality and the seriousness of what was before us.

Rolling down the hallways and watching the light fixtures pass by, one at a time, and onto an elevator, going through a few sets of double doors, I finally made it to the pre-op station. That was a busy place, nurses walking briskly, fully covered, and some barking out orders, and many following those barked orders. It looked like total chaos to me, and it was a fearful sight from what I could see. I was given an IV, and that was about the last thing I remember of that part of this journey.

The surgery lasted five hours. I was opened up from my sternum to the pubis. This is necessary for the removal of the entire colon. There was also another opening made on my left side, and an opening was created on my right side for my ileum to be pulled through the surface of the skin to create an ileostomy. Except for reading the surgical notes well after the surgery, I had no idea what went on nor how long I was on the operating table, but turned out, it was quite a long time. The actual surgery lasted for five hours, but I was in the theater, as it is referred to at times, the operating room, for about seven hours. I was taken out of the operating room and was put in recovery and was moved to ICU for the next five days.

I, of course, was unaware of anything because I was sedated and had an epidural inserted into my spine as a total block. The purpose was to keep me completely still and on my back. Of course I had a catheter inserted to drain my urine, and the ileostomy was in place to drain digestive fluids, so I was all taken care of for a four-day vacation from everything. I was in an induced coma by design because having such a large incision, I needed time of stillness so the layers of tissue could have a chance to start to grow back together. I have read about people in a coma, induced or by accident, and the experiences they have during the time they are in such a state.

The four days, for me, was quite pleasant because I had visitors, lots of visitors; most had passed away, and some were very much alive, but in this state of mind I was in, they all seemed alive. My father and my late brother, Linwood, were two of the most distinguished guests I had, and we had pleasant conversations, although the setting was a hospital room, but they were there and so many others that came to visit me, and the laughs and conversations all seemed to be real. Seeing my father and my brother, Linwood, is an experience that I will never forget, and I do have to wonder, did they really come see me? I would like to think they did. I am sticking to that story and thought out of selfishness.

I would think it was a very long four days for Becky and my children. My son was a senior in high school, and we had been making plans for him to take the next step and go off to college. He was accepted by several major universities, but he finally had made his decision to attend North Carolina State University, although he was accepted at The University of North Carolina at Chapel Hill among others, but he chose NC State. John was very bright, quite an intelligent young man, and was top in his class, and it was that way from the beginning of his starting school. Gretchen was following right along in his footsteps scholastically. How lucky can a parent be to have two children that have always achieved high grades in their courses and, for the most part, stayed out of trouble? In my work, as mentioned, I traveled quite a lot and missed a lot of their lives during the weeks I was on the road. But when I was home, I devoted as much of my time to both of them as I could.

The beginning of day 5 of my four full days of being literally laid out, I do remember the anesthesiologist actually waking me up from my slumber of four full days. The first thing I remember was being on my side and hearing his voice just talking to me, as I am sure he was doing so to get a response as that was the first sign that I was coming back to consciousness. He said—I remember this clearly—"I rolled you over to remove the epidural, and I have removed the drip that kept you sedated, and you should get some feeling back, and you will start to experience pain in your abdominal area from the surgery."

Becky was there. I don't remember saying this, but she told me later that I asked where I was and asked what time and day it was, like it mattered. I do recall the numbness and prickly feeling from my chest down to the tip of my toes, and it was what was left of the epidural that was soon to wear off. What was to come, I wasn't really prepared for or what to expect. I don't remember how long it took for the epidural to wear off, I am guessing a couple of hours, and all the while, I felt a little groggy from the IV drip that kept me out, but then I started getting some feeling back. I got really concerned when I felt the incision and how long it was, all stapled together. And my thought was, *Boy, this is going to really hurt*; however, I knew as I was told to let the nurses know, and they would control my pain with a morphine drip on a timer.

I then started feeling a lot of burning aching pain that felt like pressure was being applied. The strange thing was, the location of this burning aching pain wasn't in my abdomen area at all—although it was starting to bother me—but this burning aching sensation that felt like pressure was my right leg. My leg felt like it was on fire, and the nurses immediately got the morphine drip started. That worked quite well on my incision in my abdomen, but the leg pain was completely different and isolated within an area from my upper thigh all the way down to my foot. The nurses were doing everything they were able to do for me, but even with the morphine, my right leg was the focal point of my problem with pain at the time. Overall I felt comfortable, and my bed felt like I was lying on a cloud, or could that have been my mind making me feel that way from the effect of the morphine? Very likely.

I was still on my back and had only been awake from the four full days of slumber, or whatever you want to call it, for a few hours, but my right leg was becoming a real problem for me. I was getting a little belligerent, and as time passed, the level of the belligerence was building, and my surgeon, Dr. Larson, was called in. He walked into my room and said all my vitals looked good, and he looked at my incisions and my ileostomy and told me it was just some numbness, and it was normal and expected sometimes after surgery, and it would go away, just give it a few hours.

I asked him what the definition of numbness was, and he looked at me as if I were challenging him, and he didn't answer my question, so I answered it for him, and I told him I could feel my leg, and it wasn't numb at all; it was the exact opposite. I proceeded to tell him it felt like it was on fire and also like a severe ache, as if it had something very heavy on it along with pressure.

He again just smiled and assured me everything was fine and for me not to worry. "Get some rest," he said, but my thought was, *How in the hell can I rest like this?*

Needless to say, my first night of being back to consciousness was quite arduous. I couldn't help but focus on my right leg because that was the problem area. It seemed that my abdominal incision was doing great, although it was a bit of discomfort, but the morphine, I am sure, was doing its job. The nurses were up to the task of dealing with me during that third shift as I am sure I pestered the hell out of them. They were professional and tried to comfort me just by putting up with me. Looking back, I know I made it hard for them that night, and the following nights too, as time passed with the same thing going on.

I couldn't sleep except for short catnaps here and there, and there was nothing I could eat as I just couldn't get it to go down, and even the sight and smell of food simply turned me away from it. However, ice chips seemed to be soothing and delicious, so that became my main and only diet. When Dr. Larson found out I wasn't eating, he came to talk to me and told me he was going to insert a feeding tube if I don't start eating something.

About a week had gone by, and it seemed everything that could go wrong did, and I had some infection and broke out into an unknown rash that Dr. Larson seemed to not know what it was from. He prescribed various medications that seemed to cause unpleasant reactions. This kind of thing went on and on, and at the same time, my right leg was still on fire with very little, if any, improvement. Dr. Larson, during his rounds, would visit me and check my incisions, and I would voice my feelings about my leg. He suggested it was time for me to get up and start moving around. Needless to say, I wanted so badly to get out of bed, but there was the one real problem, and that was my right leg. I didn't seem to be able to move it freely. My left leg felt quite normal, and I had full control of movement, but my right leg just didn't seem to want to respond to my mental commands.

Shortly after Dr. Larson's visit that had a heated few moments, I decided I would sit up. It took some time to maneuver myself by using the controls on the bed and hanging onto and using the rails to pull myself into an upright position. I found myself sitting up and immediately felt very dizzy, as if I was going to faint, but it passed. So I lowered the right rail on the bed, and I had to pull my right leg over, and it just dropped off the side of the bed, and I slowly turned my bottom and brought my left leg over as to join my right leg over the side of the bed. So there I was, sitting up for the first time in days, and I had such a proud feeling and a strong sense of accomplishment.

I checked to see if I was still all together, and none of the staples were loose, so I was holding together pretty well, I thought. Then I slowly started to slide off the side of the bed. I only wanted to stand, I wasn't about to try to take a step, but just standing on my own, I thought, would be something of a milestone. What happened next happened so fast that I actually didn't realize what had transpired until I found myself on the floor. It occurred to me that I had fallen, and I just sat there with my bare ass on the cold floor—hospital gown, you know. I had three different IVs stuck in me, and I checked them all—they were still attached. I felt my incisions and checked them and was so afraid I had damaged the incisions, but surprisingly, I was still all together in spite of taking this fall from the side of the bed.

I sat there for a few moments, thinking, *Now what do I do? Well, get up*, I thought, but it seemed to be more of a problem than I could have ever imagined. My left leg was moving about slowly but freely, and my right leg was just there without any movement. Other than being in severe pain, it was just "just there." This truly was one of those I've-fallen-and-I-can't-get-up moments. I couldn't get my ass off the floor, so I then reached for the button that summons a nurse. I hit the button, and the nurse came over the intercom and said, "Yes, Mr. Beckerman, what can I do for you?"

You probably know my answer. I said, "I've fallen, and I can't get up."

I heard a chuckle, and she responded, "Really, what can I do for you?"

I told her that I had fallen trying to stand, and I was on the floor, please hurry. Two nurses came in immediately and picked me up and placed me back in bed. It felt good to get my ass off that cold floor. They proceeded to ask me what I was doing out of bed, and how did I end up on the floor? I just told them I wanted to sit up, and once I got that done, I thought I would take it a bit further and just stand up. Well, they were, I think, happy for my ambition but told me not to do that again without full support of the proper staff members. Getting back in bed was just what I needed, and for the first time in a couple of weeks, I felt like I got some rest. All that maneuvering around, trying to sit up, then trying to stand and taking a hard fall was enough to really tire me out, so I slept for a couple of hours.

My wife and children had been great during all of this. Every afternoon, my son and daughter would visit me after school, and I would put on my best face for them as now I could see worry and concern all over their faces. And I could tell they just didn't know what to expect of me lying there in a hospital for going on weeks now. Becky also came by for a while a couple of times a day. I did insist they keep up with their daily routine as I appreciated the visits, but life goes on regardless.

Chapter 6

I was now in the hospital gaining on three weeks. My incisions were healing up nicely now, and most of the unknown rashes and infections and all the other problems stemming from this surgery were getting better, except for my right leg. The ileostomy was all new to me, and I was trying hard to get a grasp on what that meant for my future and how to deal with something that was new and foreign as having an ostomy and being an ostomy patient. Do I get special recognition or perhaps a prize? I don't know yet, but we'll see.

I had been standing some with a therapist twice a day, but if I put any weight on my right leg, it appeared there was nothing there, as if I had no leg or perhaps stepping into a hole. There was just not any feeling of support because there isn't any. Dr. Larson and I now had been at odds with each other, and he was likely getting tired of coming into my room during his rounds, and I was very sick and tired of his way of playing my leg problem down. I became very demanding of him to find out what was wrong and why I was in constant pain and what was actually going on.

Early one morning, I was taken down to radiology for an MRI, and in the afternoon, I was taken down for a CT scan. The next morning, I was taken back down to radiology for more of the same. This became a routine for the next few days. I kept asking to see Dr. Larson without any luck; it had been three, maybe four, days since I had seen or talked to him. As mentioned, our conversations became heated, and I really think he was avoiding me until he could tell me something about the results of the multiple tests he put me through.

One morning, a friend of mine that happened to be on the board of directors at the hospital was in the building and was told I was still in the hospital, so while he was there, he stopped by my room for a visit. He asked me how I was doing, if I was being take care of, etc., and I told him about my problem, and I didn't hold back. For the first time, I had an outside ear, and I filled it, knowing he was a board member; I felt it was my chance to maybe get some damn answers. He seemed surprised and apologized for the pain I was experiencing and just said he would look into it.

My thought was, *I hope you do because I am not getting anywhere with Dr. Larson.* In retrospect, I think Dr. Larson truly had no idea nor any knowledge of what was going on with my right leg. By now the physical therapist had me up walking on a walker but was holding me up with a wide strap and supported me with every step, especially when I used my right leg because I still had no control and very little movement, but putting my weight on it was not a good idea because it was, as I said, like stepping in a hole.

Later that day, my general physician, Dr. Mowji, came to see me and asked lots of questions. Three other doctors came in for a consultation, and one of the other surgeons in Dr. Larson's group came in for a consultation. And then about 9:00 p.m., Dr. Sussman, neurologist, came in to see me. Becky was in my room as she was just about to leave when he came in and introduced himself and proceeded to tell me he wanted to give me a neurological exam. "Of course," I said, and Becky stayed, and I am glad she did because we both felt some kind of relief in the fact someone told us something that sounded accurate after his examination.

Dr. Sussman put me through some physical tests to determine nerve conduction and feeling, pretty basic, especially for performing something like this in a hospital room. After about thirty minutes of him doing his thing and asking me tons of questions, he told me he was pretty sure I have something called lumbar plexopathy. As I said, I am glad Becky was with me. He looked at me and said, "Mr. Beckerman, I am confident this is a classic and textbook case of lumbar plexopathy."

My response was, "What the hell is it and would you write that down?"

Becky pulled out a little notepad out of her purse, and he wrote it down. I still have that small little piece of paper with these very large words printed on it in Dr. Sussman's handwriting. It took me a while to actually get a full definition of this term, but when I heard it, well, it just didn't sound too good to me or Becky. But at least someone told us something, and the big something Dr. Sussman said was, "If you didn't have this problem before your surgery, it could have happened during the operation."

He wouldn't elaborate on it any more than that, but he did tell me he would like to see me in his office when I got out of the hospital. After he left, I finally had a feeling of some sense of knowing I had a problem—a real problem—and if it didn't right itself then, well, I didn't know anything past the "then" at that point.

The very next morning, Dr. Larson came in for the first time in days, and he said, "Well, it appears you had some visitors yesterday."

He named them off and began to tell me what they had to say in the chart notes, and all felt sure this was just what he had been saying all along. A young new surgeon was with him, and he started talking to me in a very condescending manner that I didn't take too kindly to, and I asked him who the hell he was. He proceeded and identified himself as Dr. Stevens and had joined the surgical group a few months ago and told me he assisted Dr. Larson during my surgery. And he again began telling me this was not a problem, and it was all psychosomatic. I then began my verbal attack and insisted he leave and to never come back in my room again. He started to say something, and Dr. Larson told him to get quiet and to leave the room.

I informed Dr. Larson when he named off the other doctors that came in for consultations, he left out one. He asked who he left out, as this was all that made notes in the chart. I told him Dr. Sussman came in about nine o'clock last night and gave me a neurological examination, and he told me I had a problem—a neurological problem—and he wants to see me when I got released from the hospital. At that moment, his expression changed and literally walked out of my room without saying anything at all—nothing, he just walked out. For some reason, I found that to be proof of something, but I wasn't sure what it proved, but something happened, and his reaction told me a lot, just not sure exactly what yet.

I had been on morphine now going on four weeks, and hallucinations had begun. For some reason, I didn't allow flowers in my room. Although people sent them, I just, for some odd reason, didn't want them. During a walk down the hall with my physical therapist, although a very short walk, but still I was upright and walking with the help of a walker, my physical therapist with a strap holding me up. While I was out of my room, some flowers came, and they were placed in my room when I returned. I didn't notice them until I got into bed—and as I said, I was hallucinating from time to time—and when I saw those flowers—I remember it well—there were thousands of bees flying all around that flower arrangement. I don't know what kind of flowers they were because they were covered with bees. I screamed for someone to get those damn flowers out of my damn room because they were covered with bees. I remember being asked, "What do you want me to do with them?"

I said, "I don't give a damn what you do with them, just get them out of my sight."

I probably sugarcoated that a good bit as I am sure it was much worse than that, but morphine will make you do and say crazy things. But it was finally keeping my pain to a manageable level. By now, my incisions were healing up nicely, and I was feeling pretty good, considering. And now I was into my fourth week in the hospital, and I had a surprise visit from Dr. Stanton, my gastroenterologist. We had sort of become friends during the months he treated me as he was very honest and tried to treat me as best as he could, but my diseased colon just didn't cooperate with our course of treatments, no fault of his. He walked in and sat down and told me how sorry he was he couldn't fix my problem, and he couldn't believe I was still in the hospital. The usual hospital stay for a complete colectomy is five to eight days, unless there are problems. Oh yeah, I had problems, and I told him about all the things that went wrong. He said, "I heard Dr. Sussman examined you."

I responded yes, he did, but I didn't say anything else about it because I thought maybe keeping my mouth shut, even to Dr. Stanton, might be in my best interest. He stayed for about fifteen minutes, and I was so appreciative of him to take the time to pop in for a visit.

I started thinking of things I needed to do; for example, I was a novice musician and had a studio rented, and I had a lot of musical equipment there, and I knew I needed to clear it out and get it moved home because I was quite sure I wasn't going to be able to use it anytime soon. So I asked my son, John, to go over and collect all of it and store it at the house. He surprised me and told me he and Gretchen had already done so and told the landlord he had moved it out and that I was in the hospital and wasn't sure of my immediate future. He had already turned the keys in, paid the outstanding balance of the rent by writing one of my checks, so all of that was taken care of. Wow, my two children had taken care of this for me already.

By now almost four full weeks had passed, my incisions were healing up nicely, the ostomy was becoming more and more familiar. I was still not eating, and the feeding tube was removed this morning, but I was still enjoying the slivers of ice that seemed to be my main diet. Due to not eating, and my only intake was a feeding tube that was inserted after I was losing weight rapidly, I now had lost forty pounds. I don't recommend this type of a weight-loss program to anyone, but wow, I was skinny. Not that I was overweight, well, just a little from all of the heavy doses of steroids, but not forty pounds' worth.

On the thirtieth day of my hospital stay, I was finally being released. It was one of the best feelings I have ever had, leaving that place where I had endured a living hell. Although as I was leaving, I left with the feeling I left my right leg in there some damn where. This was hanging very heavy on my mind. Yes, I was so happy to be leaving. I did feel much better concerning my illness. After giving me lots of blood during my surgery, all while knowing I was very anemic going in, all my blood work now was normal; my white cells and reds were back to where they should be. The abdominal pain was gone, but I did have an ileostomy, and it was going to continue to take time for me to get a full grip on, but I was confident it would come together.

On the way home from the hospital, I asked Becky to stop at the little corner convenience store and get me a Fanta Orange soft drink and a Reese's chocolate Peanut Butter Cup. She looked at me like I had lost my mind. Well, she had a point because I don't think I had ever had either of those little delicacies nor have I had either since. I think I had one sip of the Fanta and maybe two bites of the Reese's. But my wish was fulfilled; funny how things like that come to mind when life throws you a fast ball that you can't hit.

I was finally home after a month of, as mentioned, pure living hell. Even though I was so very sick up until the surgery, I knew what was going on and seemed like we had some plans, and those plans changed quite a few times along the way, but still some kind of plan. When I woke up after surgery from the four full days of being out, my life took a serious left turn. So many years after my life took that left turn, I am still in it and can't seem to straighten it out. Now just being home is a blessing within itself.

My first visitor after getting home was Richard Lancaster, Sanders Industries. Although he did visit me during those four days I was in an induced coma, but I had no idea he was there, but there he sat with me in my living room. He was actually sitting on my chair—well, that was all right because I was in a wheelchair. My house wasn't exactly set up for a wheelchair, but we made some changes to accommodate the various paths I would take to and from the kitchen and to my bedroom and bathroom, and that was about it. But it was great to see Richard, and once again, he told me to not worry about my position. He said business was good, but he needs me to come back whenever possible, and he was going to continue to pay me, but I don't think he thought it would be another six months. He did pay me for one more month, but then he let short-term disability take it, and that was a fraction of my income, but I fully understood.

All the while, my mortgage payments didn't stop or slow down or did anything else, and John was going to need money for college in less than a year. And I watched a lot of money go out that wasn't coming in. I guess I am just glad I had some money set aside, but a lot going out with only a little coming in is a recipe for disaster. A couple of days later, my old friend and boss Conrad Winchester of Southern Services stopped in for a visit while he was on a short business trip, and it was great to see him too. We talked about old times and all the fun and great times we had there at Southern. He still hasn't replaced me and told me he wouldn't be able to until things turned around. He is still a close friend of mine to this day.

I scheduled an appointment with Dr. Sussman, and before that, I had a follow-up appointment with Dr. Larson. I was in one of the exam rooms at his clinic, and he came in and, of course, asked how I was. I was ready for this, and I told him I was doing really good, my incisions were healing up nicely, and he looked at them and agreed. He said, "Yes, they are healing up very well, and I am pleased."

He asked me when the staples were removed, and I told him just after I was released, and it was done there at the clinic by one of the assistants. At that time was when I saw an opening and looked at him in the eye and said, "I want you to tell me what in the hell happened and why is my leg in this condition."

He stood up and said, "I don't know." And he walked out, closed the door, and I sat there for about ten minutes, thinking, well, he must have gone to get something, but after a few more minutes, I rolled out of the exam room in my wheelchair and asked where Dr. Larson was. I was told he went to the hospital. There was something very strange going on, and I had an idea that he was now avoiding me.

My appointment was approaching quickly with Dr. Sussman, neurologist, and I was looking forward to seeing him and hopefully to learn more about lumbar plexopathy. I was still not cleared to drive yet, so Becky was hauling me around, and we were now at Dr. Sussman's clinic. He told me and explained what electromyography, also known as EMG, is and what it will test for. I was on the table, with my right leg exposed, and he was sticking needles in my right thigh area to measure electrical activity in the response to a nerve stimulation of the muscle. This test is used to detect neuromuscular abnormalities. These electrodes are inserted deeply into the muscle to detect the presence or absence of neurological activity. This is a sure and proven method of detecting nerve trauma or, in my case, to put it in simple terms, nerve damage. After he tested the top side of my right leg, from the thigh to my foot, he then tested the back side of my leg. There was very good response on the back side of my leg, although there were some areas that weren't responding well, but he was happy with the results of the back side, but the top was not good news at all. On a scale of one to ten, he wasn't getting much over a one, and in some spots, it was not registering at all. In simple terms, the power has been disconnected somewhere along the line. Becky and I left Dr. Sussman's clinic with a very grim report, but he told me to come back in two weeks, and he would do the same thing to see if there was any improvement.

In the interim, I had another scheduled appointment with Dr. Larson, another follow-up after surgery. Once again, Becky took me to his clinic, and I rolled in and up to the desk to check in, and I was told I didn't have an appointment, that it was cancelled.

I said, "Cancelled, I didn't cancel it."

But her response was not very satisfying. As a matter of fact, she simply turned away from me, as if to say, *just go away.* Becky and I looked at each other and just turned around, left the clinic, and went home. The drive home was quite somber and long, not much discussion about anything until we were finally going up the driveway, and she turned to me and said, "Dr. Larson is done with you."

That was one of the most profound statements she has ever said to me on any subject or regarding anything. It hit me pretty hard because I was thinking the same thing, but until I heard it, I was trying to push it away, but it landed squarely where it hurt. I knew then I had a real problem, and he knew it too but was going to just sweep me under the rug and go on about his business.

Dr. Mowji continued seeing me, and as my GP, he was helping me with managing the constant pain in my right leg. He started me on hydrocodone, and it did take the edge off, especially at night, so I could rest. But by around ten or so in the mornings, I was reaching for more. Looking at my calendar, it was time now for my second visit with Dr. Sussman. This time, Becky had an important business meeting and couldn't drive me to Dr. Sussman's clinic, so my son, John, stayed out of school and took me. Dr. Sussman did the same type of test, and he and I both were hoping to see some real improvement. Usually with a nerve injury of this type, if it is going to improve, it will do so soon after the injury, and over a period of time—of which hasn't been determined yet—it will or could continue for a certain amount of time, and then it usually slows to almost a full stop.

We should know more after today's round of EMG testing. Dr. Sussman wanted to show me the difference in my quadriceps on my left leg to get a reading to compare to my right leg. It didn't take but just one needle going deep into my muscle for me to almost come up off the table—damn that was painful, it hurt like hell. He only did it twice, but that was all I could stand, so then going to my right leg, and I watched the needle go deep into the muscle, and I hardly felt anything, just a little pressure, but maybe not even that as I was expecting and hoping for pain because that would be a good sign. The pain didn't come, and the EMG didn't detect any electronic activity stemming from the nerves. He continued to stick me up and down my leg, but the results didn't have or show much promise. We spent quite a bit of time together as he slated the time for me as he wanted to be thorough. He was very open with me and told me he would continue to see me but not to expect him to be able to make it improve.

The prognosis was in twelve to sixteen months; whatever the improvement may or may not be that would be my window of strong, steady, hopeful improvement. But after that window of time, I need to accept whatever I may have then to be it quite possibly for the rest of my life. I asked him what could have caused it. His answer was, "I believe your femoral nerve has been compromised, meaning it suffered some trauma, severe trauma that slowed the flow of blood to the nerves and to the tissue and has damaged the femoral nerve."

Looking at the results from two weeks ago until today, there hasn't been any improvement to note. He reminded me that he would continue to see me, but there wasn't anything he could do except just keep testing, but it appeared that if there was to be improvement, it was going to be very slow. Getting back to my question of what could have caused this, he answered me by saying it could have only happened during the surgery. Then what could have happened was a nerve cut, I asked. He didn't seem to think anything was cut but more so it was just severely traumatized to the point of causing this damage. I asked him, would he put that in writing, and he quickly answered me and said, "Don't ask me to do this, I work with Dr. Larson on various cases, so please don't ask."

I wasn't quite sure how to take that, but the more I thought about it, the more I understood. He was the only one that identified the problem and informed me of what he thought happened and how. So I did have a lot of respect for him, but respect wasn't getting me anywhere except for the fact now I know what and how this happened. I knew there were way more questions than answers, but little by little, I was beginning to see what direction I might be taking.

Time continued to slip by ever so slowly, it seemed, because I was now at home, alone again, and the very dark clouds had me surrounded, sitting in my living room, wondering what in the hell was I going to do. Under normal circumstances, I would have been released to go back to work by now. I really needed to get back to work, but I couldn't even drive a car yet, and now I was watching my bank account go down every day. And Gretchen was going to the orthodontist, and that was a four-thousand-dollar bill. Becky wanted a new car, and John was just taking it all in but seeing the destruction this was causing and not asking for anything. I guess some depression was closing in on me, and I was sure it showed as things were getting tense around the home front.

Now I had monthly visits to Dr. Mowji's office because the pain medication he was writing me prescriptions for had to be handwritten and only for a month's supply at a time, and during this visit, he told me he wanted me to see Dr. Levenson, psychiatrist. I knew Dr. Mowji well, and I said, "Why in the hell do you want me to see a damn psychiatrist, do you think I am crazy?"

His response was, "No, but I do think you are depressed. Think about it, all you've been through and what you are facing, depression is expected."

I have never been depressed about anything in my life, but I said, "Sure, if you think I should."

Within two days, I was sitting in Dr. Levenson's clinic, and it felt like I was in a damn movie because in the waiting room was one lady that was talking to herself, and one man kept asking me for a cigarette over and over. I was thinking to myself if I was not crazy yet, I would be pretty damn soon if I didn't get out of there. In a few more minutes, my name was called, and I was glad to get out of that loony bin.

Meeting with Dr. Levenson was interesting. He was much older than me with a head full of gray hair and a gray beard, wearing a corduroy jacket, the kind with the leather elbow patches and leather-trimmed lapels. He really looked the part, or at least, I thought he certainly looked like what I thought a psychiatrist should look like. His speech was quiet and soft, and his movements were very slow and predictable and held a pipe but never lit it. I had to wonder what kind of drugs he was taking. Speaking of drugs, he told me he knew I had been taking hydrocodone for pain, and he told me to stop, and he was going to give me two prescriptions: one for tramadol and one for amitriptyline. I left his office thinking I was not sure about all of this as it was an experience I have never been through, and my thinking was, I might not make a return trip. The whole experience was a bit scary and unsettling, but I left and had the prescriptions filled and went home.

Regarding the prescriptions he gave me, after about a week, I was feeling like everything was in slow motion, and I didn't like the things that were going through my mind, so I soon quit taking them. I actually called Dr. Levenson's office and requested I see him again, mainly to discuss the medications he gave me. I asked Becky to drive me there and to go with me into the waiting room as I didn't know what to expect, but I prepared her by telling her about my last visit. There we were, sitting there, and that same man asked her for a cigarette at least twenty times. She became a little agitated with him and said, "I don't smoke, I have told you several times I don't have a cigarette, and please don't ask me again."

I think he got the message because he didn't ask either of us anything again. He just sat and looked at us. When I got into to see Dr. Levenson, he seemed surprised by my not liking the prescriptions, so he suggested we try a different one. So I was now in possession of a prescription for Neurontin. Becky wasn't impressed with Dr. Levenson, and yes, there he was in his corduroy jacket, as I described, and still holding that unlit pipe. I had to wonder about that, just what kind of prop was that and why? I guess I'll never know. Becky and I left, dropped by the local pharmacy, and picked up the new prescription, and during all of this time, after I was told to stop taking the hydrocodone, my pain levels were back up to an eight or nine on the one-to-ten pain scale that is so commonly seen and used by doctors and hospitals.

Within an hour of taking my new prescribed medication that was supposed to eliminate my pain, I became very sick and threw up. I didn't think the medication had anything to do with it, so that night, I was in terrible pain, and I took another one, and about an hour later, it hit me again—I was very sick and throwing up. I then took some hydrocodone and went to sleep, and in the morning, Becky left for the office, and John, of course, had a car, and he and Gretchen left for school, and I was hurting again as the hydrocodone had worn off, so I tried one more Neurontin, and in a very short time, I was very sick again, but this time it was worse.

I finally got a little better and called Dr. Mowji's office and requested I get worked in that afternoon. When I rolled into his office in my wheelchair and was quickly called to come back to an examination room, he literally followed me in, closed the door, and said, "I understand you've been to see Dr. Levenson. I hope he has done you some good, and how is your depression?" he asked.

I proceeded to tell him that I just didn't think this was for me and filled him in on all the medications he prescribed for me and what the effects were. After some back-and-forth discussion, he excused himself and came right back in with his prescription pad and wrote me out one for another thirty-day supply of hydrocodone and never mentioned me seeing Dr. Levenson again. I left his office feeling better about him not saying anything else about that as I was just glad to get another prescription of what works for me. But before I left, I asked him a very personal and hard question, and the question was, "Do you think I have experienced medical malpractice?"

I had been a patient of his for a long time and almost felt like we were friends, so I threw it out there. He didn't immediately respond, but before I left, he just quietly said, "Maybe look into it." I took that as a yes.

Chapter 7

"Maybe look into it," he said. Damn, I had no idea where to start or even how to begin, but over this period of time, without any improvement, and my life beginning to crumble in so many ways right in front of me, in full view, I started thinking, *Hmmm, now what do I do?* It was clear that Dr. Larson was through with me and wanted nothing more to do with my physical condition I felt he had left me with, and in fact, I was swept under his rug. Realizing that to be true was my first thought of just what is medical malpractice, and was this something I should even pursue.

By now I was feeling pretty good, except for the constant pain in my right leg, and the fact that I couldn't walk, along with the fact that I was still in a wheelchair. And I was now finally getting used to being an ostomy patient and being able to handle it without making too many mistakes and without having any malfunctions that result in an embarrassing moment. It had now been five months since my surgery, and I called my boss, Richard, at Sanders Industries, and I said, "If I can get clearance, I want to go back to work."

He was very happy to hear my voice and the enthusiasm to want to go back to work. He asked me, "Are you still in a wheelchair?"

I had to tell him the truth; yes was my answer. Then I quickly said, "What's your point?"

There was a pause, and he said, "You are one tough guy. Just let me know when, I look forward to it."

So we left it at that; I was to just let him know. I made an appointment with Dr. Mowji and rolled in to see him and asked him if I could go back to work. He said it really should come from Dr. Larson, but I told him why I was asking him to give me clearance, but he wanted me to contact Dr. Larson and try to see him. I did just that, but I think his staff was told to not make any appointments for me because I was simply told he would not be able to see me, and that seemed to be the end of that, so I went back to Dr. Mowji. I think he must have contacted Dr. Larson because Dr. Mowji called me and informed me that he could put it in writing for me that I was clear to go back to work at the beginning of next month, which was only two weeks away.

I was so happy and excited to get this clearance, which meant I could also drive. Well, I tried driving, and it was a real challenge driving left-footed only and seemed it could be a little bit dangerous. Ironically Richard called me the next day and informed me that in order for me to be covered by his insurance, since I was in a wheelchair, the liability would not cover me unless we installed hand controls on my car. My car was owned by Sanders Industries as a company-owned vehicle, and Richard spoke to the dealer where he buys all company vehicles, and General Motors had a promotion that on any new car, they would install or pay to have installed hand controls if needed. The ruling was if the car was purchased within one year of needing this equipment installed, they would pay for it. So that worked out well. I simply had the car taken to the local GM dealership, and it was completed, and I was legal to drive my company car.

Whoopee, step 1 was now complete of me being able to go back to work. When Becky and the children heard this news, they were all happy and seemed relieved, but Becky said, "How in the hell are you going to be able to travel with an ostomy?" And she said, "Roland, you're in a damn wheelchair, how are you going to get around in an airport?"

Oh, she went off on me. She went from being happy for me to telling me I couldn't do it and asking what made me think I could. She basically told me I was done, my career was over. At that moment, I felt again that she was distancing herself from me in some strange way, but I felt it. I was more than determined to get back to work; I had a family to provide for, and I couldn't quit. Damn it all, I was at the peak of my career, and nothing could stop me from making a living, I thought. I had already spent a lot of my savings just keeping things running, but we didn't miss a beat, not even a meal. As far as my family was concerned, it was business as usual during the entire time I had to take time off from my job. I was lucky and fortunate to have an understanding guy like Richard as a boss; after all, I was only onboard with Sanders Industries for a short period of time, but I guess Richard saw the fast growth in that short period of time and was willing to ride it out with me. But now I seemed to have a fight and some opposition on whether going back to work was something I could do, and my opposing person was my wife, Becky. Now that my company car had hand controls on it, I could finally go places on my own. I almost felt like—not that I know what it feels like—but I feel like I was just released from prison. I had only been a few places in the last six months now, the hospital and various medical clinics, and being able to get into a car and go places was a real treat.

Becky and I were invited to a friend's house for a gathering. It was one of those neighborhood things with a lot of people, and it was going to be an outdoor event, weather permitting. It happened to be a nice sunny Saturday that reached about seventy-nine degrees that day and wasn't expected to drop too much until after midnight. It was very nice, with lots of food, several coolers full of beer, and even had some live acoustic musicians entertaining us. It was a laid-back affair, and I was so happy just being out, as it was my first real night out. Something strange, I couldn't find Becky for about an hour—she was just missing. Of course being in a wheelchair, getting around in a backyard was not very easy, so I stayed on the concrete, but Becky was nowhere to be found.

This obviously was a concern, but I was trying to keep cool about it and keep an open mind. I even had the host to go inside the house to see if she may have gone inside and was just maybe talking, but when Sherri came back out and told me no, she was not in the house, I then really started paying attention to my surroundings and kept a keen eye out.

Not long after that, I saw her walking, headed my way from the front of the house, walking through the yard on the opposite side of where everything was going on, and she was alone. Several minutes later, she came to where I was, and I said to her, "I lost you for a while." I didn't say, but it was about an hour. "Where did you get to?"

She didn't answer as someone came up and started a conversation. I let it drop until we were on our way home. She never gave me any explanation about her whereabouts or anything, except she just said she went out to the car for a while and was very agitated with me for even asking. That was not what I wanted to hear, especially when just after she came through the yard on the other side of the house, I clearly saw a guy that I knew come around from the same direction not more than a minute later after seeing her. So that put my thinking into motion right then.

Now it seemed I had another serious issue that had been thrust upon me. It seemed I could see various signs along the way with Becky, since I became sick, that there was something being built between us, and the fact is, it was. So I started paying a little more attention and taking some of my thoughts away from myself and pushed my focus on what she was going through and her activities away from home. Seemed it all came crashing down rather quickly after the outdoor outing, when she was missing for about an hour without any real explanation except to turn the conversation into an argument, pushing the subject away and into what I was going to do with my life. That became the normal avenue that our conversations all seemed to end up being about. I convinced myself that Becky was actually seeing someone regularly. Me about to start back to work, still in a wheelchair, with the pressure of me knowing I absolutely had to get back to earning the income to stop the financial bleed and, at the same time, having to try to absorb all that is going on with my marriage, while keeping up the front with John and Gretchen that everything was just fine.

That was a lot on me, but I have always been one to surface under pressure and land on my feet. But that was going to be hard to do since I was still in a wheelchair, not on my feet at all. Oh well, I am sure you get my meaning, but pressure situations never seemed to get me down, particularly in a business setting, but this was different; this was personal, very personal.

It became obvious, and Becky was rather blatant by definition regarding her outside activities. Leaving the house just after preparing dinner for John and Gretchen, telling me she was going over to visit a friend or off to the grocery store, only to come back without any groceries. And sometimes coming home looking a bit disheveled and would go straight to her room. The gap was widening right before my eyes; I didn't know what to do. Now John and Gretchen had caught on, probably before, but they were noticeably becoming bothered by it. John pretty much kept it bottled up inside, whereas Gretchen lashed out at her mother several times.

It was not long before Becky walked into the living room late one day, sat down, looked at me, and said, "I have been seeing someone, and I want you to leave."

I never liked nor have I ever been the kind of person that liked an argument or any kind of fight, and I rarely raised my voice. On the contrary, I would always try my best to settle family issues calmly and was usually precise. This one really took me by surprise. The surprise wasn't the fact she admitted to me she was in the middle of a full-blown love affair, but she was asking me to leave! *No, no, hell no*, I thought to myself. I didn't say a word as I just sat there, thinking, *Damn, can anything else happen?* At that moment, I wasn't thinking so much about me, but my focus went right to John and Gretchen. Neither happened to have been home during this admission, and perhaps she planned it that way. After a long pause after she dropped that huge bombshell on my lap, I told her that I understood, and I had known it for a while. I didn't get into specifics, and at that point, why should I as it would only open the door for more arguments, one way or the other, so I just told her that this was something I needed to somehow work out.

The next day, I was supposed to leave on business for a couple of days. Needless to say, I cancelled my appointments. The first thing I did was call my closest friend, Charles Mitchell, although I had referenced this very casually to him prior when he came to see me, just after I got out of the hospital. Charles lives in Florida, and we don't see each other often, but we have been very close for a very long time, and I just needed someone to talk to. He actually had a similar situation he went through a few years prior. The situation was quite similar, so perhaps he could shed some light on maybe what direction I should take because it was time for me to take some action.

During our conversation, he put it all into perspective and told me, "I think I know what happened." He said, "You were her knight in shining armor, but it is hard to be that knight in shining armor while sitting in a wheelchair." He then added, "You've lost your luster in her eyes."

Due to all that has happened the last several months, I do think that is the simple answer, although there was nothing simple about any of this terrible situation I found myself in. Charles's first thought was for me to see an attorney. That, of course, is exactly what I did. Since I knew a lot of people around town and, of course, getting to know a few lawyers and one in particular that wasn't a divorce lawyer, I was able to see him that day to get a referral. He suggested I contact the firm of Wainwright & Bogart. He suggested I see James Bogart and to tell him he sent me. He then said, "While you're here, I'll make a call to him for you right now and see if we can get you in right away."

Sure enough, after a few words of greeting and some small talk, he informed James Bogart, of Wainwright & Bogart, that he had a potential client sitting in his office that needed his help. He also went on to say, "He is a very good friend. He is in a wheelchair, so go easy on him, will you, please? he said with a smile and winked at me, as if to let me know he would see me right away.

So driving with hand controls on my company car, I went just a few blocks to the offices of Wainwright & Bogart and rolled in and stated my name and told the receptionist I was there to see Mr. James Bogart. After a few short minutes, she led the way down the hall to Mr. Bogart's office. He greeted me with a smile and went on to say, "So you need some advice and possible representation in a divorce case."

"You know the answer, but yes, of course that is why I am here." I started off at the point of my illness and when it started to get serious and the times of despair of what was becoming to me and my family. I went right to the point. I told him just last night, she had admitted to me that she was having an affair. He, of course, asked me a series of questions, and I gave answers to every one of them. And then I told him she had asked me to leave. He smiled and said, "Don't you even think about leaving." His advice on that was to stay put and don't disrupt anything for the children involved. "If what you've told me are all facts, you might even have a case against her boyfriend."

The explanation was, or seemed, simple to me, but was that something I wanted to get involved in? I don't know. He told me to just ride it out for a few days and call him. "Let's see what we need to do."

Mr. Bogart called me two days later and informed me my wife, Becky, had contacted their office and met with his partner, Bill Wainwright, and he politely told her they couldn't speak to her about representation because Wainwright & Bogart was already in counsel with me. Bill Wainwright didn't know and was unaware I had already been in conference with his partner until she came in. So I understand she abruptly stormed out and slammed the door on the way out. Well, when he told me that, my immediate thought was, *I know what is about to hit the fan at home now, for damn sure.*

I was in the living room, knowing Becky would be home soon. John was at another Beta Club meeting, and Gretchen was at dance class, and I so hoped Becky would come in before they got home because I was prepared for the worst. I heard her car come up the driveway. She walked in, didn't speak, didn't even look my way, as if I was either invisible, or she just didn't or wouldn't look at me. She went down the hall to her room; she was only back there a few minutes, and when she came back out, she had two travel-size bags and loaded them into her new car that I was totally against buying at this time. Then came back in and sat down and said, "I can't believe you have a lawyer. You didn't waste any time, did you?"

As if I had done something wrong, and there were some other choice words that I will just leave to your imagination, but I just sat there quietly and never said a word. Actually James Bogart instructed me to keep my mouth shut, no matter what, so I did and I will continue as nothing good can come out of entering into an argument at this time. Arguments will not solve anything, so I took his advice. However, having to explain their mother had packed a couple of bags and left, to John and Gretchen was not going to be a fun job. This truly was uncharted waters again, but when they were both in, I told them together, and John got up and walked outside, got into his car, and left, and Gretchen went to her room.

There I was, sitting alone. Becky had packed some of her things and walked out, as if it was my fault, and Gretchen was in her room, with the door tightly closed, and me sitting there, wondering, *All right, now what do I do?* The first thing I did was to move my personal belongings, toiletries, to another bathroom out of the master bathroom and moved into the guest room. Being in the master bedroom just didn't seem like the place for me to be or even try to rest. In all honesty, I probably would have gladly taken her back and let what happened just go away, but for some reason, the thought came rushing back of what my close friend Charles Mitchell told me—the knight in shining armor is gone. So I knew right then and there, I would be making some serious changes.

Now remembering what James Bogart told me about not leaving the house, I called him and went back to see him the next day and told him that she had left, and that took another turn actually, in my favor. Now I was looking at a case against her new boyfriend for alienation of affection, and now she had abandoned not only me but John and Gretchen. Technically John was eighteen, but Gretchen was still a minor, but still Becky had walked out. Not knowing what to expect from her, but she was only gone for two nights and came back, as if nothing had happened—oh no, she doubled down on me leaving.

Now I was in the guest room and comfortable there. I knew I wasn't going to go anywhere. This arrangement rolled along like this for about three weeks, and I was working about three days a week. Although I was so glad to be working, but traveling while in a wheelchair was very difficult, and I had to fly to DC to see a customer there, and that was almost too damn much, trying to get on and off of a jet. I will say, they are well equipped to handle someone in a wheelchair on a flight, but it is still a problem because it needs to be announced prior to going in, and usually it takes a little longer to get checked in and then getting out of the wheelchair and into a seat and on and on, etc., etc. It was quite tiring, getting in and out of various offices, and yes, they are all handicap-accessible, but it is still extra effort, and it just takes more time, and things have to be planned ahead. But I was doing it and just glad to be producing for Sanders Industries again and earning my paycheck.

At this time, I was now really thinking of seeking a medical malpractice attorney. Going through the last couple of weeks on business trips, I realized there has got to be a better way. My thought process led me to wanting to somehow get out of this damn wheelchair. I went to see my doctor friend, Dr. Mowji, and asked him about leg braces, walkers, canes, etc. He seemed very pleased I was asking about how to improve my life and mobility; anything would be better than rolling around in a wheelchair, we both agreed. He gave me the names of a two companies that design prosthetics. He informed me they mostly design artificial limbs, but he thought it would be a good start. That was added to my immediate to-do list.

The first one I contacted and went in for a consultation was very knowledgeable and seemed to know precisely what I needed. The designer took me back into the lab and proceeded to draw out something on large graph paper, and it was drawn to scale, and he did it with amazing speed. I asked him how he had something like this in mind already. He looked at me and smiled and said, "This ain't my first rodeo, partner."

He proceeded to tell me and showed me pictures of what he did for a woman three years prior with a very similar problem. He explained what I needed was a brace, a hinged brace that will lock and unlock. When I am standing, it would be in the locked position and unlock it when I want to sit down or certainly to get into a car. He joked and said, "Have you ever tried to get in the driver's seat of your car with a two-by-four board strapped to your leg?"

I guess he thought he was some kind of a comedy act and also a prosthetic and limb brace designer. I didn't care as I laughed at his jokes because I knew then and there, right at that moment, this guy could award me with some sense of freedom. Before he could get started, I needed to check with my insurance to see what they would pay toward this; I knew it was going to be expensive. I was back two days later and proceeded to begin the process. He took several measurements from my upper thigh all the way down to my ankle. This brace would be a perfect fit, and he started with the jokes again about not losing or gaining weight. All right, I laughed and continued to go along with whatever he said because again, I must say, he was making me feel pretty confident about the fact of maybe being able to walk upright again, and I was very anxious about how long it would take for him to get it completed. He said once he fabricates the parts, a simple assembly wouldn't take long, should have it a few days because he said he just finished up a few arms and legs and one nose—there he went laughing again, and I laughed right along—but he had some time to give to my project.

A few days passed, and I was right back there to be fit-
ted. I removed my pants, and he said, "All right, let the fitting
begin." He laughed again, and me right along with him, as
usual.

I got up on the table with his help, of course, and he
put that thing on me and said, "Whoa, wait." He needed to
make a little adjustment, then again told me, "All right, let's
stand you up." He brought some rails over to the edge of the
table with locking wheels and said, "It is now or never, stand
up, young man."

He was laughing again, and me too, but I was laughing
and crying just a bit at the same time because I was standing
up—yes, that's right, I was standing up by my damn self for
the first time in several months. He then brought a walker
over to me and said, "All right, let's take a walk in the park."
Laughing still yet again, and he meant just down the hall and
back. This was a rather emotional time for me as I couldn't
believe it. There were big mirrors on the wall in that hall we
were walking down, and my reflection proved to me things
were going to get better. After all I have been through, things
have taken a turn.

When we got back into the lab, he then instructed me
on how to release the hinges because my leg was as stiff as the
two by four he mentioned earlier. I had put my pants back
on as the brace was completely hidden under my clothing.
He reached down to my knee area, and I heard two clicking
sounds, and that was the release of the hinges. Holding onto

my walker, he instructed me on how to sit down, and I sat right down on a chair, then he instructed on how to get up using the walker for support. Upon standing up, he reached back down to my knee area, and I heard the same clicking sound, and he locked it back into position to keep my leg from bending. He sold me the walker, of course, because that was my new means of transportation instead of the wheelchair. I paid him the balance of what insurance wasn't going to pay and paid for the walker, and he assisted me out and loaded my wheelchair up and me into the car, and away I went.

I couldn't wait to tell and show somebody, anybody, I was overcome with happiness and emotion. I happen to be in the same city I used to have an office in with my old friend and boss Conrad Winchester, so I decided to drive over to his office and pay him a visit. Luckily he has an elevator up to his second-floor office in his building. I will admit, reality hit again when I pulled up and stopped the car, and then it was time to get out. Well, that was a bit of a challenge, but I made it happen. Upon entering the building, his receptionist recognized me and came out from behind the glass and gave me a big hug and said, "I know you're here to see Conrad, right? You are lucky he is in, and I will go get him."

I said, "No, I will go up to his office. I want to surprise him."

So she walked me to the elevator and hit number 2 for me, waved to me, and said, "It sure is good to see you." That made me feel really good, just knowing I was about to walk into Conrad's office.

"Surprise," I said.

He looked at me as if he was witnessing something that was totally unexpected; he looked shocked. I think we were both shocked, he for seeing me, and me for being able to see him standing up, although I was on a walker and a brace that he couldn't see, but there we were, two old friends standing side by side. He offered me a seat, and we sat there for about thirty minutes or so, and I thought it was time for me to go.

When I got back to town, I wanted to see Dr. Mowji because he was the one that pointed me in the right direction to get me out of the wheelchair. Also it was time for me to get a written renewal for my hydrocodone. But I really wanted to show him my new brace and thank him for everything he has done for me over a long period of time.

Leaving Dr. Mowji's office and on my way home, all of a sudden, the emotional happiness I was celebrating seemed to start fading away, knowing I was close to home and would be going up my driveway in a few minutes to enter into a different world. Upon arrival, John was outside, shooting basketball, and when I pulled up, he came over to assist me with my wheelchair—as he often did—but I said to him, "Watch this." And I proceeded to drag my right leg over and out of the car, reached over, got the walker and unfolded it, and by using the car door to pull up on, I stood up. John looked at me and gave me a big firm hug. It was one of the best ever; it felt good.

We walked into the house together, him holding the doors for me, and said to his mother, "Look at Dad."

For just a moment, she showed her old self and stood up and said, "Am I seeing what I am seeing? This is great."

For a moment, all of the recent past seemed so far away, and just like that, she walked out of the room. Gretchen must have heard us, and perhaps what was said, and she came up the hall and stopped dead in her tracks. There I was, standing there, upright with a walker but standing. She came up and gave me the same kind of warm caring hug like I had just gotten from her brother. There I was, standing there with what was to be my only real family, and in the long run, that is precisely how it remains today.

I wanted to share my new means of getting around with a couple more friends. I called my close friend Charles Mitchell in Florida. He shared in my glory and asked me to send him a picture of me standing. Right then I asked Gretchen to take a shot of me standing in the kitchen and forward it to my cell phone to send to Charles. I told him about how the brace was designed, and it was really strange to be standing up. We said farewell, until the next time, and there would be many more next times for us for sure.

Then I called my close friend Jeff Greene. Jeff is a local contractor and constructs commercial buildings mostly. Jeff answered his cell phone. I said, "I have got something to tell you."

He immediately said, "You and Becky are back together."

No was my answer, but this was something good for sure, so I went into my detailed description of what I had gotten that day and told him I was standing up. He couldn't believe it and said, "I won't believe it till I see it."

We had lunch the next day together, as we often did, especially on the weekends when he and I were in town.

Chapter 8

Luckily I had a lot of freedom with Sanders Industries, meaning I could pretty much come and go as I please, as long as my performance was there, and I produced positive numbers, and that seemed not to be a problem. This bit of freedom afforded me the time to see my lawyer that I had retained to use for my upcoming separation and likely divorce. Still at this time, we were not legally separated, but separate we were all right, and living under the same roof wasn't any fun at all, but I wasn't about to leave, no damn way. Gretchen referred to my part of the house as Daddy's condo. Even though it was under, as mentioned, the same roof but a different part of the house, so I just went with what she called it, Daddy's condo.

James Bogart, my lawyer, just told me to sit tight and not make any moves at all, not yet anyway. Living under the same roof with a woman that happened to be your wife while she was spending time with her boyfriend, and sometimes not even coming home, was pretty hard to deal with, but it was like playing the game of chess; *it's my move, slow and methodical,* I thought.

The beginning of the next week, I went to see my lawyer, and he greeted me and immediately started talking about figuring out to somehow start a legal separation, but she was still in the house. I stopped him and said, "James, I am here for yet another reason. Yes, let's continue to work on how we can come up with a separation for Becky and me, but I have, I think, made a decision on another very important matter, and I need legal advice, a lot of it."

James got up and closed the door, sat on the chair beside me instead of behind his desk, and said, "All right, let's have it, what is on your mind?"

Being the fastball thrower I am, I went straight to it and told him I needed for him to refer a medical malpractice attorney to me. He knew all about what I had been through with Dr. Larson, I guess, through word of mouth, as it wasn't a secret that I walked into the hospital as sick as I was and fainted at the front desk, but walk in I did, only to be literally carried out a month later. Yes, they usually wheel you out of the hospital anyway, but it wasn't even a choice nor an option for me because I couldn't walk. So the word was out around town as it was obvious I was a different person in more ways than just one, as a result of what happened in the operating room.

James looked at me and said, "Do you know what you're doing?"

My answer was a clear and strong no, but I told him I was in constant neuropathic pain, I didn't know what my future held or if I would be able to continue doing my damn job. I could hardly walk, my finances were not what they once were, and my family was falling apart, and my life was just one fucked up mess right now, and damn, I was going to at least have this looked at. "Do I know what the hell I am doing? The answer is hell no, but I am going to try to figure it out," I said.

I think that broke the ice and cleared the room of smoke, so to speak. James said, "Do you know how hard this can be?"

Again I reminded him I didn't know a damn thing about this process. "That is why I am asking you."

He just sat there, shaking his head while shifting from side to side in the chair. He then got up and moved back to his chair behind his big mahogany desk, as if to take his rightful position, and he said, "I can't do this for you."

I stopped him and said, "I am not asking you to do anything, except I just want you to refer someone to me that specializes in this area that I can talk to."

James told me over and over, in different words, that maybe I shouldn't try to do this. He went on to tell me how long and expensive the process could be, and trying to sue a doctor is just so hard to do, etc., etc. I told him, "If you can't, I understand."

He stopped me and told me he would give me one name, but please just keep his name out of it, just give his office a call and ask for an appointment, as if I was just coming off the street or got his name out of the phone book. Not knowing or understanding this secrecy, I asked him, "Is there a problem?"

He simply said, "Yes, it could make my life hard here in town, I just can't have any connection."

I then started seeing things more clearly. "In other words, you don't want your name connected to this because you all work together in the same town, all right, I get it."

He wrote down the name and phone number of the person he mentioned, handed it to me, and said, "I didn't give this to you."

My answer was, "No problem. So now let's talk about how we can get a separation started between Becky and me.

He smiled and said, "Thank you."

We never did come up with how to get the legal separation started, but he thought we just should give it a little more time. We ended our meeting on a pleasant note and I left. Going home was never fun anymore because I never knew if Becky would be there, or I would have anything in the house, meaning has she taken it all, or just never knowing what to expect was becoming very stressful. Since my new method of mobility had seemed to take a front seat, things have gotten better there, and going to work was easier, and I even flew up to DC again on a business trip using a walker and taking full advantage of valet parking at the airport, which I got approved to use from our CFO at Sanders Industries. As you know, it is more expensive to use that service, and I would slide in first-class plane tickets, so I could sit up front in comfort and not have to navigate the very narrow aisles on a commercial jet. And getting around in airports on those electric carts that haul all the old people around was pretty nice, and I took full advantage of them.

The brace was really working well for me as it was really allowing me a lot more freedom, and it was a lot easier than fooling around with a wheelchair. After being in a wheelchair for all those months, I now have true compassion for those that are in one for any amount of time and certainly for those in one permanently. You just see the world from a different perspective from that vantage point of looking up to everyone and everything, it's different. I think perhaps it would be better to have been in one all your life because one wouldn't know of any other way or the difference. Sort of like being blind; to lose your sight would be pretty hard to deal with, but if you were to have been born that way, then you wouldn't know anything any differently. Maybe that isn't a good way to look at it, but it is my way of doing so.

I made the call to the medical malpractice attorney to get an appointment for a consultation. There I went to an out-of-state lawyer, and I had the thought of perhaps asking him if he was licensed to practice in other states, and he quickly named of about a half a dozen or so that he was licensed to practice law in. We met and after about an hour, he asked me to get him copies of my medical records, and he would send copies off to a medical expert for examination and asked me to send him a check for $3,000. I asked him what the $3,000 was for, he responded by telling me his experts don't work for free. I mentioned, "What about all those television ads you see, saying if we don't win, you don't pay or something close."

He answered me this way, "You were involved in a serious medical injury by a surgeon. This isn't a fender bender car accident."

Well, all right, I guess I can understand that. So within a few days, I had accumulated all of my medical records, including the surgical notes, along with a check for $3,000, and off to the post office I went. I felt a little bit of a sense of accomplishment that I had taken a step into an unknown area but knew I needed to do this. I was just so unsure of my future and my well-being, and in my own little way, I knew I was hurt financially, physically, and emotionally by Dr. Larson. My thought on it was what transpired and why, for him to have treated me the way he did. I don't think I could treat anyone the way I was treated by him. He was just downright rude and mean, with no compassion for me and my problem. To him, it never happened, but to me it did, and the results were getting louder and louder with each passing day.

And now I wanted to do something about it. I now seemed to have more questions about this process, so I made another appointment. My first question was, "By me paying you $3,000, does this mean you are taking the case, just what does it all mean? I am, as you know, very new to this process and really don't know what is next or what to do."

His answer was, he would have an answer back from his expert that has my records in a few days, and we would proceed from there. I left really not knowing any more than before I went in for my visit. But I was really getting the hang of walking using the walker and my brace on my right leg that keeps it, as I've mentioned, as stiff as a two-by-four board. The problem with my leg is if I put any pressure on it, my knee flexes, and it is like I am stepping in a hole; there is just nothing there to support me. But with the brace, as long as it is in locked position, I am good to move forward, slowly, but I am walking stiff legged but walking upright.

The medical malpractice attorney called me and told me he had favorable news that his expert thought there was a case but wanted to send my records on to someone else for examination but needed two thousand more dollars. Of course my immediate question was why he was asking me for more money. He reminded me, "These services of these medical experts didn't work for free, and if we are going to proceed, then he needs two thousand more dollars."

I tried to weigh it out in my mind quickly, and hearing that the expert gave him favorable news, I thought, *Well, all right, I will get you a check in the mail,* and I did.

Upon my arrival at home, Gretchen was home alone and was very upset. She was in her room and had been crying. I think the whole thing with her mother had hit a peak when she told me that when she got home, her mother was packing up more of her clothes and said she was leaving. I knew this was just really upsetting my children, and I asked where John was, and her response was, "I don't know, he just got in his car and left." And she started really crying again.

I was sitting on the edge of her bed, trying very hard to come with some magical solution without much luck. So the only thing I could think of was this—I told her to call her brother and tell him to meet us at a particular restaurant downtown for dinner. And after a little more of me trying to soothe my daughter, she then picked up the phone and spoke to John and told him where and when to meet us. He was just pulling into a parking space as we were, and the three of us walked in, me with my walker and leg brace and my children on either side, and it was a good feeling to be with them, but what we experienced wasn't in the plan at all.

We were halfway into the building, and there they sat, Becky and Russell. My daughter's emotions got the best of her as she burst into tears and started for the door. My son turned and walked out right behind her, and there I was, standing alone with the happy couple, staring at me. And all I said was, "Well, this is a bit confusing." And I turned and walked out.

Gretchen rode home with John, and when I walked in, they were both just sitting there quietly, not knowing what to say. For the first time, they had actually seen their mother with Russell. They knew who he was as I, and they were well aware of what she was doing, but they had never witnessed the two together, and I think it was quite a shock, understandably. I sat down and just said to both of them how much I loved them, and that nothing or anyone would ever separate us, and I would always be there for them, no matter what. That was the truth as I meant it and feel this way today. I told them this was an unconditional promise. We all sort of did a group hug, and well, we went out to eat but not at that restaurant.

I went to see my lawyer, James Bogart, the next day and told him what happened the night before, walking into the restaurant with my two children. He was quite surprised the two of them—Becky and her boyfriend—were that bold; after all, we weren't even legally separated. And he proceeded to tell me he had been contacted by a colleague of his other lawyer and informed him that he had been retained by Becky Beckerman, Roland Beckerman's estranged wife, and he would be in touch soon with some proceedings. He told me he thinks we should be aggressive now that she had secured a lawyer. I jumped in quickly and told him I did not want to leave and wanted to keep my house. My son, John, would be going off to college in the fall, but Gretchen was the one I was more concerned about because she still had a couple of years before she would be going off to school.

Due to my physical condition, I just didn't want to be faced with me moving or going anywhere. James looked at me and told me the only way to accomplish this was to buy her out. Since the house was almost paid off, there would be quite a bit of equity to share. He asked me what my financial status was, could I afford to pay her half of the value of the house, and would I be willing to give her half of everything else to stay in the home and keep things as they were, physically of course, as nothing will ever be the same in that sense. I thought for a minute; I have never been afraid to make a decision, so after some quick thinking, I told him yes, I was willing to do all of the above. Seems at certain times, during crucial times, sacrifices have to be made to obtain long-term objectives, and this certainly was one of those times.

So Becky was out of the house again, living, I guess, with Russell and would come to get various personal belongings only when I was away and, most of the time, when John or Gretchen were there. My lawyer, James Bogart, sent a draft of what I wanted to do to her lawyer, and I couldn't believe it, but she was quick to accept the plan, pending on the amounts, etc. After having the house appraised and getting my finances together, we were able to come up with an agreement. There is an old saying, "The reason divorces are so expensive is because they are worth it." I guess that is true, although I would love to be able to erase all of the things that led up to this, including the illness. Her losing her knight in shining armor was just a bit too much for her to live with, I guess.

So within a week, we were at the offices of Wainwright & Bogart, sitting in the conference room with James Bogart, waiting on Becky and her lawyer. They arrived on time, and we began to dismantle my marriage. It was a sad and somber moment for me, and it really was more involved, and all I could think of was John and Gretchen as I could see what it was doing to both of them. As I mentioned before, John handled it much differently than Gretchen. I could see John slipping away, little by little, and Gretchen's bitterness toward everything was just getting worse, understandably of course.

As we navigated through the paperwork and exchanged signatures, it was time for me to part with some money. There was one document I paid particular attention to, and that was the quit deed on the house, noting she was signing off of the deed, and a new deed would be filed with my name only. I had four checks prepared that I had given to James when I got there prior to the meeting, and he proceeded to hand them over to Becky's lawyer. Her lawyer took one look at them and sat back in the chair and just laughed and said, "Do you expect us to take personal checks for these totals? We expected certified checks."

My generosity, goodwill, and my good nature got the best of me at that point, and I exploded. I unleashed months of anger, frustration, humiliation, and a temper I rarely showed, at him. "Take the fucking money, the checks are good, and that is all she wants anyway, is my fucking money."

I felt I had been stepped on abused and had two fronts against me, her and Dr. Larson, and I had all I could take at that moment, and I am not sorry for my actions. I got up as best I could, locked my brace in place, walker in my hands, and left the room. A few minutes later, James called me and asked me to stop back by his office. He greeted me at the door, and we went into his office, and he sat down beside me, as he had done before, as I really felt empathy and compassion for me from him as he knew all of what I had been going through the last several months. And he told me that everything was all right, they took the checks, but only after contacting the bank, but they took my personal checks, and all papers were signed, and at that moment, I was legally separated, and a settlement has been reached. There were some items of furniture in the house I had agreed to that she could get at a later date that was written in the agreements, but the main parts were in place and dated.

That was the beginning of the end of that part of my life, but I wanted to do my part to put all animosity behind because no matter what, she is the mother of my two children, and I don't want to go through life with any hate or ill feelings for their sake. A separation has to be in place for one year before the divorce can be finalized. I felt a small sense of accomplishment, but I also felt broke, and I was damn close to it for sure, but I remembered that old saying, "The reason a divorce is so expensive is because they are worth it." I understood the full meaning of that old saying particularly at that time. I forgot to mention, I had all the locks changed on all three doors at the house by a locksmith while we were at the offices of Wainwright & Bogart because that property now belongs to me.

Here we go again. I got home and was going through my mail, and there was something from Dr. Larson's surgical clinic. I opened it up, and it was a statement for $28,000 and some change. I damn nearly had a heart attack and a stroke at the same time. I literally think I was hyperventilating and having an anxiety attack. I am glad I was home alone; it was something I couldn't believe. I called his office to inquire, and they transferred me to the billing department, and all the lady would or could tell me was it was for services rendered. I tried to explain that my insurance had already handled the charges from Dr. Larson's surgical fees a couple of months ago, and all she would tell me was the insurance company paid their part, and this was more fees that were due and payable.

Peaks and valleys for me were all I seemed to have, and the valleys were very deep and dark. Maybe it was time for me to go back to see Dr. Levenson, psychiatrist, because I think I was now going completely damn crazy. Twenty-eight thousand damn dollars and some change. What is this all about? I just couldn't believe Dr. Larson was sending this bill to me, everything had already been taken care of, I thought. I was really perplexed over this, and all I knew to do was to contact James Bogart, and I did the next morning.

I took a chance and just stopped by his office. He was just before leaving for court but said he had a few minutes. I showed him the $28,000 statement. His immediate response was, "Welcome to the legal world, word must be out that you are having a medical malpractice attorney look into your possible case, and this is probably his way of showing you two can play in that arena."

I asked him what I should do. Again he got up, closed the door, came and sat beside me. It must be a thing with him and his clients when he sits beside them, but he said, "I didn't say this, but just ignore it. He can send you all the statements he wants, but collecting it is another issue. Unfortunately he can bill you for whatever he wants, but if I were you, I wouldn't worry about it, he is just trying to scare you off."

I thought, *Well, he is doing a damn good job of it*, but in another sense of the idea and thought, I now think, *Well, if he is trying to scare me off, then he must feel and/or know maybe he has done something wrong.* This was all so new to me. I was just trying to learn as I go, and so far, I had $5,000 invested in a case, I had no idea if I even had a case at this point.

I got back home, and Becky and Russell were in the driveway, and I got out of the car, carefully and slowly as usual, and Becky came over and told me she couldn't get into the house, what was wrong with the door. I thought, *Oh boy, this is going to be more fun.* The locks were changed. That was all I said, and she went into a rage, and then Russell jumped into the circle of rage with her.

At that point, all I wanted to do was just fall into a hole and cover myself up. I don't know how I had kept my sanity through that day and many other days, but I did politely but firmly tell Russell to go get in the car as this was not any of his business. Luckily he did just that, and I opened the door for Becky and politely told her that she could come get the other things, along with some furniture, anytime she would like, but just let me know, and I would make arrangements for someone to be here to let her in. I probably shouldn't have, but I also told her she now had enough money to buy her own damn house and furniture, and that took us down yet another avenue of thunder and lightning, so to speak. But things eased off a bit, and she got what she came for. She and Russell left, and I didn't see or hear from her for a couple of weeks. The children were in contact, and I think had lunch or dinner with their mother, but I had a nice break from it all.

I had to go to a staff meeting at Sanders Industries, and before the meeting started, Richard wanted to meet with me privately in his office. It was a good meeting; we went over a P and L statement from the previous month, and our numbers were not only holding up well, but they were increasing, and we went over the statement line by line and made some decisions on how to cut this and add this, and well, you know what a P and L statement is all about, profit and loss. Stop the losses and amp up the profits, just that simple. After we got the business off the table, he said, "Let's talk about you, how are you doing and how are the hand controls working for you? You are looking great. How are you feeling, is your health all right?"

He had a one-million-dollar insurance policy on me, so I guess he had a vested interest from two different fronts. He seemed to want to talk about Becky and that whole situation, and I really didn't want to discuss it with him or anyone. I just told him that we had come to terms, and things were pretty much settled, and I kept my house. He said, "How in the hell did you do that?"

My answer was, "You can create magic when you start writing checks." And I left it at that, and I changed the subject. Thank goodness it was time for us to go to the conference room for the staff meeting. It was the normal slow-moving meeting with lots of questions and comments, and some really weren't even relevant to the issues that needed to be addressed, but I sat through it and let middle management have their three hours of glory. I didn't care for wasting time in meetings that lasted three or four hours that could have been completed in about ninety minutes, but hey, that is just me.

I did some more research on medical malpractice attorneys, and I stumbled upon one that is a former surgeon that went back to law school to get his JD to practice law, specifically medical malpractice. I was still in touch with the firm I had invested in, and I knew that contacting another firm might be a bit unethical, but I thought, *What the hell, why not?* So I got an appointment with Dr. Franklin Parker, MD, JD. I thought, *Wow, this guy might really be something, having both a medical degree and a law degree.* It was a four-hour drive away from home, and I planned it around a business trip, so it all worked out nicely. He had a very nice office. It was not a large firm, it was just him and two ladies with him; one was his secretary/receptionist, and the other was a paralegal.

I had already sent him a copy of my records, along with the surgical notes. He seemed very prepared with a plastic model and showed me all the parts of my anatomy and the areas of concern; he was quite impressive. His receptionist brought us coffee and cute little tea cakes, bite-sized, and they were delicious. In our discussion, he told me he thought I had a very strong case, and he would like to help me. He said after going over my records and the surgical notes, he could draft up a formal notice to Dr. Larson pointing out his faults and demanding settlement immediately. He said he would have to have another medical expert such as himself to join him in this effort to use as ammunition to get Dr. Larson to do the right thing here and settle the case. He certainly had my attention. I had to ask how much money he would ask for. In my mind, I was thinking, *Oh, maybe 500,000,* what did I know about this stuff?

But when he answered me and said, "I will demand a settlement of 3.5 million," I almost fell out of my chair. He said, "Look at you, here you have recently graduated from a wheelchair into a walker with a brace on your leg"—by the way, he was impressed with my brace—"your neuropathic pain is through the roof, and your family has been split because of what Dr. Larson did to you. He needs to take responsibility and allow his medical malpractice insurance company to take care of this and move on. They all have insurance for this reason, and he should ask them to just settle it. And they will because they don't like court cases, and neither will Dr. Larson."

Wow, all of that sounded so good—great, as a matter of fact. Our meeting lasted a little over two hours, and I was thinking just how much was this going to cost. I asked him the question, "Just what do you need from me at this time?"

He laid out an extensive plan of attack, as he called it, including bringing in his other expert, and told me he could get this taken care of for $5,000 and would take a 30 percent share of the $3.5 million. I asked, what if they didn't agree on the 3.5 million? He responded by saying, "Oh, they will because they don't want it to go to court."

I quickly did the math and thought, *Wow, that sounds like a good deal to me*, and I told him I would get him a check out. In less than a week, he sent me a copy of what he had sent to Dr. Larson, and again I was impressed, and it was a very demanding letter; it appeared to almost be a threatening letter, but again, what did I know about this legal language. I just knew it looked very good to me. Here I was again, riding another peak, and on the way home, all I could think of was to wonder what I was going to run into when I got home this time as some kind of troubling thing meets me there every time.

I walked in, saying to myself, "I walked, it is so nice to walk." Even though I have to use aids to walk, but it is a far cry from that damn wheelchair that was now folded up in the back of my car, just in case I needed it. Hope I never do again, though, but still it is there if needed. Gretchen was doing some of her schoolwork on the dining room table, and John was in his room with headphones on, reading a book. This was so pleasant, almost like the Cleavers on *Leave It to Beaver*, the old TV show that was so wholesome and everything good, with one exception—it was the remnants of our family minus Becky. I remember coming home over a span of years that I truly had that warm feeling of coming home to a family—wife, two kids, cats, and a dog. The house smelling like Thanksgiving or some other holiday that requires cooking a lot of great scrumptious delicacies, fire in the fireplace, enjoying all that is good with the world or our world. Those days are long gone, but the memories will always be there, no matter what.

After a few hard days of traveling, I was feeling very tired and thought I was just coming down with something, didn't feel like any flu-type symptoms, but I did have a low-grade fever, and I noticed some kind of mucus discharge in my underwear; not much, just enough to notice. Everything was doing great finally, after a lot of trials and lots of errors getting things under control with my ileostomy in that department, I was doing pretty good. I thought I was doing good, but that discharge startled me.

By the next morning, I was sick and throwing up. It was a beautiful sunny early spring day. I went to see Dr. Mowji and told him what was going on. He called Dr. Stanton, my gastroenterologist, got me right in, and by then, I was really feeling badly, and thank goodness the throwing up had stopped for a while anyway. Dr. Stanton looked at my records and asked me why Dr. Larson didn't do a proctectomy. I said, "What in the hell is that."

Upon examination, he found that my anal canal was diseased, and that was why I was having a discharge from my rectum that was still in place. He couldn't believe Dr. Larson left diseased tissue inside of me, and I was thinking someone was trying to kill me, what was going on now, I asked, and I asked again, what in the hell is a proctectomy? Dr. Stanton explained to me because my entire colon, inclusive of the anal canal all the way to the rectum, was diseased, and he assumed Dr. Larson did a proctectomy to remove all of the diseased tissue out to the very end, but apparently he didn't. He handed me some antibiotics and said he was going to call Dr. Calabria again on my behalf and ask him to take my case and that I needed a proctectomy as soon as possible.

So now I was taking a step backward again. *How am I going to handle this with my boss at Sanders Industries? What does all this mean? Where do I go from here? What is next?*

So many thoughts going through my head, and the main thought was John and Gretchen, they have been through enough. At least my children weren't babies, not that they couldn't take care of themselves but close to it. John was about to graduate from high school and is pretty responsible, and I knew I could count on him, but I needed to find out more before making any decisions about their care. The fact of making a decision to get this handled wasn't an option, it was about to take me down.

The very next morning, Dr. Stanton called me and told me Dr. Calabria would be happy to take me this time and had a slot for me day after tomorrow. So I made arrangements with a family of a girl Gretchen was very close friends with that knew of the family situation very well, and Gretchen's friend's mother immediately said, "Of course, Roland, we can take care of John and Gretchen for you. How long will you be in the hospital?"

My answer was, "I really don't know, but I should know something by late tomorrow."

She said, "Maybe I shouldn't ask, but is Becky around or is she—"

I stopped her right there and said, "If either of them want to stay with her, sure, but I don't think they will, and it is all right if they want to sleep here or at your house, I just need a watchful eye. Gretchen can ride to school with John, but perhaps dinner with you, and again just a watchful eye."

I really didn't know what else to do because neither of us had any family nearby. She understood and told me she would take very good care of them and for me not to worry. I went up to the university hospital and met Dr. Calabria in his clinic for an exam and some tests for pre-op. What a great guy, very personable and friendly and full of questions. He did remember Dr. Stanton contacting him several months ago about performing a complete colectomy on me, and he apologized several times for not being able to fit me in. He recalled, "It sounded like you were a very sick man. I am just sorry I couldn't get you in, but I am glad you are here now, and I am going to make you better by getting the rest of the diseased tissue out of you for good this time. Yep, we are going to take good care of you."

He continued the examination and spent several minutes feeling and poking around my very large incision from the surgery Dr. Larson performed on me, and he kept saying, "Hmm, hmm, hmm."

Finally I asked him what did "hmm" mean. He responded by saying, "Interesting," and there he went with that *hmm* again. He said, "I want to send you down for some scans. I am interested in your incision and just want to take a look."

"What are you looking for?" I said.

He answered, "I am not sure, but we will know in the morning, but first things first, let's get this diseased tissue out of you, then we will look at your abdominal area."

Well, that left some unanswered questions, but as he said, first things first. So here I was again, being rolled into surgery. I was surprised by my brother Carl; he came for moral support. It was great to see him, we only had a few seconds, as he got to my room just as I was being rolled away. He said, "I will see you on the other side."

A proctectomy is major surgery, indeed, and it is a hard one to recover from. Aside from the anal canal and the rectum being removed, a lot of tissue has to be removed, including the sphincter muscles, and then tissue has to be pulled together to close up where the rectum was. This is great dinnertime conversation. You should try it sometime at your next dinner party; your guests will love it. It is just facts of more of what I have had to do to continue to live as normal of a life as I possibly can. The main thing here is to live, and at one crucial point, I wasn't sure if I would be seeing another sunrise and sunset again, but I made it through a lot, and I plan on continuing to see those sunrises and sunsets and to see my children continue to grow and prosper.

The surgery, from what I was told, went well, but it was another very long one, another five hours just a bit more, but I was in recovery, and Dr. Calabria was standing right beside me and said, "Mr. Beckerman, you have three visitors."

I was so out of it, but I was awake and could see my brother, Carl, my son, John, and my daughter, Gretchen. I was so overcome with emotion I think I sort of passed out, but I do remember it. I had tubes down into my stomach, keeping me pumped out. I had so many things going on and realized I really couldn't talk, but Carl and my two children spent the night at a local hotel and was there the next morning when I was awake, and this time, I didn't faint. I really couldn't talk well at all because of the tube in my throat, but I asked my kids why they were not in school. They said, "Come on, Dad, this is important, and you're our dad."

My brother, Carl, looked at me and said, "Hey, they care about you and so do I. You just get some rest and get better, and when they talk about releasing you, call me and I will come pick you up and take you home. Just let me know, little brother."

So they all left, and seven days later, I called Carl and said, "I will be ready in the morning. Dr. Calabria just left my room and told me to make arrangements for someone to come and get me out of here."

Dr. Calabria was great. I just wish so much he could have taken me in the first time for my complete colectomy because I am thinking he wouldn't have caused the lumbar plexopathy that I was diagnosed with by Dr. Sussman. So now that I was going to go home tomorrow, my mind seemed pretty clear, and I was still dealing with the pain from the surgery, but it was managed well with the morphine drip. I asked Dr. Calabria for some of that to go. He laughed and said no, but he would prescribe something for me. Of course he knew I had been on a diet of hydrocodone for months now, but he said he would step it up just a little so I could rest until more healing could occur. He prescribed oxycodone; he told me it was a higher dose than hydrocodone, and it might help a little more with the constant pain in my leg. This was a little different as it was not cut with any acetaminophen, and if I were to have any issues, please contact him at the clinic. Just before he walked out of my room, he paused and said, "The scans I had done of your abdomen the day before the surgery resulted in what I was afraid of." Hence all of the *hmm* sounds he was making while feeling and poking around on my incisions from the complete colectomy. He said, "I will schedule a follow-up to take a look at how you're healing up and see your progress, and we will discuss those scans then."

I asked if there was a problem. He answered, "Quite possibly, but I don't think it is anything we need to look at just yet, but I am afraid it could become a problem for you. We'll talk when you come back for follow-up, all right."

So I was discharged, and Carl was so nice to offer to pick me up and transport me back home. I had been gone for a total of ten days, and it was a hard ten days, to say the least, but another step toward wellness has occurred. After trying to recover at home, I made a few business calls to customers and cheated my way through getting various things accomplished, and once again, Richard at Sanders Industries was really good to me and understanding. But I felt he was eager for me to get through my medical issues, and believe me, I wanted them behind me too.

I was well into my recovery, and I got a certified letter in the mail from Franklin Parker, the other lawyer/doctor. My son happened to be home and saw the mailman with the letter and signed for it and brought it in along with the other mail to me. I thought this could be really good. As I opened it, all I could think of was, *Maybe he is sending me a check or a partial payment*, or I just knew it was good news. The letter was short and very upsetting. It was from an attorney representing Dr. Larson, and all it said was they refuse to pay any amount for any reason to Mr. Roland Beckerman as Dr. Larson had done nothing wrong. "If you feel the nature of this matter should take another course such as a court case, simply let it be known."

I think I lost my breath. I was once again thrown back into the darkness. My son asked me if I was all right. My answer was, "Sure, just another hurdle."

I needed to be alone, so I went to my room. Hey, I was back in the master bedroom again, but it didn't seem to matter; at the time, nothing seemed to matter. John must have read the letter as I probably just got up and left it on my table beside my chair. He came back to my room and just sat there with me, didn't really say anything, just sat there. For how long, I don't know, but I appreciated it very much. By the time Gretchen got home from either dance class or cheerleading practice, I don't know, I had sort of pulled myself together again. I was really getting tired of pulling myself together, it was getting old, very old. Once again I was feeling defeated, and I just ready for a change—a real change—one that would free me of everything except John and Gretchen. They were the only things I felt I needed to live for, everything else had been drained away into a cesspool of reality. Suicide was a thought—a strong thought—one that I contemplated a lot, but it seemed just when I was deep into that thought, Gretchen or John seemed to always get into my sight with something so good and real and pure that it would steer me into another directive of thought.

The next day, I contacted Franklin Parker's office and had to leave a message. I asked his secretary to ask him to call me as soon as possible as it was urgent. I called his office every day for three days and finally got through to him. He asked me if I had heard the news from Dr. Larson's attorney. "Well, yes, that is why I am calling you. What does all that mean exactly"

He said, "Why don't you come to the office, and we will discuss it."

I pushed everything aside and got there as soon as I could. Upon arriving, he complimented me on how well I was getting around. That wasn't anything I wanted to talk about; I wanted to know what this all meant from a legal point of view. He told me they just didn't take him up on his demand to settle for $3.5 million. His demeanor and tone of his voice didn't seem to match my hopeful interest. Rather it was more like, *Well, it's just business and the way it goes sometimes.* I was having a panic attack because I just couldn't understand, he made it sound so damn easy and simple. Write a letter requesting settlement, and *boom*, check in the mail. I asked, "So now what do we do?"

He proceeded to tell me about how strong of a case I had, and if we kept turning up the heat, "We will wear him down, and he will settle, but we will have to build your case before we can file an actual lawsuit against him."

Now once again, I was in uncharted waters, and I could feel the sharks swimming all around me, biting my wallet. Mr. Parker began telling me he would have to reel in a couple of experts willing to testify and build a team to go after Dr. Larson, then we had to get depositions, and I would be deposed too. I stopped him right there and asked him to explain what depositions are. He then explained what that meant and how long it would take, and it would be rather expensive. That was what I didn't want to hear. I was in deep already for thousands of dollars, so now in my mind, I was thinking, *How in the hell is this going to work? Can I do this? Should I do this?* So many things bouncing around in my head, what a confusing state of mind I was in.

I left not knowing what to do next. And I still had the other law firm that I had a total of $5,000 invested in that seemed to be fading away because they seemed to have put things on hold, and I had lost confidence that they were really doing anything for me, just couldn't get any answers from them.

Chapter 9

Over the last couple of weeks, I had been really practicing standing and walking around inside my house by holding onto various pieces of furniture and especially in the kitchen, being quite large, and there are lots of countertops I can use for support. I was determined to graduate up to using a cane instead of the walker, along with my leg brace of course, and thought maybe this would be a good time for another visit with Dr. Sussman, the neurologist, and have another EMG test done to see if I was getting better. It didn't seem that I was, but I was being optimistic.

He seemed happy to see me, and I was happy to see him too. He asked me about my pain level, and I told him it was about the same, but now it seemed to be preoccupying my thought process. I told him I have missed a few exits while traveling the interstates on business trips. The pain just seemed to be wearing me out and, at times, consuming my thought process in some strange way. He wasn't surprised and proceeded to get the EMG test started. Here we go with the needles again, poking the top side of my right leg. This time I asked him not to prove anything to me, like the last time, by sticking my left leg to show the difference between the two; it hurt like hell. He laughed, told me not to worry, he hadn't planned on it this time because we proved it last time.

This time the testing went a lot faster, or maybe to me, it just seemed that way, perhaps because I knew what to expect and was much more relaxed, and I had allowed reality and past experiences in his clinic to lead my way instead of the unknown. The EMG revealed very little improvement, if any, below my knee; however, above my knee, the quadriceps showed only one area that showed a very small uptick in activity, but nothing to get too excited about.

In the privacy of his office, Dr. Sussman asked me if I was having what happened looked into from the legal side. He then answered his own question and said, "There are rumblings around with some of the hospital staff that you had an attorney send Dr. Larson a nasty letter demanding he agree to a settlement, or you'll sue him."

Wow, I was like, whoa, now I was seeing clearer that this was indeed a fraternity of sort as I hadn't told anyone about this, and it only actually occurred a few days ago; word travels fast. I answered him by saying, "Well, yes, I have had it looked into."

And I knew he had sent a request to Dr. Larson. I was almost afraid to ask him this burning question, but here goes, I asked him, "Do you think I have a case?"

He quietly said yes but would not elaborate except to say, "You were injured under his watch."

That was about all I could get him to say about that. He then steered the conversation to the question I had about trying to stop using the walker and try a cane with the brace in place of course. He walked out of the examining room and brought a cane in and handed it to me and said, "Get up, lock your brace into locked position, and let's give it a try."

I did so, and it just worked. There I was, walking with a cane. This was yet another milestone, I could do this. Dr. Sussman had been great to work with, and he was the only doctor, other than Dr. Mowji, that had taken real interest in my injury and had helped me in many ways. He wrote something down on a pad. I thought perhaps he was writing a prescription, but he wrote down a name, tore if off, and handed it to me. I looked at it, and it read *Atticus Wentworth, Wentworth & Wentworth Law Firm* and told me what city he was in and said, "Look this guy up, he might be able to help you." That was all he said, and that ended our time together.

Although I didn't get good news about the electronic activity in my right leg, but at least, it wasn't getting worse, so that was good, but what I did get was the name of Atticus Wentworth, another lawyer. I went straight to a local pharmacy that sold medical equipment and bought the ugliest cane, but that was all they had, but I just had to have one; it was one of those don't-care-what-it-looks-like moments because it wasn't a fashion statement, I got to have one now.

As soon as I could, I researched Atticus Wentworth, Wentworth & Wentworth law firm. I discovered he was the senior partner and specializes only in medical malpractice cases and had been doing so for quite a while. I went deeper into his credentials and his scholastic records and saw he has been the recipient of several awards and achievements in his career. This guy was really a who's who in his profession and is recognized by his colleagues and has been awarded the prestigious ranking of top lawyer a few times over the span his career. I was also able to find a few of his past cases by researching, and he has been involved in and has had many successes over the years in the medical malpractice area. My first thought was, *How in the hell am I going to be able to afford this guy? He is going to be expensive, and I thought so far, I have just been playing in the minor leagues, but this guy is a major leaguer.*

For the next couple of days, I couldn't get this guy off my mind. Still haven't heard anything more from either of the two lawyers I had invested in, and I wasn't feeling too good about them either. And now I felt like Franklin Parker might have really pissed of Dr. Larson, and I was wondering if Dr. Larson was going to come after me for the recent statement I received from him for additional costs of services, totaling over $28,000.

Atticus Wentworth just wouldn't get out of my head, and I was thinking, *Damn, I wish I had heard about this guy sooner.* Every single day in my mind was remembering getting sick, smelling death, having surgery, watching the destruction of my family, losing income, but lucky to have a great boss to hold my position open twice now, all while knowing my wife, Becky, was screwing around behind my damn back. At times, I was convinced my life was just fucked up as it can be. My saving grace was John and Gretchen. I think they were supporting me as much as I was supporting myself, and that was a good feeling, just knowing we had each other. Without them, I really don't think I would have kept moving forward during all of this as they were the glue that held me, and if the truth were known, all of us altogether.

I got up the nerve to contact the offices of Wentworth & Wentworth. They were located in Richmond, Virginia. I didn't get through to Atticus Wentworth, so I just left a voice mail asking him to return my call. I was just before walking—yes, walking—into the office building of a potential client with a cane, and I did buy a much-nicer-looking cane—the first one I bought would have won the ugly cane award—and my cell phone rang; it was Atticus Wentworth. He identified himself and simply said, "How can I be of help to you, Mr. Beckerman?"

I just stopped in my tracks. There happened to be several chairs and sofas in the lobby of the building, and I went over to the one in the corner, away from everyone else, and I was really afraid to even begin as I knew I was talking to a real professional, and I wasn't sure where to begin, but money was at the top of my list, but I knew not to mention that at that moment. So I simply and briefly told him a little about what had happened, and I just touched on my personal life regarding my family but told him it was all connected. He asked a few pertinent questions, and I was able to answer them all with vigor, and he asked me my age and the age of my wife and children. I informed him I was legally separated, and the children were living at the house with me. He sort of giggled and said, "Your children are living with you at the house, where is your wife?"

My answer was, "Well, it is a long story."

So we went on with our phone interview as I felt as if he was sizing me up, and I fully understood. He asked if it would be convenient for me to go to Richmond for a consultation. I told him it just so happened I had some business in Richmond the end of the week, and I could work around that and go in then if it was convenient for him. He asked me to hold and came right back with a day and time—Friday afternoon at two o'clock. I told him I would make it work.

I went to Richmond and met with my potential client, and it all came together. I had signed up another very large account. That is real security—job security right there, *boom*! Another new piece of business I was able to secure for Sanders Industries. What a great day so far, and then I started getting really anxious about my two o'clock meeting with the heavy-duty lawyer Atticus Wentworth; just his name intimidated me almost, but wow, what a strong name, and it just seems to demand respect. But I was thinking I was not going to be able to afford this guy. I found myself walking slowly with my sporty looking new cane, with a stiff right leg up, one step at a time, to get to the front door of his office building, walked in, and the reception area was loaded with leather furniture, Persian rugs on the floor, nice art on the walls, and a great-looking receptionist, smiling at me, asking me, "How can I help you, sir?"

I said, "I am Roland Beckerman, here to see Mr. Atticus Wentworth."

She welcomed me to the offices of Wentworth & Wentworth and asked me if I would care for anything to drink. "Coffee, tea, or water? We have bottled water," she said, continuing to smile. Now this was all right with me—oh, and I noticed two Jaguars and a BMW parked right out front, and I was betting they belonged to the people there. In just a few minutes, the receptionist said, "Mr. Wentworth will see you now."

She took me into the conference room, with mahogany walls, big mahogany conference table, and the bookshelves were full of reference books. I guess that was what they were, hell, I don't know but I knew I was where I wanted to be. Mr. Wentworth walked in wearing a very nice tweed sport jacket with just a shirt on without a tie, khaki pants, and looked like scuffed-up brown bass weejuns, holding one of those yellow legal pads. We shook hands, and I unhinged my brace and sat down, and no more than a few seconds of small talk, he said,

"Tell me about you, where you're from, what do you do for a living, hobbies, that type of thing."

So there I went, but all the while thinking, *Does he really want to know this kind of stuff?* But I continued on for a bit, and then he asked me to tell him about my illness, and when I was telling him, Dr. Larson was brought in, and we discussed the surgery. That was when he asked me to give him every detail of the conversation and to be very specific in my choice of words. Then he finally started writing notes on his yellow legal pad. Although we didn't request anything, that really nice-looking receptionist brought in some coffee on a tray, still smiling. Oh man she was so nice and very pretty. I looked at my watch, and we had been in there for ninety minutes, and it seemed like about thirty minutes as we covered quite a bit, and time just flew.

During our coffee break, I just asked him what he thought. He said, "I don't know yet what to think, but I would like to see your medical records, all of them, and include the operatory notes that Dr. Larson dictated after the surgery."

I didn't tell him about the other lawyers, but he asked me if I had spoken to any other lawyers about this matter. I had to answer him, and I said yes, I had, as a matter of fact. "Have you signed anything or has anyone filed a lawsuit on your behalf against this Dr. Larson?"

My answer was a definite no. I did, however, feel the need to tell him about the letter Franklin Parker, attorney, sent to Dr. Larson demanding a settlement. Mr. Wentworth said, "What? He sent him a damn letter demanding him to settle?"

I sort of shrugged my shoulders and said yes, he did. He just muttered some words, and what I got was that probably wasn't a good idea. Then he asked me again if I had signed anything or were any suits actually filed. My answer again was no. I didn't volunteer this information, but the only thing I have signed were some damn checks. We ended the meeting, and again he told me to send him all of my records, and he would take a hard look at all of it and perhaps have someone else take a look at it. At that point, I stopped him, and I asked, "What is this going to cost?"

He said, "Cost, it isn't going to cost you anything for me to look into this."

I said, "You mean today's consult is no charge, and you will look into it and not charge me, is that what I understand?"

He said, "Yes, that is correct." He then went on to inform me that if and only if he finds that we have a case, then we would start to build the case and bring in expert witnesses that would testify in court if necessary, and if it did end up going to court and if we were successful enough to win either a settlement or a full court case, as in a trial with a jury, then and only then will any money be paid to us on a contingency basis.

I wasn't sure I was hearing this properly. "So only if we get anything out of this will I owe you any money."

He said, "We will sign a contract if and when I take the case, with the percentages spelled out and agreed to and signed as a valid contract. Send me your records, and we will see what we can do."

The meeting was over, and I had a long drive home but felt good about my entire day. I picked up a half-a-million-dollar-a-year account for Sanders Industries; my boss, Richard, was quite happy with that news when I called him prior to going to see Mr. Wentworth. And I felt like maybe, just maybe, I was finally starting to get somewhere with trying to build a case against Dr. Larson, but I just wish I hadn't muddied the water by having Franklin Parker send that damn demand letter to Dr. Larson. What was done was done, and Mr. Wentworth didn't say too much about it, at least I didn't hear exactly what he muttered. Maybe he was talking to himself, hell, I don't know, but what I do know was I had a great day.

During my drive home, I called John and Gretchen and told them I would be home about seven thirty that evening and asked if they would like to go out to dinner. Gretchen informed me her friend Michelle was coming over to spend the night and asked would it be all right for her to go too. "Of course it will be just fine," I said.

Michelle was a year older than Gretchen, and I think John sort of liked her, so that made for a great night out, eating dinner, and there were no unwanted surprises like we had before. I asked John to drive us because I knew I was going to have a few drinks to celebrate my day.

Saturday I got up and made French toast for our breakfast as that is Gretchen's favorite breakfast item. Michelle had never had French toast. The girls loved it, although Michelle put way too much maple syrup on it, but that was all right; I bet she couldn't taste how great my French toast was, though. My French toast was one of Gretchen's favorite Saturday morning treats I made for her, while John never showed too much excitement for it. I was afraid to tell anyone about my meeting with Mr. Wentworth as not to jinx what I thought had some strong potential.

It was Saturday, and I called my usual Saturday lunch partner, Jeff Greene, to meet me for lunch. When he saw me walk in without the walker, he was quite surprised and very complimentary and congratulated me on the accomplishment, and we proceeded to have another great lunch at the little sandwich shop we seemed to like. Speaking of like, I am not sure if our lunches together were because we liked to eat, or to me, it just seemed like it was a way for two good friends to just get together and hang out and solve the world's problems for an hour or so, and it just happened to be during lunch on Saturdays. I think it was the latter, meaning it was just a convenient time to do what we do.

Later on that day, my close friend Charles Mitchell called me just to say hello and to check to see how I was getting along. I told him the good news that I had really stepped up and have gotten away from using my walker and onto a cane. He seemed really pleased and happy for me, then he asked about how my pain was, hoping it was getting better. Well, actually it wasn't really any better, it now seemed to have peaks and valleys. It usually peaked late in the afternoon hours with the valleys being first thing in the mornings until about lunch. But I also said, "It never goes away, and it is really starting to bring me down."

Charles knows me very well and continued the conversation by asking if I had seen any of my doctors about it lately, and I told him about my recent visit with Dr. Sussman and about my results of another round of EMG testing that wasn't very encouraging. Since we were on the subject of Dr. Sussman, I ventured out to tell him about him giving me the name of Atticus Wentworth, senior partner of Wentworth & Wentworth in Richmond, Virginia, medical malpractice specialist. The first thing he said was, "How much money did he ask you for?"

He could hardly believe it when I told him it looked like he had some kind of contingency fee that we would agree on regarding a percentage of the amount gained. But that whole idea was a long way away because I don't even know if he would take the case. "I am sending all my records to him on Monday. He said he will review them and have someone else review them too. He didn't say who, but I am thinking he maybe has a doctor, either on staff or maybe has one retained for such services, I really don't know."

Charles thought it sounded pretty good and mentioned, "Well, what do you have to lose?"

My response was, "I don't have a damn thing to lose. I have already lost enough."

He asked me about Becky and the kids, and I told him we were legally separated, and so far things seemed to be working out, but trying to keep John and Gretchen taken care of and me trying to travel some with my job was about all I could handle. "I need some damn help, you want to come up here, at least until school is out?"

Charles responded, "You're kidding, right?"

"Yes, of course I am, but thought I'd give it a shot." We both laughed.

It was great to talk to him for a little while. He always seems to have a way of bringing me up, as if it is almost an escape for the time we are talking. His dry—very dry—sense of humor and his wording is always interesting, and I never know what he might say as he isn't predictable at all; that's what makes him fun to talk to. Plus he is the one, if you recall earlier here, that put what happened with Becky and me into perspective when he said, "You are no longer her knight in shining armor."

And from that I have concluded that there are two types of women. Married women that think they have their knight with the shining armor, but when a serious problem occurs, such as a serious illness that renders that knight in a very negative manner and/or seems to place them in more of a liability position in a sense, they are either runners or fighters. If it appears the knight's armor will never shine again, they reach out for something else and/or someone else to escape from that possible liability of that tarnished armor, and they become a runner. Or when something happens, such as a life-changing illness occurs, the other type of woman proves herself to be a fighter, one that stays by the side of that knight with the tarnished armor, thinking perhaps, *Well, together we can make it shine again. It might take a lot of work, but together we will do our best.* That is what I believe, and it has come from my own experience—firsthand experience, not hearsay.

I hoped when things settle down some, I would like to plan a trip down to Florida to see him again; we don't get to spend a lot of time together. Actually it isn't often we see each other, but close friends can remain close, even though they don't see each other often; however, we do talk from time to time to stay caught up, so I guess that was what today's call was all about—to catch up—and we did, until the next time of course.

Headed to one of my accounts, my cell phone rang; it was Franklin Parker, the lawyer/doctor that sent the demand-to-settle letter to Dr. Larson. It surprised me a bit as we started talking, and he asked me if I wanted to proceed. I hesitated to say anything. He said, "Hello, did I lose you?"

"I'm here, but what does all this involve?"

He informed me he had another expert that wanted to review my records. He said he'd like to start building a case against Dr. Larson. While he was talking, I interrupted him and said, "Is this going to cost me more money?"

He answered, "Why, yes, it is, just the cost of doing business and part of building your case against Dr. Larson, but I think we can get him to review your records and give us a recommendation for $2,500."

Thinking back about how wonderful my whole day was that Friday on my business trip to Richmond that resulted in a half-a-million-dollar-a-year account I picked up for my company, Sanders Industries, and later in the day, my meeting with Mr. Wentworth at the offices of Wentworth & Wentworth, and leaving with a good feeling, and he didn't ask me for a dime, I thought perhaps I needed to sit on this for a while. So I responded to Dr. Parker or lawyer Parker—I really don't how I should address him—but I told him I would have to give this a lot of consideration because he's asking me for more money. He said, "It is only $2,500, and it could be the key to building a case for you against Dr. Larson. That is what you want, isn't it?"

"Of course it is, but I have to think about it." I ended the call.

First thing the next morning, he called me back and asked if I had had time to consider continuing with him. He must have thought he had a live fish on the line; maybe I was a live fish, but this fish ain't biting this time. I told him I would have to give it some serious thought, but I thought in truth, I might be shifting my interest to Mr. Wentworth. He just seemed to have it all together, and I just hoped he would take my case.

I was driving down Interstate 95, heading south to a large customer of mine in Savannah, Georgia. It is a federal training ground, and I had to get clearance to enter, so it must be some serious stuff going on within those walls, but the guy I dealt with there was really a neat guy. He was a big duck hunter, and I have shot a few ducks myself, and I happen to like roast duck quite a bit.

My good friend and old boss Conrad Winchester called me to check to see how I was doing. It was good to hear his voice. It just seems there are some that know what I have been through and just are genuinely concerned about me, and I appreciate them all, and it proves they are my friends. Conrad and I talked for about the last thirty minutes of my drive. I told him next time I was up his way, maybe we could have lunch. He said, "Hey, man, I understand you're walking a lot better."

Jokingly I told him, "Damn, man, give me a break, even a baby can learn how to walk." We both got a chuckle out of that one. I did hope to see him again soon, maybe he would buy my lunch next time. I think I picked it up last time, but who's keeping score.

Toward the end of the week, I got a call from Becky, and she wanted to stop by to tell me some news, of course, when she responded by saying as soon as it was convenient. She stopped by on Thursday night, walked in, and we had a rather civil verbal exchange, and I was determined that no matter what, I was not going to get into any kind of argument or confrontation; I just couldn't do that. Being late in the day, my pain level was pretty high, so I popped two oxycodone tablets just before she got to the house. After about twenty or thirty minutes, we were just sitting there in the living room, and it felt a little awkward actually, and I spoke up and said, "What did you want to tell me? You said you had some news."

She started crying and proceeded to tell me that her relationship wasn't going to work out, and she was going to leave Russell and move out. *Oh, hell,* I thought. I felt something coming that I just couldn't handle, there had been too much that had happened now, I just couldn't think of her. Then she said, "I am going to get an apartment for a while and live by myself."

All of a sudden, that giant elephant just got up off my chest. I had to get my thoughts together as that wasn't at all what I was expecting, and at the same time, I felt relief that the elephant had gotten off of me, but for the moment, I felt some compassion; after all, she was my wife for a long time. And the fact is, she is John's and Gretchen's mother, and we had so many great years together, so I did allow those emotions to come through again, but I knew where the line was, and it had been drawn.

So now back to the conversation. I didn't really know how to respond because it was up to her and not me; it just wasn't any of my business. The thought rushed into my head. I just hoped that was really what she wanted to do. As I mentioned, I just couldn't do this, too much had transpired. I couldn't go back now. She got up and just said, "Well, this is what I am going to do, and I am going to need the furniture that we agreed on that I could have, and I will make arrangements to pick it up as soon as I can find an apartment." There was a bit of relief when she left, although I think my inner feelings for her were still there, but I also was absolutely sure that since I had lost the shine off of my armor, and my physical condition had gone through some drastic changes, it was over, so I allowed those feelings to go right out of the door with her when she left.

Chapter 10

My pain levels were about the same, but after this period of time, meaning months of constant burning, aching, and just dull pain in my right leg all the damn time was really wearing me down and was just, in general, hard on me. It seems time just slips by at a very brisk pace. I haven't had anything more to do with the doctor/lawyer Franklin Parker, and his calls had finally stopped as I just marked it off as a loss, and another lesson learned. My son, John, was just before going to North Carolina State University. Gretchen was a rising junior in high school, and life was pretty good, except I was just tired all the time because getting a full night's rest just didn't seem to come anymore.

I continued to see Dr. Mowji monthly mainly because by law, I think he had to literally see me to write my prescription for oxycodone because it is a controlled substance and is high up the ladder in that regard, and he told me again, "Roland, you need to slow down and take care of yourself. You are just working too hard, and the travel is wearing you down. We keep a close look on your blood work, but the fatigue you have is becoming chronic, and I am concerned."

Wow, none of that sounded good, but Dr. Mowji has seen me at my best, and he has also seen me at my worst. He has been great, and I have full confidence in his ability and medical knowledge as my GP, but how can I slow down? I have to keep working; I have a lot of responsibility and need to continue to provide for John and Gretchen. I love them so much, and I so enjoy watching them continue to grow as John is becoming a young man and is becoming independent, certainly in his thinking, and he is and always has been extremely bright, and Gretchen is, as I mentioned earlier, following right in his footsteps scholastically. They are both such bright and wonderful young people.

Something strange occurred today. I received a phone call from the Social Security office, and the lady on the phone said she was calling me on behalf of my disability claim, and she had some questions. My response was, and I hesitated and said, "Why are you calling me?"

She came right back with, "I just need a few questions answered so we can finalize your claim because you are due to receive full disability because of your medical issues, a full medical benefit. It was filed four months ago, and you will start receiving full benefits soon."

I asked her who she was, and I said, "I need to meet with you."

I went first thing the next day. She proceeded to tell me I had been approved for full benefits. I was so shocked because all I did was visit the Social Security offices because

I was told to do so by Dr. Larson at my first follow-up visit that didn't end well, but I do recall him telling me that, and I did go in and discussed disability. I don't remember actually filing for it, so therefore, how did it get this far into the system? That was the only time it was ever mentioned. I said, "Don't send me anything. I can't do this, are you going to pay my bills? I don't think so."

She was as shocked as I was, and she said, "Do you mean you are turning full benefits down?"

My response was, "I will take it only if you will increase the amount by four."

She looked rather strangely and said, "Well, I will just hold the file open."

I got a call from her a few days later, and she said, "I have never had anyone to turn down full disability benefits, are you sure?"

I thanked her for calling but told her, "Yes, I am sure, as I mentioned, unless you can increase it by four, I can't accept it."

She told me to have a nice day, and I think I did. To this day, I am unsure of how the Social Security office got involved in my well-being and/or even my future. It is still one of those unsolved mysteries, but I have an idea how it moved or who had it moved through the system, but I know I will never know for sure, but it could have only been pushed by one person.

Time continues to slip by, by my standards, way too fast. Becky seemed to have settled into her own in her apartment and was seeing someone else. Her new knight in shining armor, Russell, tarnished, so she moved on. I didn't like the SOB anyway, especially when he attempted to tell me what great children John and Gretchen were and how he was getting close to them. I stopped him right there and told him I didn't need him to tell me anything about my damn children. Little did he know, Gretchen hated him, and John, I think, wanted to cause some kind of physical harm on him, which I thought were normal reactions of both of them, and as I mentioned, I didn't like the SOB, even before he and Becky started having their love affair. For Becky, I think it was an escape, and for him, I think it was just fun. There wasn't any love at all as it didn't last long before she left him and moved out on her own into her apartment, and I am glad she did, and I really want her to find happiness and prosper. As I have mentioned before, she is John and Gretchen's mother, and that will never change, so I will simply remain civil and just do the best I can with the whole fucked-up mess.

I got a call from Atticus Wentworth, the medical malpractice attorney that was working on my case, and he asked me if I would be in Richmond anytime soon as he would like to meet with me, and he also mentioned if I didn't have any business trips up his way anytime soon, he had something he needs to take care of in my area, but either way, he said, "We need to meet."

I didn't want to waste time, sensing a high level of importance, so I planned on going to Richmond the very next day, and we sat down, this time in his office instead of the conference room. He seemed to have somewhat of a somber look, and he got right to the point. He told me that he was sure I had a very strong case, one that can be won, and he said, "It is one I really want to take, but in order to even file the case, I have to have some team players." He went on to explain what "team players" really meant. "In order to have any strength and validity, I have to have two of doctors that understand the problem, and more importantly, they have to be able to clearly explain what Dr. Larson did wrong that caused the nerve damage to your femoral nerve."

He reminded me of the demanding letter that Franklin Parker sent to Dr. Larson and explained just how damaging that was because the letter was just a demand without anything to back it up. I knew what was coming next, and it did. Mr. Wentworth paused and said, "I don't think I can help you because it will take more time than we have left for me to assemble the proper experts to help us with your case." He then asked me if I knew there was a statute, laws called statute of limitations.

My response was, "Statute of limitations? What the hell does that have to do with medical malpractice?"

He took the time to explain it to me and said he just didn't think he had enough time because of the amount of time that had already passed. I then asked what was the time limit we're talking about here. His response was, "Three years from the date the injury occurred, and you are pretty deep into it already, and I just don't want to waste your time." He went on to say, "I don't think it would be fair to you, even though I am confident you have a very strong case for me to get into it this late in the time frame. I am sorry and I wish you the best," he said.

His assistant handed me a box with all of my files neatly tucked inside and marked on the outside with my name with identifying numbers written on the top. Once again, I kept saying to myself again I was faced with and had to accept defeat. This one seemed to cut quite deep; my emotions almost took over while we were walking out of the office together as Mr. Wentworth walked with me to my car and loaded the heavy box into the back seat. He noticed my wheelchair folded up back there and said, "You are getting around a lot better and I am glad, and I wish you all the best, Roland."

We shook hands, and he again wished me all the best and apologized again that he couldn't be of help to me. I think being in shock was a good way to describe my mental status at that time as I just sat there while Mr. Wentworth walked back into his office building. I didn't know whether to be upset, mad, disappointed, or just plain pissed off, but I think perhaps I was all of those combined. It was a very long drive home, and the memory of that day, long ago, in James Bogart's office, my divorce attorney, when I mentioned looking into a medical malpractice lawsuit just to get his opinion and his reaction was as if I had said something vulgar and/or nasty. Then he proceeded to tell me how hard and nearly impossible the process truly was, and that was something he really didn't think I should do because of all of the difficulties involved, I then realized, well, just maybe he was right.

Continuing to do, or I should say try to do, my job was steadily getting harder and harder. Dr. Mowji continued to see me, and now he was prescribing 120 oxycodone tablets in each monthly prescription he wrote for me. We were becoming friends, but if the truth be known, I think our friendship started quite a while ago, but he seems to genuinely care about my health, both mental and physical. I am glad to say he hadn't pushed or even suggested I see the psychiatrist again as my experience there wasn't very successful or pleasant, and aside from the fact, he found out just how mentally strong I was from the manner I had handled all of the adverse situations that life had thrown at me since my medical problems started. I had somehow held it together, but it was continuing to become more and more of daily challenge, and Dr. Mowji clearly saw this, and every time I saw him, he spent a few minutes talking to me about slowing down, but now he was advising me to get off the road and maybe find something else to do that didn't require the rigid schedule of traveling and try to unload some stress.

The fact is, he was right, but what in the hell would I do? This is all I know. Sales, marketing, and business development is what I do, and these things aren't performed sitting in a comfortable office with nice beautiful green plants, a comfortable chair, and a nice view out of the office window. Instead my office is either looking out of the windshield of my car, traveling at seventy miles per hour, sometimes a little more, or watching the runway pass by just before liftoff and, upon arriving at my various destinations, setting up my laptop computer to catch up on the day's messages and responding to the ones that required attention. That was pretty much the type of office I have, sort of a roving office. I didn't know what else I could do to earn the income I had set myself up for that was needed to stay afloat.

My mind was starting to think maybe Dr. Mowji was right, maybe I should find a way to slow down. Going through two periods of time that I couldn't work and had to accept—not depend on because it wasn't enough, but it did help—was the small short-term disability checks that came from Sanders Industries and medical bills and money I had given to a couple of lawyers. I really needed to keep earning the income I needed. I think the reference of a catch twenty-two could be used here, sort of like, am I coming or going, or am I spinning my wheels, or more importantly, am I just wearing myself down.

After long thought and consideration of everything, I concluded I was just wearing down physically and mentally. I hope it didn't show as I did my best to hide it, especially wanted to hide it from John and Gretchen. John was away at college, and it was just Gretchen and me at the house. I must say, having Gretchen there was a wonderful thing; we really had a good time together. She now had her driver's license, and of course her own car, and that really awarded her with a lot of freedom and really made it a lot easier on me. John was busy with his schoolwork and just being a college kid, but I think he felt the need to come in on weekends, not a lot but he came, and I encouraged him not to burn up the highway as I wanted him to enjoy college life, and I am sure he did just that. Enjoy it while you can, son, because one day, life will hit you, and reality will be firmly planted in you. Words of wisdom there, I'd say, coming from dear old Dad.

I continue to stay in touch with my close friends Conrad Winchester, Charles Mitchell, and my local lunch buddy, Jeff Greene. If I am not reaching out to them, they are contacting me. I am sure they knew I was under a lot of stress, trying to work and keep things balanced and just trying to stay up on everything. Their support really meant a lot to me, and I know they were genuinely concerned, but I was the only one that could make needed changes, but I just couldn't do it right now, just couldn't.

I had mentioned before how time has a way of slipping by, and that hasn't changed. It seemed I went to sleep one night and woke up two years later. I didn't know where the time had gone. Dr. Mowji seemed to think maybe I should try to back off of the oxycodone for a while and maybe try something else. Was I addicted, didn't really think about it, and Dr. Mowji would say, when I asked him about that was, "Roland, you're using this in a therapeutic way, not for recreational purposes, and I think you could back off, but it does seem to manage the pain in your right leg."

I mainly used the oxycodone at night so I could get a few hours of uninterrupted sleep, so I was thinking he was right about my therapeutic use.

I was now cutting deep into the statute of limitations, and I hated to admit it, but I had been back in touch with the attorney that sent the letter demanding settlement to Dr. Larson. In my travels, finding myself in various cities with some time on my hands, I got in front of several lawyers, all with medical malpractice experience, and it seemed they all told me I had a great case, and they could likely help me, and some even used the term *slam dunk. Yeah*, I thought, *the only slam dunk is on the basketball court, not in the medical malpractice arena*, I had learned the hard way. But I just couldn't let what happened to me go for some reason, so I continued to search, thinking and hoping I would come across the right lawyer and could get something done.

By now it had become much more than money; it had become quite personal and was becoming more and more about plain morals, justice, and human decency. I had crossed paths with Dr. Larson a few times, only to get a glaring stare with sort of a smirk look. Of course I didn't speak, mainly because speaking to him wouldn't satisfy my need or wishes, as neither my needs or wishes would have been very nice. But as I said, I had reached back out to doctor/lawyer Franklin Parker, still not sure how he should be addressed. Sitting in his office, he said, "We need to get to work."

For the first time, he mentioned the statute of limitations, asking me again when the injury during surgery occurred, the exact date. Yes, we did have to move quickly now, so there I was, feeling like this was the best there was, and knowing I couldn't let it go, I just had to stick with it and him to hope something can get established before the statute runs out, and if they did run out, well, it would be over forever, and that damn Dr. Larson got away with fucking up my damn life. Sorry, that was how I felt. Franklin proceeded to tell me he now had a few medical experts/doctors that wanted to take a crack at my medical file, so here we go again. Yes, you guessed it, he told me he would need $4,000 for consultation fees. I felt like, well, this is it, if I don't, then it doesn't go anywhere, and time isn't on my side. So I agreed to get him a check for $4,000. This was hard to swallow, but I just bit the damn bullet and did it with a clouded conscience. I knew this was going to be the end, if he couldn't get some results from these experts of his. All I could do now was to wait.

Chapter 11

My son, John, was doing quite well in college, and Gretchen was just before entering into her first year as a college freshman. My divorce had been finalized, and my physical health was getting worse. The fatigue and pain was becoming so hard to deal with, and traveling was becoming a real chore. I was still depending on and wearing my leg brace and, of course, using a cane. It was getting to the point of just dreading having to get out of bed and hit the highway or get to the airport, but I continued to just do my best, and my boss, Richard, at Sanders Industries mentioned a few times for me to take a day or two off here and there, work at my own pace, and to take care of myself. I knew he was just concerned, but I continued to grind away as best I could.

And Becky just announced she got engaged. She called and told me just after, said she wanted me to hear it from her first and not anyone else. She and I had been getting along pretty well, considering, but if you recall, being civil and not engaging in all the negative stuff that came along with a separation and ultimately a divorce was important to me to keep it that way for the children's sake, didn't really care about anything else. I was genuinely happy for her and wished her all the best. She told me there wasn't a date yet, but she was thinking before the end of the year, which was fast approaching.

I was getting anxious about the statute because it was now down to just having three months left until the three-year period would be up, and I seemed to be bugging the hell out of Franklin to get it filed. *What is going on, do we have what we need, are we going to be able to get the lawsuit filed in time, what about our experts, are they onboard, and so on.* He always appeared like everything was going to be all right, just-hold-on-and-hang-in-there-with-me kind of thing, but hanging on was getting very hard because the clock was ticking now faster than ever. I had just decided in my mind that I needed to just let it go; as hard as it was going to be to do that, I really didn't have any choice. I had met with every lawyer I could find that would consult with me. Now time was really against me, and Franklin didn't seem to be so upbeat, and I wasn't getting those positive vibes from him. As a matter of fact, I wasn't getting any vibes at all from him, so there it was, I was done with this whole damn lawsuit bullshit. Just as my divorce lawyer tried to tell him, "Medical malpractice is a very hard thing to try to do." I guess I should have listened, and the money I laid out trying to make something happen was haunting me pretty hard, and now was the time to really beat myself up, and that was what went on for the next couple of weeks.

I get a very surprising phone call from Mr. Atticus Wentworth of Wentworth & Wentworth, the medical malpractice lawyer in Richmond, just before checking into my hotel in Lynchburg, Virginia, on a Monday night. He asked how things were going along regarding my health and said, "You're divorced now, aren't you?"

I answered yes, I was, as a matter of fact. "I will get to the point of my call, would you be nearby any time soon? I have something I want to discuss with you, or I could perhaps meet you somewhere, whatever would be convenient, but I would like to meet as soon as we possibly can."

I told him, "I am in Lynchburg now, I have an early morning meeting but free after that." And he told me he could clear a couple of hours for me and asked if I could be there, say, by lunch, and we could have lunch together. Knowing Lynchburg was only about a two-hour drive to Richmond, I said yes, lunch it is.

I went to my business meeting first thing, and it turned out to be quite a successful meeting that resulted in a very large order. I phoned my boss, Richard, at Sanders Industries and gave him the good news. He said, "Great, this is one of those champagne celebrations, Roland. You did it again. Congratulations, great work." Incidentally I don't even like champagne, but I didn't tell Richard. Then he said, "I am going to schedule a staff meeting next Thursday, and I want you here."

I said, "No problem. I will be there, Richard."

While driving over to Richmond from Lynchburg I was surfing on a high wave from the success of my early-morning meeting and the anticipation of why Mr. Wentworth wanted to see me was getting the best of me. I pulled into the parking lot in front of his office building, and as I entered the office, I was greeted with a smile again, and the receptionist said, "Hi, Mr. Beckerman, Mr. Wentworth is expecting you and will be right with you."

Just a short few minutes, Mr. Wentworth came out and greeted me warmly. We shook hands and told me how nice it was to see me again, and after I took a step or two, he added, "Damn, Roland, you're getting around a lot better now."

I responded as I had before, "Well, even a baby can learn how to walk."

We both chuckled and walked out, and he said, "I'll drive." And we got into one of those beautiful Jaguars; this one was the silver one, and it was a very nice quiet smooth ride. We pulled up in front of this upscale seafood restaurant in downtown Richmond that had valet parking, and we walked in and were seated immediately, as he had made a reservation. We were seated in the far corner, away from everyone else, and after a couple of minutes of small talk, he asked me how my case was going and did I have anyone working on it. I jumped right in and told him about getting back in touch with the attorney that sent the demand letter, but it didn't appear anything was moving to my satisfaction or expectation. Mr. Wentworth said, "Well, I have something to offer you. We have two expert witnesses and a possible third and fourth, and we all have been in discussion about your case."

And I just stopped. I almost choked on the tea I was drinking, and I said, "Go on, please."

"I would like to take your case and get a lawsuit filed, if this is something you'd want."

I couldn't really speak at the moment as my emotions were flying all around the room like a paper airplane in a windstorm and just felt this was just a dream, just a dream, and I would wake up in a minute, and it would all be over. I said, "Mr. Wentworth—"

He stopped me and said, "Call me Atticus."

I said, "All right, Atticus, what does this all mean? And yes, I would love for you to take this and do whatever you can do to make it happen."

Getting a lawsuit filed—hell, yes—finally something looked positive after almost three long damn years of a lot of expense, pain, defeats, and suffering. Atticus said, "You will have to notify the attorney you are working with, in writing, that you are firing him, ceasing your relationship, and you need to do it by registered mail before I can ethically and or legally take the case over. And in the essence of time, I can send you the necessary paperwork for you to hand deliver to the courthouse in your county and have the lawsuit filed." He said, "There will be a fee of probably one hundred dollars, find out, and I will send you a check."

I said, "Just send me the paperwork, and I will file it and take care of the fee, don't worry about it."

He said, "Fine, then I will get the documents drawn up, and send them to you overnight via FedEx."

I even remember what he had for lunch that day but couldn't tell you what I had. He had fried flounder. In all the excitement, I don't know or couldn't tell you if I ate what I ordered or not actually. But I do know—here I go again—riding a very high wave, the highest of the high ones of all so far into this crazy journey. If I recall, the fee was ninety-eight dollars, and that was all of the money I spent on this case during my entire relationship with Atticus Wentworth. He never asked me for another dime, he didn't ask me for this. I insisted I take care of it, but of course, I wanted it done and knew time was very important. This was the very best ride home I had experienced during so many disappointments in almost three years. Atticus told me, "Let's just get the lawsuit filed, and then we will have time to build our case and start putting it all together. It's kind of like assembling a puzzle as all the pieces have to be there, and more importantly, they have to fit."

Just as we were driving back in that beautiful silver Jaguar, he informed me, "Once we will get our ducks in a row, we will start the process of getting depositions scheduled, and we will likely depose you first." The last thing he said to me that day was, "We'll be in touch."

The adrenaline was really pumping, and I think I made it home in record time. First thing the next morning, I drafted a letter and e-mailed it to Atticus for his stamp of approval. Hell I haven't ever written a letter of this nature, although writing letters and memos were a specialty of mine, but I had never fired a lawyer before, certainly not by registered mail. He only made one small adjustment, and in truth, I think it was an error with my grammar. Oh well, no surprise there. As soon as the item was corrected, off to the post office I went and sent it off via registered mail to Franklin Parker, MD, JD.

Within the next couple of days, I received the paperwork from Wentworth & Wentworth. It was, or appeared to be, a simple legal form with all the spaces filled out with notary stamps and a few signatures spelling out what the intent was, and the intent was to notify the county clerk of court that a medical malpractice lawsuit was being filed against Dr. Larson on behalf of Roland Beckerman, me of course, all duly filled out, and here it is to be notice of this instrument on this day. We only had less than two weeks before the statute of limitations were going to run out, and after that, as I mentioned, the doors would close on it forever. I notified Atticus Wentworth of Wentworth & Wentworth that all was filed and told him I dropped a copy of the receipt of ninety-eight dollars in the mail to him, and it was now in the clerk of court's offices filed away. What an accomplishment. For the moment, my pain and fatigue seemed to be far away and just how special an event like this was to actually take over your physical and mental state for a while. This felt good.

Chapter 12

Now just less than two weeks before the statute of limitations would run out, my case had now been filed with the clerk of court in the county where the injury occurred. It was so nice to hear the lady at the courthouse say, "Here is your receipt for the filing fee, Mr. Beckerman."

I smiled and just said thank you and walked out, and it was one of the most proud moments of the entire period since the day this all started, which was in the operating room under the care of Dr. Larson. It is now up to Atticus Wentworth to build my case to prove Dr. Larson failed to administer the standard of care that is due every patient. Over this period of time of consulting with and working with various lawyers, I have learned a lot about how this works. It was now time for us to assemble our experts. It was now time for us to gather any and all remaining informative facts related to our case. It was now time to build this case, and it was now time for us to go to work. I just had to ask Atticus why and how he concluded to become involved again to make his entrance back into my life because if you recall, he had told me he didn't want to waste my time, although he stated clearly he believed I had a very legitimate and strong case. He was concerned about not being able to assemble precisely what was necessary to file a case in time; after all, I had already burned through about a third of the time allotted prior to the statute's expiration date. But Atticus plainly and clearly stated, "I never could let it go, so I remained interested, and as I found more promising information, I would file it."

The first medical expert that was fully onboard was a very well-known doctor on staff at one of the most well-known teaching universities in the country. He has had countless speaking engagements literally all over the world, written four books on various avenues of surgery, a member of a long list of medical associations, has gained the recognition as being one of the best in his area of expertise, and has taught thousands the proper techniques of performing various surgeries while instilling the innermost value of being a surgeon, and that was to give every patient 100 percent as it is a moral duty. I was honored to learn Dr. Spencer asked to meet me, so we arranged an appointment at his clinic, and he not only wanted to meet me, but he wanted to examine me, I guess, to see for himself the extent of my injury and to just get a feel of what I had been going through and to witness my mobility or lack of mobility.

Meeting and spending time with him was a pleasure, to say the least, and he was such a gentle-minded human being and treated me with much respect while regarding me as the subject of hopefully helping me to right a wrong, in some way or the other. He told me he was sure of where the mistake was made as there was no other answer to the question. He said, "In reading over all of the CT scans of you from head to toe that Dr. Larson had ordered for you during your time in the hospital, he actually ruled out all of the other possibilities, so he really did us all a favor as the scans would have found the problem if there was any to find. So by his ruling all other suspects out, it made my assessment and prompted my decision that only the constant pressure of the retractors used to hold Mr. Beckerman's tissue aside for clear view and working space as noted in his operative notes declared could have been the only thing that caused your injury.

"The testing Dr. Sussman did was quite thorough, and the results of different EMGs performed at different times revealed within range of each other, not showing any improvement in gained activity has also helped me with pinpointing the location of the area of the injury. His diagnosis of lumbar plexopathy is, in my opinion, correct. In Dr. Larson's operative notes, he clearly stated, 'Once the retractors were in place, I didn't move them.' But it is common practice during operations, when retractors are used, the surgeon must monitor them and release the pressure to simply give the tissue a break from compression that can and has, as it has been proven, to cause nerve damage by either cutting off blood flow or slowing it down, or to say to traumatize the area by strangling the proper flow of blood supply to the nerves, and in this case, it was your femoral nerve that was literally starved. There wasn't anything severed but nerve damage can easily occur even without being severed and in this case it was just starved of proper blood supply."

Upon leaving this meeting, I felt a lot more knowledgeable about what happened. He did ask me about the pain I endure, and I explained just how it has affected me in my daily routine and how it seems to take over at times, meaning it occupies my mind to the extent of missing things I shouldn't miss, and even days start to run together, and I seem to get confused of even which day it was without looking at my calendar.

After my very eye-opening meeting with Dr. Spencer, I secured another appointment with Dr. Sussman because I wanted to discuss pain management with him again. I hadn't seen him in a while, and he seemed glad to see me and, of course, asked about how I was getting along, not just my mobility. I think he really did have concern for me. I remember so well, like it was just last night, when he walked into my hospital room late that night, while Becky was still there, and gave me a basic neurological exam and diagnosed me with something I had never heard of—lumbar plexopathy. He was the only doctor—and I had been seen by several that particular day while still in the hospital after my friend and board member went to the administrator and informed him of my problem, not from the surgery of the complete colectomy but because of my right leg and what was going on—who addressed my problem and took me seriously and at least gave me something to ponder. I guess it was a great diagnosis because now, today, it seems to be as true as ever.

But we talked about how I could manage my pain a little better. Together we went over the list of prescribed medications I had been given in the past and discussed each of them and concluded again the opiates were the only thing that worked without the crazy side effects, but the opiates were something that was dangerous for me to continue because of my work and travel. About the only thing he could say was, I really should try to get off the road. He said, "It just might save your life or the life of someone else."

That hit pretty hard. Then I was asked if I was still seeing Dr. Mowji, and I told him yes, we have a great relationship. Dr. Sussman said, "He is a fine doctor, and I suggest you continue to allow him to help you with your pain management."

I was just before walking out, and he stopped me and asked me to follow him into his private office. It was nice, all leather furniture, it was dark except for one lamp that was lit on his large desk. He asked me to have a seat. He opened up a drawer or two, as if he was searching for something, and he pulled out a piece of paper with a name and phone number printed on it. He said, "Don't misunderstand me, I will be delighted to continue to see you, as I have said before, but I want you to see someone with more gray hair than I have."

It only took me about a half a second to understand his meaning. He wanted me to see another neurologist with more experience than he has and/or just wanted me to be seen in an effort and in hopes another neurologist might just stumble upon the answer of how I could improve. He not only gave me a neurologist's name, but he gave me the name as being the head of neurosciences at another major teaching university. I thanked him and told him I would give his office a call, and he interrupted me and told me Dr. Hyatt was expecting my call. Dr. Sussman informed me he and Dr. Hyatt had discussed my case over the phone a couple of times, and he expressed an interest in seeing me.

In just a few short days, I was sitting in Dr. Hyatt's clinic, this older gray-haired short man with thick tortoise-shelled glasses came in, and his hair looked like he had just walked in from a terrible windstorm, and I immediately thought, *Oh yeah, this is my kind of guy.* Turned out he was just what I had hoped for. He was very similar in his approach as Dr. Sussman—very kind, easy to talk to, and just had a gentle way about himself. And he was full of information as I asked him to slow down some as I wanted to take some notes to research later. He seemed to know my case quite well and told me he and Dr. Sussman had spent some time on the phone, and I said, "Yes, he said you had conversations regarding me."

He asked me if I would mind if he did his own EMG test, my answer was sure, let's do it. This would be the third EMG, so we went into another room, and he had an assistant—I think a student—administer the test while he just stood and watched. While monitoring the meters and shaking his head in a manner I had seen before, I knew the results weren't anything encouraging. So after this and our conversation and exams were about to come to an end, the only thing he did differently than Dr. Sussman was to extend the hopeful time of possible recovery by a couple of months. His explanation was that neurological injuries have a window of quick improvement which is normal to expect and, in most cases, hopeful improvement. He did tell me something I think I already knew in my mind, as he told me, "Because of the amount of time already passed since the injury occurred, I don't think you will ever recover. Not to say you will not gain some back, but I really don't think you will ever fully recover, not even close."

He went on to explain that neurology is more of an art than a science because there is so much we don't know, and it is a lot of assembling facts and guessing. So I left there with more negative thoughts regarding my problems, but I left there also feeling a little bit liberated in just knowing this was it, so let's just move on from here. No more questions, no more thinking, "*Yeah, I will be all right, just give it more time, etc., etc.* It fueled my fire now, more so than ever, to be even more of a team member with Atticus Wentworth, especially now after having the lawsuit filed and after my meeting and exam with Dr. Spencer, head of surgery.

I informed Atticus Wentworth about my meeting with Dr. Hyatt, neurologist, and he stopped me and said Dr. Hyatt, head of neurosciences, was now onboard with us. That news traveled fast, and I was not sure how that transpired, but Dr. Hyatt had joined our team of experts, so now we had Dr. Spencer, head of surgery, and Dr. Hyatt, head of neurosciences, with others about to come onboard too. That roller coaster in my head was at it again, with the highs and lows, but it seemed the roller coaster was hovering mostly around the high side of the waves for a change. Things were really looking up for my ever-changing journey with so many mixed emotions that seemed to spring up and slap me right across my face, more often than I want to recall.

It was now that two well-known department heads of two of the most respected and prestigious teaching facilities in the country were onboard with us as others were surfacing and expressing interest in assisting. It seemed now some of the doctors Atticus made contact with and/or paid to have my records looked at in an effort to assist in finding where the fault of Dr. Larson was and because of the reason—the one ever-so important reason—Dr. Spencer had openly given as the only cause of my injury. Because of that, it had sparked a lot of interest. It seemed we were all learning something here, and it took Dr. Spencer, a man with decades of experience, to identify so clearly and plainly just where and how it occurred. But he did it by deduction, meaning all other possible reasons were ruled out at the hand and effort of the one that caused the problem himself, Dr. Larson, by completing several scans of Mr. Beckerman from head to toe. It just took someone like Dr. Spencer to open his eyes and mind to the facts in the case of how I was injured, and more importantly, how simple it would have been to avoid this mental mistake in the first place.

I recall Dr. Spencer stating he teaches the importance while using retractors to hold tissue back and out of the way during, in this case, abdominal surgery to always release the pressure every ten minutes or so to allow the stressed tissue to relax and regain full circulation of blood flow, just in case the flow had been unknowingly put in a compromised manner and/or position to avoid nerve injury. His approach has gained notoriety and has earned merit with many colleagues. Within the next few days, another well-known surgeon that Atticus had been in contact with reached back out to Atticus Wentworth. After reading some material Dr. Spencer had written, he too had agreed to come onboard with his full support of precisely how and where the injury occurred. Dr. Durst, head of surgery at a well-known hospital in the northeastern part of the country, concurred with Dr. Spencer and Dr. Hyatt.

Within a couple of a few short weeks from my filing the case at the local clerk of court's office, in the county where the injury occurred, we now had Dr. Spencer, head of surgery, Dr. Hyatt, head of neurosciences, and Dr. Durst, head of surgery, signed on as the beginning of our team of expert witnesses willing to testify against Dr. Larson on my behalf. The list, however, did continue to grow, much to my delighted surprise because it seemed this whole idea of getting a case filed was not going to happen. But thanks to the ongoing efforts of Atticus Wentworth and his diligence to find a way to make this a reality for me, we had made giant steps. It all seemed to be happening quickly now, but Atticus had informed me, "Now the process has started, we will have periods of time that due to our efforts, things will move at a rather rapid pace, and then it will slow down as events have to materialize as we go along."

So he had prepared me to hurry up and wait. I liked the hurry part of that, but the waiting was hard, but I knew sort of how the process works now. So hurry up and wait it is. I was continuing to work and to visit with my two children while they were away at school, you know, doing what parents do, as in bring them food, some cash, and little gifts that can make their lives a little more enjoyable while being a student. And of course, being sure their cars were being maintained. Oh boy, speaking of cars, I asked Gretchen what happened to her trunk lid and roof of her car. I said, "It looks like someone with golf shoes did a tap dance on it."

I am not sure what her response was, but whatever it was didn't suit me, but I just let it go. John's car was in a little better condition, I thought, until I looked at the inside. It was a mess, but I expected it—oh, and the inside of Gretchen's car wasn't any better. I had kept both of them informed of the recent happenings regarding my medical case and the building of it, finally. They both seemed relieved that things were starting to move along as they know how important it had been to me for a long time now. And by the way, both were doing very well in school, and so I could overlook the fact they were trashing their cars. However, after looking around the parking lots of other students' cars, I determined both of their cars weren't the worst, so there.

I spoke to Atticus, and he told me he had gotten a few more phone calls from other doctors who wanted to take another look into it that he had spoken to before. As I said, when Dr. Spencer put his thoughts together, others seemed to latch onto his expertise in identifying exactly what it was. It made it easier for others to see clearly what the truth was in this matter. Another doctor from the northeastern part of the country injected very interesting concept that added quite a bit of strength to Dr. Spencer's conclusion, not that Dr. Spencer's conclusion needed any more strength, but it was very much welcomed. His name was Dr. Rabbinowitz, head of surgery at his respective hospital, and he went deeper into how the injury occurred.

When Atticus and he were conducting a phone interview, and later a video deposition, he began to explain in detail how he could add something of importance in the way he interpreted what happened. His way of explaining it was, again, quite simple, as you know sometimes the complicated issues have simple solutions if you'll just look in the right places. He said, "By the stress that was put on the tissue, it is very similar to a knockout punch by a boxer."

My thought was how that could be related to me and what caused the injury. Atticus went to tell me what else he said, "Just like a boxer throwing a knockout punch, even though he has a boxing glove on, the energy from the pressure delivers the blow. So looking at it like that, by the pressure from that was forced, even though there could have been surgical sponges between the blades of the retractors, maybe, and the tissue, the fact is the pressure is still there to cause enough trauma to stop and or slow down the flow of blood, and there again, that is what caused your injury. This solidifies the only thing it could be, and that is due to the retractors not being monitored or ever released during the surgery. The forced pressure was just too much to allow proper blood flow, and it literally starved the nerve tissue, causing enough of the slowed or stopped flow of blood to inflict serious and, in this case, permanent damage to the femoral nerve."

So now Dr. Rabbinowitz had joined the team. Atticus and I met at his offices to go over everything so far, and he informed me of some of the next things I could expect to occur. He told me there would be a short hearing at the courthouse, just as a formality, basically to announce a formal beginning of the lawsuit that could lead to a jury trial. He said, "Before it could travel as far as going to court, all of that wouldn't or couldn't happen until we will start taking depositions from everyone—"

I interrupted him and asked him to please define, although I thought I knew what a deposition was, I wanted a full definition and explanation of what it was and the process; after all, this was my first rodeo here, partner. Atticus smiled and said of course, and he gave me a crash course on it, as he often gave me crash courses, but he did them in a fashion that it was easy for me to understand fully what everything meant, well, almost maybe. He then said, "Just hang on because it is going to take at least sixteen months for us to get all the depositions finalized."

And my immediate thought was I know this was going to be expensive, and I also was aware Atticus had already put out a lot of money assembling everyone so far, and there was much more to accomplish, and he still hadn't asked me for a dime. If you recall, I volunteered to pay the filing fee when I took the paperwork to the courthouse in an effort to speed things up because the statute of limitations were about to run out. And I knew he already had a bundle invested and a larger bundle to go before this was all over. That made me feel very good about all of this because if he was that confident to put out this kind of money up front, then I was thinking our chances were pretty damn good that we would win either a settlement, or if it were to happen to go to court, then we would certainly win in court.

Of course now, well over three years had passed, and so many things had changed in my life and my attitude toward Dr. Larson was becoming increasingly bitter toward him as a human being. Atticus informed me that he was contacted by Dr. Larson's attorney, and they would begin their own depositions and would like to start with me. This was to be held at the offices of Wentworth & Wentworth, and the date would be determined soon. The deposition was scheduled two weeks from the day we talked. Atticus asked me to go to his office the afternoon before the morning of the deposition, and he would inform and prepare me as this was all new to me. I had no idea how these things were done, who all were involved or anything related to being part of a deposition.

Arriving at his office, I was again greeted with a smile, and coffee or water was offered. After a short wait, I was ushered to the conference room. Atticus came in and proceeded to educate me on what my deposition would be about and the reason(s) they were conducted. He simply said, "Just tell the truth and keep your answers short and to the point as there isn't any need to elaborate." Then his assistant walked in and handed Atticus a file. He opened it up and said, "Roland, here is the contingency contract that spells out how the award is to be split after either a settlement is made or if it should go to court, how the award from court proceedings will be split between you and our law firm."

It was just as he had explained, so I signed it; he signed it too, and it was witnessed by his assistant. The signing of this contract between Wentworth & Wentworth and me gave me a sense of truly being part of something meaningful, substantial, and certainly something big. So that was now completed, I asked him what would be the nature of the questions. He answered by saying, "They will ask you all about what you've been through and how you've maintained your current lifestyle and about your various doctor visits and the outcome of each."

Then we did a little role-playing which was most helpful, so I was ready. The next morning, at nine o'clock, I arrived at the offices of Wentworth & Wentworth. I was thirty minutes early as we were set to start at nine thirty that morning. I must admit, I was just a bit nervous, but I was also ready for it to begin. One of the attorneys for Dr. Larson arrived, then a court recorder/notary lady walked in, and they went into the conference room to get things set up. Atticus then came out of his office, and there we were, about to begin something I had never experienced.

At first it was just a basic introduction of who everyone was and why we were all assembled. And of course, it was all being recorded, and everything any of us were to say would be on record. Dr. Larson's attorney, Jane Delany, said she remembered meeting me at the motions hearing a couple of weeks ago and started off by asking me just simple identifying questions like who I was, family information, and then she switched gears and went straight into my illness, leading up to the day of the surgery and when I noticed there was a problem with my right leg, and all of this lasted just under two hours. I think I did pretty damn good for my first rodeo, and Atticus was pleased, and I was really happy to get this under my belt and over with. So that was just the first step of many steps before anything can be done. These are just the steps necessary that are set up in the legal system. And again, this is just one, the first one, with many more depositions to be completed on my side, the side of the plaintiff and the defendant; me being the plaintiff, and Dr. Larson the defendant in the case.

Time seemed to really slow down for a change, and my fatigue was now being officially called chronic fatigue by Dr. Mowji, and I was still taking opiates daily. My work was becoming more bothersome because of the fatigue, and I was seemingly spending more time stopped at a rest stop along the interstates than before or sleeping in airports. I just couldn't get the proper rest because I would wake up every hour or so, not to go to the bathroom, rather I would wake up to change positions or to get up and walk around a couple of minutes to return to bed to try to find a comfortable position that would allow me to fall back asleep. Life was getter harder because of the constant pain, and I just didn't know what else to do.

Dr. Mowji continued to strongly advise me to make some changes and pushed me to file for disability. He said, "You know you'll get it, so please look into it and just do it." He then said, "You really need to take care of yourself."

He was right. I also wanted to, but I needed to take care of my two children. Due to medical expenses, a divorce settlement, various fees paid to a few lawyers, two kids in college, and while I was out of work for months, my income was compromised; my bank account wasn't looking very healthy anymore. So I was really in a hard spot.

One of my closest friends, Charles Mitchell, came for a visit. I picked him up at the airport, and we arrived back at my house, and he just said, "I wanted to come see you because I know you've been through a lot, and you have a lot on your plate, and I know from our conversations, you have got some decisions to make."

Night came and we had a nice dinner, several drinks, and the next day, it seemed my troubles were far away, just having my friend in my house with me and having open conversations. He was to leave the day after to go back to Florida. On the way to the airport, he started asking me about the kids in school and mentioned the costs of various things, and he was aware I was pretty much taken by a few lawyers. Just as we were approaching the airport entrance, he reached into his shirt pocket and pulled out a check and proceeded to write a check for $10,000 and handed it to me and said, "Pay me back when you get rich." And he smiled.

I almost wrecked the car and was overwhelmed with emotion. I stopped and got out with him while he unloaded his bag, and I told him I couldn't take this and did everything short of stuffing it in one of his pockets. I think I tried, though. He said, "Yes, you can. I hope it will help you."

We quickly said our farewells as I needed to get out of the way of others at the drop-off space at the airport, and he walked away, and I left and I had to just stop when I could find a suitable stopping place and take this all in. There I was, just handed a large check written out for $10,000 from my close friend Charles. I think he planned to give the check to me as were we departing, knowing we wouldn't have time to discuss it. He just wanted to present it to me and move on. That was pretty much what happened.

Chapter 13

The next deposition was set up for Dr. Larson. To accommodate him, Atticus agreed to have it set up in the conference room at his clinic, which I thought was very thoughtful, perhaps too thoughtful. I will not make any further assessment regarding that, but I guess it was, as he said, accommodating. Oh well, here we go. However, Atticus surprised me again. This time he brought in a colleague of his that had worked with him before on various cases. His name was Larry Schloss. Here we go with another doctor/lawyer situation. He had a colorful past; he actually was a professional Major League baseball pitcher and injured his throwing arm, then went on to medical school and was a practicing surgeon, but sometimes life throws curveballs, and later he went to law school and became a lawyer. So he has seen both sides of the law regarding medical malpractice.

In we went into the very clinic. I felt as if I wasn't welcome in, and we proceeded to go into a conference room in the basement of the clinic. It was fairly well appointed; however, I thought it would have been a little nicer, considering it was a surgical clinic, but that's just my thinking. It really didn't matter because we were there to do some fact-finding through taking the deposition of Dr. Larson, not for me to critique the decor of the damn conference room. I am not sure what to call Larry, so I will stick with Mr. Schloss since his last degree was in law, but Mr. Schloss started off deposing Dr. Larson in the normal fashion, just getting the facts or who was present and the reason we were assembled, as again it was being recorded by a court recorder and notary. Mr. Schloss did introduce himself to Dr. Larson and his attorney as Larry Schloss, physician/attorney.

During the lengthy deposition, Atticus and Larry went pretty deep into the questioning process, and Dr. Larson primarily said nothing, except to answer with very generic answers as I am certain he was coached. The one question he was asked a few times in different ways was, "What do you think happened to Mr. Beckerman to cause his lumbosacral plexus injury?"

Dr. Larson's answer was always the same—"I don't know." Dr. Larson kept saying over and over, a little differently each time, "It is impossible for this kind of injury to have happened because of anything I did or didn't do."

During this series of questions, Dr. Larson appeared to become agitated and frustrated with most of the questioning. Larry and Atticus were holding their line tight, and his was coming undone, or it appeared it was. He kept trying to answer questions with answers that would point in other directions, such as he mentioned a few times the epidural could have been the cause of this problem. Another line of answers he used was his thinking it was something going on presurgery in an effort to put him in the clear. And he would often answer, "I am not sure I follow the question." And I think this was a simple move to buy some time to think, perhaps, who really knows? He was on the defensive during the entire deposition, and it was quite clear he was pushing in every direction he could, except in the direction of himself. The one thing he said that really told the story was, "When I get the retractors in place, I don't move them again."

There were many "objection to form," meaning Dr. Larson's attorney didn't like the question or felt it was being too invasive, but we were just trying to get to the root of the problem, and the problem was Dr. Larson and wasn't anyone else. He was in charge, he was the lead surgeon, he was the captain of that ship. He and his attorney knew what this was all about, and their defense was up, but our offense was being aggressive, and we were gaining strength because of how he evaded questions and didn't give direct answers because if he did, those answers would have opened the door for him to admit what and how this happened, as there was only one conclusion of how that has already been determined by our team of very experienced surgeons.

After a couple of hours of a lot of back and forth, and at times, it seemed to become a bit heated, more from the defense than our side, and I think that came from Dr. Larson becoming irritated by the line of questioning we threw out at him as they were quite direct and pointing to the area of concern—the time and point of injury. Since Larry was a trained physician/surgeon, he used more medical terms than I have ever heard in my life during the questioning, and I am sure that was the reason Atticus brought him in to assist with this deposition. Another crash course for me, no doubt, it was very interesting to witness such a process. Deposing me, the plaintiff, was quite a different picture than deposing the defendant, Dr. Larson. This one seemed to be more about discovery, while deposing me was more about the facts of what I had experienced, meaning it was two very different approaches to reach the expected results.

After the deposition was over, we went to a park. It was a beautiful day and just got out in the fresh open air and had, I guess, a short meeting to summarize what just happened. The notes were spread out on the hood of that nice Jaguar, with a slight breeze blowing, and we used a couple of briefcases to hold the papers down. But it was such a nice day, being and holding a meeting out in that weather was something out of a movie or perhaps a dream, my dream. Larry was quick to say, "Dr. Larson knows what happened and how, but of course, he wasn't going to admit to anything at all."

Atticus and Larry were a great team as I think the areas Larry didn't cover, Atticus did, and that was why Larry was brought in—to zero in more directly with medical terminology. There isn't any doubt, this cost Atticus a good bit of money to fly Larry in, and I am sure there was a fee involved for his professional services. These guys are professionals, and they don't work for free. But I still have only ninety-eight dollars tied up with Wentworth & Wentworth, and I am so happy to have them representing me in this case that continued to build by the day, or it sure seemed as if it was. Even though it was hurry up and wait, as Atticus had pointed out to me before, it still had the appearance this train was moving along just fine.

And moving on to more depositions, I was only present for my own and Dr. Larson's, but now Atticus informed me of approximately how many more there were to be. I was shocked by the number. Dr. Larson had as many or more on his team than what we had up to this point. Atticus told me there were going to be more to join our team that would add to his list of experts to be deposed. It was beginning to become very clear why it was going to take about sixteen months or so to get all of this work accomplished. I was continuing to learn more and more about this process, no wonder the stakes were high, just look what was involved.

Since I have never been involved or been part of a medical malpractice lawsuit, I had no idea of all of the hours that goes into not only just building a case, but once the fact is established there is a case, then all of the hearings, depositions, and meetings just seem to continue, but there is an end to all of this. It is called a trial, and I was in hopes it didn't make it that far, but Atticus said, "If they want to take it to trial, then that's what we'll do."

After witnessing how Dr. Larson handled himself, I wanted to close the door on him because of a few lies he told about me regarding what went on at his office and just in general. He seemed to look at me like I was at fault for accusing him of hurting me. What! This was just not going to fly with me, and my anger had set in more since being in the room with him and having to listen to his manner of speaking about something that was very real to me. And not once—not once—had he even uttered a word of compassion to me about any of this, not even an apology. I think that was what any considerate human being would have done under almost any circumstances, but maybe he thought he was just above that, and he was on another level. If that was what he thought, then he was wrong, and I wanted to push now harder than ever. It was so obvious now to me, and the team at Wentworth & Wentworth would do everything within their power and within the law to seek justice in the case for me and to hold Dr. Larson accountable for his mistake, made on me that day in the operating room.

Time was clicking right along. I was working, but damn it was hard. Every single day seemed to become a little harder, but I had cut my appointments down, and making the ones I did keep more important and certainly more profitable for Sanders Industries, and Richard, my boss, continued to support me in my efforts. Business was good, and our distribution had grown at a staggering rate. We were now in several states, and Richard couldn't be happier. I continued to attend staff meetings from time to time to go over our numbers and look over the P and L statements, and it seemed almost all line items were in the black, and that is great terminology and what you want to see on a P and L statement.

Having lunch on Saturdays with my good friend Jeff Greene, keeping in touch with my old boss and friend, Conrad Winchester, and of course staying in touch with Charles Mitchell just seemed to keep me motivated to keep pushing. All three certainly had my best interest in mind as they all were aware of just how difficult things were for me physically, and of course, we joked about my mental state, and all we seemed to do about that was laugh about it, as if to cover the fact maybe I am a little crazier now than I was a few years ago. The time had really flown.

Becky did get married, although I didn't know her new husband, but I was very happy for her, and since she was now married, I felt the connection between us is John and Gretchen; as I mentioned before, she is their mother, and nothing can or will ever change that fact. Gretchen was spending a little more time with her mother now than before, and perhaps it was because Becky had settled a bit and lives more normally, whatever the hell that is, who knows. John was still a little distant, and perhaps still hesitant for some reason or another, but I didn't question that nor do or would I question Gretchen on their feelings toward their mother.

What we went through early on wasn't any fun for any of us. Becky was in a difficult spot mentally of how to work with and deal with a husband in a wheelchair, and I give her that, but she is the one that pulled everything apart, just a fact. And due to that, I don't question nor try to influence either John or Gretchen in that arena. But Becky is married, and that is a good thing, and I wish them a lifetime of happiness and just don't bother me, did I say that? I guess I did, so let's just let that be our secret.

Deposition after deposition, it just seemed they were happening more often now, but they were getting done and getting closer to hopefully all being complete. One of the many depositions taken there was one that stuck out as unusual. The designer of the retractor used is a practicing physician, and his design comes mainly from his style of surgery and what he thought would be most useful, particularly during abdominal surgery, so Atticus thought it would be prudent to depose him regarding his very own design, certainly not to attack him in any way but to get a feel for his way of using it. He was very open to being deposed, and it was done by video conference. I was present at the offices of Wentworth & Wentworth and witnessed the video conference, my first by the way.

It was, in general, the usual deposition of introduction and then on to business. He explained in detail how the instrument was to be used. A little deeper into the course of questioning, Atticus started a little different line of questioning, and all of a sudden—*boom*—there it was again. He said, "Of course during surgery, the retractors must be released to relieve the tissue from any kind of compression that could lead to damage." Atticus asked for him to be more detailed and to clarify what he meant by damage. He went on to say, "There is a lot of tissue, and the psoas muscle located in the lower sections are all connected and could be affected, and lots of nerves throughout that could be damaged by compression, putting or causing trauma and slowing—or even stopping—blood flow to keep them healthy and alive. When this occurs, it starves the nerves of blood and can cause nerve damage. Sort of like if you stop watering a houseplant, what happens to it, the answer is simple—it dies."

All sounded pretty clear to me, and it must have given Atticus what he needed because he moved on with his series of questions. Another crash course for me, and I seemed to have had lots of them in the past four years now, and I enjoyed every single one of them as I have always been a sponge for knowledge. My father once told me, he said, "Son, you are full of knowledge. Some maybe useless but don't ever stop learning." I took his advice and I am still a sponge.

I keep mentioning how time was flying by, and now was no different. It occurred to me that because of my opiate use, I seemed to lose or partially lose my sense of time because when the pain was hitting me hard, it alone seemed to occupy my sense of being aware of time, and then when the opiates kicked in, time seemed to not even matter as much, and somehow it all started to run together; therefore my internal clock was pretty fucked up most of the time, but I continued to push forward as I had no other viable choice. I continued to miss exits at times while traveling on the interstates, but I never seemed to miss an appointment. I do have my priorities still embedded deeply in place. But pain had become a large part of my life and the management of my life just to maintain the level I expect out of myself. I don't need someone or anyone to tell me what or how to do my job. I know better than anyone because I use an infallible method of measurement regarding my performance in my business. It is called revenue; as long as I continue to increase incoming revenue to Sanders Industries, then I know I am doing my job, whether I work five days or two days a week, as long as I get it done, that satisfies me and seems to continue to keep Richard pleased.

Richard and I were recently attending and displaying at a regional trade show, and just before the opening bell, we were standing around in a circle with a few of our colleagues from various parts of the Southeast, and there I was, standing there, still wearing that brace on my right leg under my pants with a cane, and the cane jokes were flying, and I was the one mostly spouting them off. We were all laughing and carrying on like a group of guys could do. And Richard spoke up and referred to all of our joking and kidding around and said, "You guys are cracking jokes, and they all seem to be centered around Roland, but I am going to tell all of you, I would rather have him than any three of you guys combined. Mr. Roland Beckerman gets more done in one day than most of you guys get done in a week." And he turned and walked away.

We all looked at each other and just laughed a bit. I think there was some truth to that, but how much, I don't know, never will, but the jokes stopped. The bell sounded, and the trade show was open, time to go to work. It did, however, make me feel ten feet tall for a few moments. I thanked Richard later for his profound statement he made concerning me. He quickly answered, "I meant it." It was never brought up again.

I kept in close contact with Atticus, and it seemed I received copies of more progress he had made in the case of more copies of depositions from Dr. Larson's side of the aisle. And I would get a call from him at least once every week or two with verbal updates to confirm some of the copies of documents he had forwarded to me in the mail. I looked forward to each and all correspondence as I looked at it like they were building blocks, and the building was getting taller and taking shape. I would cross paths with Dr. Larson from time to time around town, and he would always look at me with a definite stare, and if eyes could talk, they were saying, *What are you doing to me, and why are you trying to ruin my life and reputation?* And my immediate thought would always be the same, *I haven't done anything wrong, but you sure as hell have, and you have damn nearly ruined my life.* Then I would just go on about my way, and sometimes I would see him and just imagine he wasn't even there. It is a small town, and we both have to live in it together, so I would just block him out of my sight, and he can stare at me or whatever he chooses to do, but I was through with him just as he was through with me, except I wanted him held accountable. And an apology, as I have mentioned before, would be nice, not that it would be accepted because too much water has gone over the dam now for me to ever accept it, but I would love to just hear it for the sake of knowing he finally offered it up. It would be meaningless except for me to just hear him say it.

I once asked Atticus how I should react to my crossing paths around town with Dr. Larson. He pretty much summed it up the way I was already looking at it, and he reminded me it was a small town, and we're going to find ourselves either in the same room, on the same side of the street on the sidewalk downtown, in the grocery store, or in various functions and/or events held in town for the community. He was right, and I continued to find myself in all of those situations, but I just blocked him out as if he wasn't there. That was my mechanism of not wanting to see or be near him at all, not because I was afraid of a confrontation but more like if there were to be a confrontation, I don't think it would end well for him as my rage would very likely surface; unlike me for that to ever happen, but I do have my limits, and he had pushed me to the edge, so I don't need a spark. And the fact I carry a cane that, well, I guess, could be used as a weapon—I hate to even have such a thought, but I do so I just needed to keep doing what I was doing and just stay clear, and if I did stay clear, then nothing like that would ever happen.

I was curious of how many more depositions needed to be taken now as it seemed I had a large stack of correspondence from Atticus with copies of several of them. In no way was I questioning Atticus's reasons for doing so many as I was only curious because I certainly didn't know or had any basis to think or know otherwise, just curious that's all. So I did ask him about that, and he calmly said, "We are getting to the end of this tunnel, and the light is getting clearer now, so maybe just one or two more, then we can move on to the next step in our process. Roland, just continue to be patient, and we will find some common ground soon."

Not sure what "common ground" meant, but I had a good feeling about it, and my confidence level and trust in Atticus and the law firm of Wentworth & Wentworth and of course our team was at an all-time high. It just seemed like everything I had hoped for was coming together wonderfully well. And my children, John and Gretchen, were doing well. As I mentioned, Becky was now married, the medical malpractice suit was falling into place; however, the one thing that wasn't going so well was me. Continuing to keep up the front—and it was a fake front—that everything was just fine with me was getting harder and harder. I was having thoughts of even crossing over the line, just thoughts, although thoughts they were, indeed.

The one thing that would always pull me away and out from under the very dark clouds while having those dark thoughts—I said one thing, but the truth was there were two—were John and Gretchen. They didn't really know this, but just the thought of them pulled me through more very bad times that led to dark thoughts than I would like to admit. I so wanted to see them continue to grow and prosper and become fine young adults. And I wanted them to have a great life and mainly to live life to the fullest and have some fun along the way. They were, and still are, the only thing I truly care about, in every way, combining every human instinct in a protective way. I will go on record and say they kept me alive so far, and it looks like these two will continue to give me my life because in the end, they are really all I have. They are part of me, and when I look at either of them, I see great things, and they are continuing to show me just how wonderful they both are. This is truly a never-ending story about them, and I will keep it alive and well as long as I live. They just don't know what they've done for me during this fucked up mess, but they continue to be there for me, and I will always be there for both of them, unconditionally.

Chapter 14

Atticus and I continued to stay in touch, and he was keeping me updated on everything that transpired. Still a learning curve for me, and until anyone has direct involvement in a case like this, one has no way of knowing just how deep things like these are. Filing a lawsuit, yeah, no problem, just do it and go from there. No, it isn't that way at all, and I would have never imagined the depth of this process until now as I found myself more than knee-deep with a long way to go before we even approached the end.

Atticus had been great in keeping me informed, and more so, his level of professionalism was off the charts. I couldn't have asked for a better partner. I did feel we were sort of a partnership in this because we both shared seemingly every move together. There must be things he did that I was not aware of, and that was all right with me because I had put my complete trust in him. He was the only lawyer I met with that I know had told me the truth from the very beginning, even the time when he told me he didn't think he could help me and for me to seek counsel elsewhere; he was being truthful. That was a big blow to me at the time, only to later get that phone call from him, inviting me to go see him and have lunch together when he asked me for the case. That is just one example of his professionalism and his worthiness of earning my complete trust. Plus, the fact he still hadn't asked me for a dime. That alone right there heightened my feeling toward him and his law firm. His entire staff has always treated me with utmost respect and decency. It was always, "Hello, Mr. Beckerman, how are you, can I get you anything, Mr. Beckerman?" And asking me if I was comfortable, probably because it was obvious by the way I walked and squirmed around while sitting, me just trying to find a comfort zone as the pain was always there, but still they all made me feel welcome.

I was scheduled to attend a staff meeting at Sanders Industries and asked Richard if we could have dinner the night before, as I usually come in the night before those meetings anyway, and Richard responded sure, he'd love to, and told me to pick a restaurant. Well, I wanted a quiet one, you know, not one of those loud chains full of people trying to see who can talk and laugh the loudest, as if it were some kind of contest, because I had an important subject to bring up and discuss. The subject had been on my mind and had gotten quite heavy, and I thought I would just throw it out there to Richard to see what his reaction would be. It was a bit like rolling the dice, not knowing the outcome or even the level of the result, but I thought the time was now.

The subject was, I wanted to think about truly working just a couple of days a week but no change in doing the various trade shows. I know he was somewhat aware I was not working exactly full-time anyway, but it had gone sort of untalked about and not really officially discussed. Working from home and only going to the corporate offices except for meetings did have its advantages, but I was becoming more fatigued, and I just wanted to be up-front and completely honest with the man that signs my check. So I entered it into the conversation by just coming out and saying, it seemed, all in one quick and long sentence.

Our dinner hadn't arrived yet, and as he sipped on a bourbon and water, he looked at me, as we were eye to eye, and began to tell me how much he has enjoyed working with me and thanked me for all the business I had brought to Sanders Industries. And at that point, I just knew what was next. I felt as if he was building up to a stopping point to tell me, well, it's been nice, and to discuss a severance arrangement and a time frame for me to leave Sanders Industries, but instead the complete opposite happened. He had been expecting this for some time now, and he wasn't going to bring it up. He was just waiting on me in my own time to bring it up, but he expected it. So no surprise to him, but the surprise was he told me if I could give him a couple of days a week of solid work that would fulfill my duties, as I have since I came onboard with Sanders Industries, he would be

happy. And he added, "But of course I do expect you to continue with the trade shows as usual."

My response was no problem there. Trade shows for me
were quite easy, getting the booths set up for display, I always
had help and support staff with me for that, and a trade show
usually lasts for three days. So all I had to do was show up,
check in my hotel, spend time on the showroom floor, and
since my mobility was compromised, Richard allowed me
to have a comfortable chair in the booth, which we never
allowed before, but I had a special need because standing for
eight hours was just not possible anymore.

So we continued our conversation in an effort to sort of
finalize our new agreement between the two of us, and once
again, I was riding high, just knowing it was now all out in
the open with my employer. The thought came back in my
head from the time we were standing around at a trade show
floor with a few of our colleagues, and Richard told them he
would rather have me than any three of the guys combined. I
knew then he meant it, and of course, I reminded him of that
moment and what he said. He responded by saying, "Yes, I
do, and yes, I meant it."

All right, dinner was over, and he ordered one more
drink. He had his usual bourbon and water, and mine was,
as always, scotch on the rocks. Afterward we walked out
together, simply said see you in the morning at the staff
meeting. Richard paused at that moment and told me to
keep our conversation just between the two of us because,

"I think you'll agree, this is a different kind of arrangement, not very normal, wouldn't you say?" Both of us had a good feeling about our conversation, and I simply walked across the parking lot to my hotel, and he got in his car and left.

I was going to be back in Lynchburg, Virginia, again soon on business, and I contacted Atticus, thought perhaps since I was close by, we could meet. He began to inform me that he had just drafted a letter to me, asking for a meeting, along with some other important information that included copies of another deposition for my review. So we settled on a day and time. Walking into the offices of Wentworth & Wentworth was no different; a smiling face met me, and by now, I had become a regular, and everyone there seemed to know me, and each time I visited seemed to become a little warmer. It was just a pleasure to visit. But I was there not to socialize, but it was business as usual with Atticus.

This time he brought his son, Atti, in the conference room. Atti had recently joined Wentworth & Wentworth when he graduated from law school and passed the bar exam. Atti was a very nice and personable young man, and his father, in my opinion, would be the perfect mentor. I never really knew who the other Wentworth of Wentworth & Wentworth was, but now maybe they called the firm that with the anticipation of Atti coming onboard one day. Who knows, and I never asked. I do know there were a few other lawyers in the firm, I think five in all, and now six with Atti. I did ask, I had to ask Atti if he was a junior. He answered,

"Why, yes I am number 2, the second, junior, whatever you want to tag me with is fine, but yes, I am a chip off the old block, name included."

Atticus had a very large file brought into the conference room and spread it all out and briefed me with a few short but to the point sentences on each of the items he picked up and/or pointed to and proceeded to tell me we now had a total of fourteen depositions. I was shocked as I was aware we had deposed several doctors on both sides as experts in building the case, but fourteen depositions, that was a lot. I guess I hadn't been keeping count, and it also was proof of the time, effort, and, of course, money, the amount of money it took to get all this accomplished, I knew, was a consider- able amount, all coming out of Atticus's coffers that belonged to Wentworth & Wentworth. To me it seemed written in stone—they were all in with me and my case, no doubt.

He continued speaking about everything on the table and said, "Now that we seem to have assembled and accom- plished all of the necessary depositions of everyone, I feel we've developed a very strong case on your behalf, but we still have a long way to go."

Atticus carried on and got to a point and informed me that Dr. Larson's attorney had contacted him and mentioned perhaps having a meeting of arbitration. Here we were taking it to the next level, and I don't even really know what arbi- tration is. I think I know the basic definition of the word, but I didn't know how it would fit into what we were doing.

Atticus explained it perfectly and made it quite understandable. He simply told me it was the process of both sides getting together with attorneys present with someone from the court system, most of the time a judge, in an effort to make presentations and perhaps to make suggestions for reaching a possible settlement. Atticus continued, "But in my experience," he said, "it is more of a sparring round or two that reveals how things could go if it were to be carried on into the courtroom. But for whatever reason, I am glad they called and have suggested we look into having a meeting of arbitration."

Still a bit unclear, I asked, "What does this mean exactly? Is it a good thing?"

Atticus answered by just saying it was all part of the process, but yes, it was a good thing. So leaving it at that, I had a feeling of yes, we were continuing to move forward. I still found it hard to believe or even imagine fourteen depositions, just amazing. We had a few minutes of general conversation as Atticus asked me about my health and how my pain was and how I was managing it, and he always asked about John and Gretchen. Since my association with Atticus began, we seem to have learned a few things about each other out of the conference room and away from the legal arena, and he seemed like a really neat guy and great father, and he had learned a lot about me too. I don't want to push things or paint a picture that isn't there, but I almost felt as if we've become friends. Atticus is a few years older than me and worlds apart professionally, two totally different worlds we

work in, but still I felt strongly there was a friendship building between two men that understood each other; however,
one is simply helping the other. It could easily be the other
way around, but it wasn't.

Our time was about to end for that meeting, and I was
fully aware of everything as Atticus covered it all, including
the probability of a meeting of arbitration that could occur
soon. As usual, in closing, he said, "We'll be in touch."

I always took him at his word as he was always in touch
with me and kept me in the loop seemingly on almost every
move. I was always getting something in the mail from him,
just copies of everything that occurred. I had built a file, and it
was growing rapidly, especially since the depositions started,
and I would review it mainly out of astonishment, but also I
knew I wanted to keep up with all of the happenings of what
Atticus was doing, and he was going well beyond any point
of expectations I had ever had in building this case. But that
is the deal, when you need legal help, you seek out the best
lawyer you can find and hand him the ball. He had proven in
so many ways he is quite the professional, and I am so grate-
ful I was given his name, even though he pushed me away
early on but later to reel me back in after, and only after, he
had a very strong heavyweight medical expert that identified
where and how the injury occurred and wanted to help, Dr.
Spencer, head of surgery, at a very prestigious teaching hospital, one of the best in the United States.

It seemed every move Atticus made was calculated and was executed with such precision. It was really quite impressive, at least he impressed me, but I also realized he was simply doing his job. That was so obvious he loved what he did, I doubt he will ever retire. From my costly experience, particularly in the recent past, I found just like in any other profession, you have good doctors and bad doctors, good schoolteachers and bad schoolteachers, and in this case, I found there are good lawyers, and yes, there are bad lawyers. But in what I said above, I want to clearly state when I said you have good doctors and bad doctors, I wasn't, in any way shape or form of fashion, referring to Dr. Larson. As far as I am concerned, he is likely a good husband, father, and probably a good doctor. I was merely speaking in general to make a point. But I will make it clear, I have witnessed good people doing bad things unintentionally, bad deeds do occur, and when they do, good people allow themselves to be accountable because it is the moral thing to do as a human. It doesn't always happen that way, but I for one think it should.

Chapter 15

Atticus contacted me and asked me to find a conference room locally to rent for an afternoon, from one to five, in the afternoon of a certain date that was two weeks out for a meeting of arbitration. Dr. Larson's attorneys had requested this meeting, so Atticus would be coming here for this purpose. We talked a bit, and I told him of a couple of possible and suitable places for us to all meet, and he just told me whatever the cost was to let him know who to send a check to for the rental. He also requested beverage service. I inquired what types of beverages, he chuckled and said, "Just water and coffee, maybe a few soft drinks." Chuckling again, he said, "But not a full bar, just coffee, water, and a few soft drinks. We'll celebrate later if there is anything to celebrate."

So I went to work on finding the right spot for this meeting. I called my friend Jeff Greene, my Saturday lunch buddy, I knew he had lots of contacts with the banks in town and was on the board of one. I thought maybe he could help me with finding a suitable conference room to rent. He was knowledgeable of my case and knew what arbitration was and said he would look into it for me, and I reminded him of the date and time. Just the next afternoon, I had gotten in from a day trip seeing a potential customer. He stopped by my house and told me he had the perfect conference room with private restrooms and a full bar area that could be stocked with whatever we needed. It was located at one of the banks downtown, upstairs, and there is a private entrance, an elevator in the rear of the building, he went on to tell me. I did ask if this was the bank he was on the board with, and he said yes, it was. Then I inquired what the cost would be. He didn't really answer the question; we talked on a bit, and the subject was changed, then we realized it was cocktail hour, so we sat out on my porch and had a cold beer and ate peanuts. Isn't that what two old friends do, sit around, drink beer and eat peanuts, and throw the shells over the rail into the bushes; organic matter, I think we called it, good for the soil. After we finished our beer and ate all the peanuts, he got up to leave, and I asked him again what the cost would be, and he said, "Don't worry about it, it's free for you, my friend."

I know it wasn't free, but he wouldn't give me a number to give to Atticus. He just said it wasn't being used that day anyway, so we could use it at no charge. What could I say except wow, thank you very much.

I called Atticus the next morning and told him we were meeting downtown in an upstairs conference room over a bank that even had an outside entrance in the back of the building with an elevator. And it has a private restroom and a full bar area that would be stocked with just what he requested—coffee, water, and soft drinks. It was totally private. Atticus asked me what the fee was so he could get a check cut and sent and who to send it to. I quickly replied and told him there would not be a charge. I informed him my good friend and board member of the bank, Jeff Greene, secured it for me and wouldn't hear of accepting any payment. Atticus said, "That is nice of him, sure is wonderful to have good friends like that in your town and be sure to thank him for me, please. And thank you for your efforts in securing this space, and it sounds just perfect." The conversation continued. Atticus said he would get all parties on the same page and confirmed for the meeting set for that time and date. Once again, Atticus said, "We'll be in touch." That must be a thing of his, but he means what he says and says what he means.

That seemed to be a quick two weeks in anticipation as I think I was getting a bit anxious about this meeting. I had been deposed myself and had witnessed the deposition of Dr. Larson, taken by doctor/lawyer Larry Schloss and Atticus Wentworth. Schloss, as mentioned, was brought in by Atticus in an effort to speak in more medical terms and to fully understand anything or any medical term Dr. Larson could possibly throw out during the deposition. But now, much later, here we all were assembled in a super nice conference room. It had a very large mahogany table, seemed these type of rooms like mahogany conference tables with lights that seemed to spotlight each chair at the table with a nice brass chandelier hanging over the table that was turned very low by a rheostat. Acoustically this one was quite special as it seemed you could hear a whisper from across the room and certainly from across the table. The reception area was well appointed too, except it had hardwood floors and a big Persian rug, but the conference room was carpeted with a short tight pile as the chairs rolled effortlessly, and perhaps the carpet had something to do with the acoustics in the room being nearly perfect.

It was now one o'clock in the afternoon and seemed we were about to begin. Starting out, it seemed very similar to that of a deposition, only it was a step further into the legal system itself as it was another piece of the legal puzzle that was necessary. After all of the introductions, Dr. Larson's team was on one side and our team on the other side of the table with an older man at the head of the table. He was to be the presiding judge, in case there were any differences that needed to be decided upon. He really hardly spoke; I guess it wasn't his job nor his place to speak unless there was an issue that would demand his attention.

Dr. Larson's team pretty much laid out bits and pieces of their case, and Atticus laid out more than just bits and pieces. He was, in my opinion, rather aggressive, and me being an aggressive businessman, that suited me just fine. I could see exactly what he was doing and what the other side wasn't doing. Atticus was establishing his or our ground, and he was doing so quite firmly. The defendants were seemingly playing catch-up, meaning they were attempting to respond to Atticus's facts as he laid them out on the table. I had determined that arbitration is, in fact, a meeting to settle disputes as I could clearly see, but it was just as Atticus said, "It's like legal sparring." And as the meeting progressed, that became more evident.

In the back of my mind, I was in hopes that Dr. Larson's team would walk in and just make an offer to settle and be done, but that didn't happen, and deeper in my mind, I really didn't think it would, but one can hope and hope I did, but that wasn't in the cards that day. It was just back and forth all afternoon. It was getting close to four o'clock. We had been at it pretty hard with only one five-minute break, and we all attacked the bar area; some got coffee or water, and I had a Pepsi poured over ice, Atticus had a Pepsi and coffee. I couldn't tell you what anyone else had, but we all sort of took turns gaining access to the area. It was purely two teams, so we didn't chitchat, and being in the same room with Dr. Larson for me was strained, to say the least. But all remained very civil and cordial, but there were no words spoken between Dr. Larson and me. Other than a greeting, I don't think Atticus had much of or maybe nothing else he said directly to Dr. Larson. All of his speech was directed to his attorney.

Well, as I mentioned, it was getting close to four o'clock—perhaps just after—and Atticus started winding the meeting down without any opposition from the opposing team. I think they were worn out and ready for it to end. And truth be known, I was ready too because my hopes weren't going to happen, and I was aware of it early on, and it was quite a grueling afternoon spent in the conference room of a bank arranged by my good friend Jeff.

The opposing team vacated the room first after packing up a few briefcases full of papers and documents. And after they left, Atticus and I stayed for a few minutes just to debrief and decompress a bit, and oddly enough, the older man, a judge I think, held up and offered up his opinion. I don't know if this was customary, unusual, or even ethical, but he stayed a few minutes and said, "I think you'll be offered a settlement in this case because of the strong facts you submitted today, and I don't think going to court would be in his best interest."

Atticus agreed but made no comment. He then punched the elevator button, and the doors closed behind him, and he was gone. In summary, Atticus told me he thought it went well, but now they were even more aware of what they were up against from what he threw out on the table, and he threw plenty of hard facts that came directly from our expert medical witnesses. It was just worded differently by Atticus to fit the legal language he used and did so quite eloquently, again proving to me just how high his level of professionalism truly is.

We left together going down in the elevator and parted ways in the private parking area behind the bank. There wasn't any celebration; there wasn't any reason for that, not yet anyway. Another step now is behind us, so I was wondering what was next, and during a phone conversation with Atticus, I asked him what was next. He calmly said, "We wait."

We talked on for a few more minutes, and as usual, he asked about John and Gretchen, as he always does, and I know he was genuine in wanting to know. And more so now, I felt a friendship was continuing to build. We've learned a lot more about each other and have spent a lot of time together. Of course, the bond was the case, and without it, I would have never met this guy but just seemed we were on the same avenue in more ways than one.

I didn't know it, but we have a mutual friend; so strange because he lives very near me. Atticus and he have known each other for a while. As a matter of fact, he was part of a lawsuit that Atticus had won in a settlement a while back, and they developed quite a friendship. I had no way of knowing this until Atticus called me and said he was going to be very near and asked if I would like to have lunch with him and a friend of his. I said of course, then had to ask if he is local. He responded by saying, "Yes, he is local, and you probably know him. His name is Robin Jenson, Dr. Robin Jenson."

I immediately responded, Yes, of course I know him. He is a friend of mine, I know him well, what a great guy he is. Sure, I would love to have lunch with you guys. How do you know Robin?"

He answered, "We will talk about it later, but I will be there next Thursday. I told Dr. Jenson to pick out a quiet restaurant and secure us a table out of the way and to give you a call."

I thought how damn cool was this, and then my mind started turning, all the while thinking what this was all about, could it be about the case, couldn't be or could it be? *I shouldn't second-guess or stress over it. Damn, let's just go have lunch together and see what it is all about.* I did get a call from Robin, and he seemed excited that Atticus had invited us to have lunch. He had already picked out a place that was out of the way, a diner-type place out in the county. I had eaten there once a while back, great food, and it was indeed quiet, just seemed like the perfect quiet type of place Atticus asked for.

So there we were, three guys, a lawyer, a doctor, and me. The lunch turned out to be more than just lunch, but I can tell you, Atticus ordered fried flounder again. He seems to really like fried flounder. Robin happened to have the same. I couldn't tell you what I had and seems I am quite observant, always have been, but just not observant about myself, just my surroundings. I think that might be a good trait of mine, being observant and attention to detail, I'll take it.

During the time we were actually eating, the subject of a trial from a few years back came up in conversation, and bits and pieces of my case entered into the conversation. I was mostly quiet, not making many comments, just observing and taking it all in. Robin looked at me and said, "This is one of my cornfield conversations."

I looked around and didn't even see a cornfield, and I said, "Robin, what is a cornfield conversation?"

He laughed looked at Atticus and said, "Roland, it is a conversation you want to have but don't want anyone to hear a word of it. In other words, a conversation about topics with only the ones you trust."

I thought I got it now, and the conversation shifted toward me and what happened to me. But first I was told a while back, Atticus filed a suit against his medical practice, not him personally but one of his partners, and Robin actually was active in pushing for a settlement for the plaintiff early on in the case. Robin told me he had utmost respect for Atticus, and Atticus was quick to speak up and say the feeling was mutual. He told me making a settlement doesn't necessarily admit that someone was wrong and certainly doesn't mean they did anything wrong intentionally, but bad things happen to good people on both ends. He said his partner did something wrong, not intentional, but he was the responsible one, and he took it upon myself to persuade him to allow his med mal insurance agent to handle a clean and clear settlement. It was done quickly; it didn't make the news, and the main thing was it was over.

I was shocked with this testimonial. The whole time, Atticus just sat there, finishing up his fried founder. Atticus then began telling me they have had a lot of conversation about my case, and early on, Robin knew the case was ongoing pretty much from the beginning, about the first time I met with Atticus prior to him leaving the case. I found more respect for Robin, even knowing something and speaking about me but not ever mentioning it to me out of respect for the man he was conversing with, Atticus. They were discussing this in confidence because Robin is a colleague of Dr. Larson. Although he isn't a surgeon, he still refers patients to him and works with him on cases and literally pass each other in the halls of the hospital almost daily. However, Robin is a realist, and Atticus knows he is, and this meeting again turned sharply in my direction, and he was onboard, not officially, but he had assisted Atticus by consulting, and Robin told me he had studied the files, charts, scan results, and operatory notes, and he was in total agreement with Dr. Spencer, the first expert to pinpoint the problem and to ask to assist with my case.

I learned a lot that day, first about Robin's own case; well, the case didn't name him as the defendant, but his partner was named, so that's pretty close, and what it resulted in and why. And I felt I had a closer friend than I ever would have known by him consulting on my behalf with Atticus, all the while keeping it secret until I was invited to the cornfield conversation. This seemed to have started something; there seemed to be more cornfield conversations with Robin in my future. Well, we were both living in the same town, which made it easy for us to meet for lunch, and it seemed the diner out in the county became the restaurant of choice, simply because if we arrived after, say, the lunch crowd rush, we could sit quietly at our chosen table in the back and hardly be seen by anyone, not that we didn't want to be seen together. On the contrary, we were seen together many times, but to have private conversations, this was the perfect spot. We did it so often we even got to know Mary, our wait person. I think she liked us because we tipped her well, and she kept the iced tea coming.

These conversations meant so much to me, and it just continued to build a bond of trust and, of course, a stronger friendship as he knew something about me, and I knew something about him that was related. It was definitely cornfield-conversation material that we discussed there, not to be heard by anyone, just between two friends, and he had compassion for his fellow man, and it showed through by him pushing for a settlement within his own firm, and that compassion was passed right along to me, and I was appreciative.

Another meeting of arbitration was requested by Dr. Larson's team after a six-week gap since the first one. I learned of this in a letter from Atticus. It was a very brief letter, more in a memo type, as he often speaks it on paper, but the message was clear and asked me to call him at my convenience. I called, was put on hold only for a minute or maybe two,

Atticus got on the phone, and said, "I guess you got my note. They want to have another meeting, and I will arrange it with someone to preside."

I was thinking maybe the same older guy, a judge, as last time. Atticus asked me if I could secure the same conference room, and he said, "This time tell your friend I insist on some kind of fee for the use of it. But let me know if the date and time will work, and if so, I will let everyone know that it is a go."

My curiosity was running wild, and I asked, "Why do you think they are asking for another meeting?"

He answered by saying, "Well, you know what arbitration is designed for, and from what I can gather, from all of this, is maybe they think it is time to offer a settlement. Otherwise why would they want to assemble all of us again, and I was told their medical malpractice insurance agent is going to be present this time around. So again maybe, just maybe, they will offer a settlement."

I asked, "What makes you think they might want to offer to settle? I am very curious."

He responded by saying, "The person in charge is actually Dr. Larson, maybe he sees what he is up against. He doesn't have a single expert witness on his team that has offered any suggestion or fact of what could have caused this injury. But we have, as you know, several respected expert witnesses that have testified while being deposed and will testify again in court, if necessary, to those facts, and they all point to the same reason—compression and trauma caused by the improper use of the retractors that Dr. Larson used. They just don't seem to have a case or good defense in my opinion. Therefore, they have asked for another meeting." Atticus went on to say, "Stranger things have happened."

So I truly didn't know what to expect. I only hoped they were ready to make an offer. He went on to say, "Even if they were to make an offer, we don't have to accept it, but if they make an offer, that is ammunition for us to negotiate until we can both agree, and you will be a major part of making decisions of and during that process. I also think Dr. Larson is taking advice from his counsel, and I think they see what we have and clearly see what they don't have, so having said that, I think we are in a good position. Do you think you can get the same conference room?"

Responding back, I told him I would check with Jeff Greene and let him know as soon as possible. He then reminded me to tell my friend Jeff to let us know what the fee would be because he expected to pay this time around. He chuckled and said, as always, "We'll be in touch."

I reached out to Jeff Greene about securing the conference room. He happened to be out of town but told me he would be back day after tomorrow, and he would stop by the bank and look at the conference room schedule. He told me there were two conference rooms, but he had let me use the main one with all the nicer amenities and went on to say he would check as soon as he got back. As a matter of fact, he got back the morning of the day he mentioned and suggested we go to lunch and then we'd stop by the bank. So we picked a place just down the street from the bank and met there for lunch, and afterward, we made a short walk up the street, Jeff a fast walker and me not so fast anymore, to the bank.

When we walked into the lobby, I told Jeff I had to sit down for a minute as I was wreaking with pain and felt I couldn't take another step. Jeff understood, he had seen me like this countless times. He asked me if wanted some water. I snapped back at him and told him I didn't want any fucking water, I wanted to stop hurting. I felt bad and apologized. He responded by saying, "Oh hell, man, don't worry about it. Come on, man, let's go look at the conference room calendar."

So upstairs we went using the main elevator, of course, but we made it up there, and my pain was just piercing in my right leg, but what the hell else was new. I took my seat in a nice leather chair up in the reception area where the booking calendar is kept, and upon looking at it, Jeff informed me it was wide open for the whole day, as sometimes two meetings can be held in the same day, one in the morning hours, which leaves the afternoon hours open for meetings. But the whole day was open, so he penciled me in for one o'clock on the day Atticus requested, and I asked again about the cost.

He said, "Well, it is actually $500 for a full day with refreshments. Lunch is extra, but for a half a day, it would be 250, but don't worry about the cost."

I then proceeded to tell him that my lawyer insisted he pay a fee but was also very appreciative of the favor of not charging the first time, but he just told me to get a number from you. Jeff said, "Hell, man, tell him to send a check to you for $200 made out to the bank and just give it to me, and I will slam it through."

Slam it through, not sure what that meant but Jeff had a strange sense of humor, so I just went with it. I called Atticus the next morning and told him we were all set again and for him to drop a check in the mail to me for $200 and make the check out to Southern National Bank. I said, "Jeff told me to have it sent to me so I could give it directly to him, and he would 'slam it through.'" And I laughed, not sure if Atticus caught the humor but I did.

I wasn't getting much sleep at night, as usual, waking up every hour or so, only to hear my alarm clock yelling at me to wake up and either get on the road or get to the airport to get to my next appointment. It was just getting harder and just more difficult. I later called for an appointment with Dr. Sussman, neurologist, again and asked for another EMG. The appointment was made, and after a cordial and quite pleasant entrance to his examining room, we had a nice conversation. He asked about John and Gretchen, and I proudly gave a positive response on both of them. And he asked me some general questions about my health and why I wanted another EMG. "Do you think it will show some improvement?" he asked with a hopeful expression.

I responded by saying, "Not really, I just want to see if I am any worse."

He then changed his look and said, "All right, let's get to it and see what you have."

After going over the results with me, he, along with Dr. Mowji who continues to advise me to get off the road, said, "You should really try to slow it down."

I went through the short version of my last meeting with my boss, Richard, at Sanders Industries and told him I was doing as much as I could to keep my job, and my boss was continuing to work with me, but now it just seemed that was getting to be too much for me to handle. I really didn't know what to do. But the results were in, and I hadn't shown any real improvement regarding the EMG we just did. To speak of, yes, there was some slight improvements that occurred over the recent years, but not anything to be celebrating. He looked at me and just said, "Roland, I am afraid that we, Dr. Hyatt, the head of neurology I referred you to quite a while ago, are right. Especially now that more time has passed, I am afraid it is definitely permanent, just as we suspected from the very beginning. But I am glad you allowed Dr. Hyatt to work with you some. As I said, I wanted you to see someone with more gray hair than I have."

Here's the irony; Dr. Sussman, even though he is younger in years of age, he has more gray hair than Dr. Hyatt, but I wasn't going to tell him that or make mention of his having more gray hair. I left, and as always, it was a pleasure to have seen him again professionally, and I always feel welcome there, and he really seems to care for me as I am sure he treats his patients the same, but he makes me feel special.

I received the check from Atticus and dropped it off by Jeff's office downtown for him to slam it through—still don't know what that means, just one of Jeff's sayings. I guess he gets lots of checks. But upon opening the envelope, I noticed the check wasn't made out for $200, rather Atticus had it made out for $250, which was the actual rate for half a day. He wrote out a note on the memo attached to the check, and it just said, *Tell Jeff thank you for waiving the fee the first time.*

Chapter 16

Enter round 2 of arbitration, and I was welcoming it to happen and was very anxious. Atticus was continuing to enter this with extreme caution and kept telling me to just sit back, remain calm, and to not say a word or answer any question without first consulting him, even if I were to have a question directed at me, not to answer until he would not only approve but approve of the answer. Atticus was being very meticulous in the plan of how we were to conduct ourselves. I had met Ben Rosen, one of the partners at Wentworth & Wentworth, a few times during my many visits at the offices, and he was going to assist him at this meeting, and his son, Atti, came along to watch his father work and do what he does in this environment. I don't know if he has witnessed this in real time, as I am sure he has been through this in law school, but this isn't law school; this is where the pedal hits the metal in real time. We had the same older gentleman presiding over this meeting, while Dr. Larson and his team was on the same side of the table as before, but this time, I was introduced to a lady carrying a large briefcase and handed me her business card, and on the card I read, "Eastern Medical

Insurance of Boston, Massachusetts," and her name was Elizabeth Brainard, Special Agent Settlements.

So I was thinking, *Well, we're getting off to a good start.* As usual, the beginning of the meeting was cordial except Dr. Larson and I didn't speak. I think Atticus spoke to him only to say hello or something very brief at the most. The meeting started out with Dr. Larson's counsel starting the conversation out, thanking us for assembling here on this day. The question was directed to Atticus, if he had more parts of the case he wanted to add and wanted to discuss anything more that he had wanted to enter in as part of the fact-finding mission we all seemed to be on, and of course, Atticus brought more facts and statements from our team, and what a great team we had of medical experts.

Atticus took the floor and started laying out more facts and statements that was in addition to the previous arbitration meeting of what he had already laid out for discovery. There seemed to be a little slower method being performed on the other side of the table this time around. They didn't seem to have the fire and lacked the vigor in their approach, or maybe that was what I wanted to see in hopes they were there to offer a settlement. I was just doing as I was told, keeping my mouth shut and sitting back and being calm unless I was spoken directly to, so I sat.

Not a word was spoken to me, although there were plenty of questions and answers. They were flying back and forth across the table from both sides. At one point, it was like I was witnessing a ping-pong match, there was so much back and forth. I seemed to have gotten lost in all of it because it now seemed to be reaching a point, almost a standoff of sort, and Dr. Larson's team sort of huddled up for just a few moments and said, "We are at a point of wanting to offer a settlement."

There was a very long pause, and the presiding judge spoke up and said, "I think this is a good time to take a ten-minute break."

We kept our seat, and the opposing team walked out into the reception area. Atti went to the bar and came back with bottled water for us, and we were just sitting waiting on them to return. My heart was about to beat out of my chest, thinking this had been a very long journey in the making, and thanks to Atticus and his firm, here we were, approaching what appeared to be the finish line. But all of a sudden, it sounded like they were all in some kind of argument, or perhaps some kind of dispute, but voices were raised, and we shut up, trying to listen in, but it was unclear, but it sounded like they really were at odds with one another. None of us could piece it together and noticed Dr. Larson walked down the hall alone, only to return to the huddle. More than ten minutes passed, and then it approached almost twenty minutes, and they finally came back in, took their seats at the conference table.

The first person to speak was Elizabeth Brainard, who represented Dr. Larson's medical malpractice insurance company. She started out by saying, "It was our intent today to offer a settlement to Mr. Beckerman for his injury. However, just now Dr. Larson has decided against it and wants to take it to court."

The darkness just found me again and threw me into a very deep dark hole. I am not sure what all was said at that point for a few moments, but I distinctly remember—and this is something I will never forget—Dr. Larson spoke for the first time that day and said, "I think the community will bail me out."

At that point, Atticus spoke clearly and said, "We will see you all in court."

And the meeting was over. They quickly left the conference room, and Atticus, Ben, Atti, and I stayed for a while. Atticus seemed to be the only one of us that appeared to be all right with this crap that was just thrown at us. Perhaps in his world, this was part of the process for an end result, but I felt the end result was just ripped away from us. Atticus just said, "We are very prepared, and our witnesses will participate in the courtroom, and we will present our case but with more emphasis on the facts since we will be presenting to a jury." He looked at me squarely in the eye and said, "We are ready to take it to court."

All I could think of was what Dr. Larson said, *I think the community will bail me out.* In my mind, that was a very guilty admission. Atticus and Ben Rosen picked up on that very thing but said he wanted to take his chances there because he wanted to try to get away with this. He simply got cold on the idea of offering a settlement, so we'll just prove it in court. We've already proven it here, so court it is. He knew what happened but wanted to find a way out, but we're not going to let it happen. We tossed our conversation around a bit more as it turned out to be a much shorter meeting of arbitration than the previous one, and we used that time to start discussing—what else—court.

Now getting a court date was the next thing to get done. All the depositions had been done and recorded, two arbitration meetings had come and gone, the next thing was court. It was fascinating in many ways of when this all started and following every step I took in this process, lots of bad steps and many steps backward in an effort to take forward steps, but there I was with my team, getting ready for war in the courtroom. The only time I had been in a courtroom was for a speeding ticket many years ago, but I just didn't feel this was going to be anything like that. This was the kind of stuff you see on television or even at the movie theater, and here I was in the middle of it and once again taking another step into the unknown. But I knew I wouldn't be in the position I was in without the knowledge, help, and expertise of Atticus Wentworth of the prestigious law firm of Wentworth & Wentworth and his team of medical experts he had assembled. And let's not forget the amount of money that I had no idea how much it might be, but the amount of money he had invested in this so far had to be a staggering figure. I was astonished and amazed at how much it might be, but I knew, without a doubt, it was well into six figures, and now it would continue to mount. There would be much more money spent to bring in our team from various locations when it was their time to be called as a witness in our case.

I felt good about our chances, and I wanted Atticus to get all of his expenses and more as he doesn't do this for free, I am sure. Now it seemed my focus was on the moral end of this because of the way Dr. Larson treated everyone, particularly me. It was a known fact the reason the meeting was called was to start the settlement process. That was why the insurance company representative was present and why she was called in. Dr. Larson made the decision to settle, and we all assembled, and right at the last minute, he changed his mind and not doing the moral thing here but tried to continue to wiggle out and continue to sweep me under his damn rug. It became personal a long time ago for me, but with all I had been through and continue to go through every single day because of him, yeah, it's personal, you're damn right it is. I try so hard not to dislike anyone and always give everyone a second chance, and *hate* isn't a word I hold on to, but right now, Dr. Larson was making it very hard for me not to fully hate that son of a bitch. Who the fuck does he think he is? All right, rant over, for now.

To say I have learned a lot during the past few years is an understatement, but the interesting thing here is I have learned a lot about people in general, much more than I ever thought possible, I guess, but I have learned there are people that have closed minds and people with open minds. Yeah, everybody, including me, already knew that, at least I hope so. I am taking it to another level here, and I am going to put it in terms of a fraternity. And by definition, the word *fraternity* refers to a medical brotherhood and/or relation of a brother or between brothers with liberty and equality associated by being tied to a brother or brotherhood with a common interest, goals, expectations, etc., etc. I interpret this to mean one group, perhaps, has certain things in common that maybe the other group of brothers has something a bit different in mind. Not to say who is right or who might be wrong, but still different opinions or ways of approaching various topics will prove to be different from fraternity to fraternity. They all can't be on the same page. On the contrary, if they were, then there would only be one fraternity, therefore, rendering that thought preposterous in nature and in fact.

Where am I going with this? I will tell you where I am going with this, but it will take time for me to put it into words. I had seen clearly by reviewing all of the depositions, all fourteen of them, there was a divide. The divide came in the illustration of opinions by two sides, and in this case, the plaintiff on one side and the defendant on the other side. One was obviously pulling for their team, and the opposing team was certainly pulling for their team. So now we have established two fraternities who happen to have very different mindsets of what has occurred in a particular situation.

This situation is how an injury occurred to a victim while being operated on by a surgeon, a likeable guy, a man the community admires and sort of put on a pedestal. Why, I don't know, but that is the way it seems sometimes. And now a certain fraternity all rally around this particular member of that fraternity. The mindset here is we are all brothers, one-for-all-and-all-for-one type of mentality.

So now this brother has been accused of malpractice, not giving the standard of care expected, but oh no, he couldn't have done anything wrong; he is a brother, and we will not allow this madness to gain any access into his life. And we will defend our brother at any cost. The cost here is the victim and all that is attached, yet oh no, our brother did not cause any harm. No way, it is impossible for this to have happened on his watch, he is incapable of making a mistake or error of this kind. So one by one, his brothers came to his rescue and are defiant in defending him by turning a blind eye to some cold hard facts. Turning an eye to the cold hard facts is easy to do because even though there might be facts, yet they can easily be construed, twisted, and made to be confusing by entering in various theories that are far from facts, or perhaps far from the truth, but still it is a way to help defend a brother.

Now on the other side of this coin is a rival fraternity, and this bunch has gathered together and have gone over the facts of the nature of the problem and have looked at every possibility or probability and ruled out, one by one, possible causes, and going through a meticulous fact-finding mission, these brothers have pinpointed the problem. Now they are digging deeper into all of the *how* to determine the *why*, basically working backward now, all the while continuing to rule this and that out as possible issues that contributed to the problem being studied. So now we have the two very different groups with very different opinions, but the major difference here is one side is based on confusion and possibilities, while the other side has dug deep into the basics of problem-solving for the good of the issue without the subject, a human being, in mind, and more importantly, who it might hurt professionally.

This fraternity is about right and wrong, and the other fraternity is about protecting a brother. It was so obvious in all of the depositions on the side of the defendant in this case; it is, to me, a revelation. As an ongoing process of leaning hard into the psychology of the meaning of my interpretation while reading each word of our team and the opposing team, this was the only conclusion there could possibly be from accumulating and understanding each deposition. There is always opposition, in sports, on the playground, or in this case, in the legal system. There are always two opposites that go against each other. It is the negative and the positive, and in the case, it is the positive on the side of the plaintiff and the negative poll on the side of the defendant. It just seemed to work in every case or situation if one will just look hard and deep as I have. They both can't be right, but the side that is based on facts and truth should come out on top.

I am curious by nature, and I want to know the *why* of damn near everything, so I dug until I found out and discovered these are two fraternities that are going to argue until the bitter end. One side is fact-based, and the other is based on what ifs or could be this or that and smoke and mirrors. You don't have to agree with me on this, but I think it will be hard for you to discount it in any way or stretch of your imagination. To put it into perspective from a different angle, as we all know, we operate on a two-party system politically. Don't worry, I am not going to get into politics here, but using the two-party system will bring this all together, perhaps, and make my thoughts and theory on the fraternity system more clear. As we look at political opponents, one side is for their candidate, and the other side is for their candidate, and when things get tight as they do in a medical malpractice lawsuit, there are indeed two sides. These two sides are the plaintiff and the defendant. All of the sparring back and forth between the two is much like two political opponents sparring verbally, back and forth, pleading for votes. Here is where it gets clear. Each side has a favorite, and it seems nothing can change the minds of anyone on either side to support the other, so it comes to a vote, and in politics, it comes down to the people going to the polls to vote for their chosen candidate. And in a medical malpractice lawsuit, when it goes to court, the jury are the voting population, and there are only twelve. But there are always facts that have been openly discovered and discussed, but still the brotherly protection of the bond of the brothers of certain fraternities remain strong and intact, regardless of facts. However, there are always others that bring cold hard facts that challenge the brotherhood. Once a side is chosen, each will stand by what they do and/or say, regardless of facts.

All right, back to Dr. Mowji because it was time to get my prescription for 120 oxycodone filled for another month. I was not sure if the fatigue was getting the best of me or a combination of the pills and not getting the proper rest but just seemed I was falling deeper, but the pain was ever-so present, and there wasn't anywhere or anything I could turn to. Just seemed all had crashed down on me at this time. But Thanksgiving was approaching, and Gretchen has planned a nice Thanksgiving dinner for her brother, John, and, of course, me as she had given me a list of stuff to pick up at the grocery store. And of course duck was on the list as that is and has been our thing for Thanksgiving for a very long time, so why break a tradition. I say let's keep it going.

That was something for me to look very forward to, and having them home with me and the three of us together meant so much to me, and as I have said before, I think they are my lifesavers. Literally they have saved my life and kept me looking ahead instead of allowing the dark clouds to accumulate too often. Don't misunderstand, Thanksgiving at home with me isn't some huge feast of everything imaginable. Who needs all of that? But it is a great dinner with duck, wild rice and vegetable, and some good bread, and just because it is Thanksgiving, we'll offer up some sweet potato pie or a pumpkin pie—but not both, either or—and that rounds it out. That is enough for us, always has been.

Soon after the Thanksgiving holidays were over, and I was at home alone again. I made some hard decisions but not until going over what I wanted to discuss, so I called Charles Mitchell, and he sensed the urgency in my dialogue and simply boarded a jet and came to see me. For two days, we discussed me filing for disability, but this time, I was going to accept it. I didn't know how or what was going to happen especially financially to me, but I just didn't think I had much of a choice nor did I care. It would mean I would have to resign from my position at Sanders Industries, and the tough part was, there is a six-month waiting period before I would receive my first disability payment. Charles told me not to be worried about the gap from the time of resignation from Sanders Industries until the first payment started. My response was I was already worried about it. This was something I must do, but I just didn't know how it was going to work. During this interim period, you can't work, per the federal rules, for the six-month period, and all I could think of was, *How am I going to stretch and make it?* Charles just looked and me and said, "I will help you with some income every month until you start getting your disability payments."

I laughed and told him maybe I could be a Walmart greeter if they would pay me cash and kept laughing. Charles wasn't laughing, and I think my laughter was just coming from nervousness. He said again, "I will help you get through this." There was some back-and-forth conversation directed at the subject, and after a while, he just said, "No more talking about. Let's just stay in touch and let me know when you file for it and when you resign or, in this case, retire from Sanders Industries, and we will work it out." What he said next was something I had heard before. He said, "You can pay me back when you get rich." And we both laughed together on that one.

My decision was made now knowing it looked like I was going to be able to make this all happen. Just by me getting off the road and slowing my pace down even more than I had already would improve my quality of life so much. And I thought it was going to make Dr. Mowji very happy because he had been suggesting I do this, and in the last couple of years, he had really pushed me pretty hard. I know he cares about me and my well-being, that's why he never ceased to let up on me retiring on disability every time I was in his office, and it was monthly.

I snuck up behind him in the grocery store one evening, and he had some snack cakes in his grocery cart, and I scolded him about buying some junk food. We laughed about that for months. And another thing we always laughed about, every time I would come out of the examining room, I would say to the staff, "Doc says I'm a goner." Only this time, a couple of patients heard me, and they didn't seem to find the humor that I shared with Dr. Mowji and his staff.

So off I went to the Social Security office to officially file for disability benefits. As I waited for my turn to speak to a staff member, I kept thinking how fortunate I was to have the close friends I had and the support of all three of those close friends. We all have lots of so-called friends and a lot of acquaintances, but for me to call out three close ones, I think, is pretty neat in many ways. Charles, Conrad, and Jeff, these three guys are just great and wonderful to me in many ways. They always seem to show up at the right time when I find myself in the dark places. Now my number was called for me to go to a window and let my intentions be known. The nice lady was quite nice and accommodating and got all my paperwork filled out, and she asked me if I was still working.

I answered yes, but I knew I couldn't be working for a period of six months, and she proceeded to inform me that she could not file the paperwork until I had stopped working. Not a problem, I told her, and she said she would simply put a hold on it until I notified her of my last working day and date. I walked out feeling good once again, but now, oh boy, I had to resign, literally walk away from a very good-paying job with tons of freedom. Richard had been so good to me to just keep me onboard during all of this. But I just couldn't continue because I had lost so much of myself physically, and the quality of my life was just going away; therefore, I didn't think I had any other choice. Life is full of choices, and this was one of them, and I had made a decision, thanks, in large part, to my good and very close friend Charles Mitchell.

I called Richard, my boss at Sanders Industries, and told him I would be in the area, and I wanted to stop by the office and meet with him. He responded, "Sure, Roland, when do you have in mind to be nearby?"

We set a time day after tomorrow, and of course, he said make it around lunch and laughed. I said, "Sure, Richard, thanks, and I look forward to seeing you."

I arrived and entered the building from the staff entrance in the back of the building and knocked on his office door. He opened it and greeted me with a smile and said, "You hungry?"

"Sure," I said, "I can always eat something."

As we were walking down the hall toward the exit, I stopped and quickly spoke to everyone in the front office, as I always did. We pulled up in front of one of Richard's favorites, Outback Steak House. Not my favorite, but hey, he was buying, so no problem. Once we sat down and placed our drink order, two iced teas—mine half and half, just too much sugar for me, yeah, I know we're in the South. He started telling me about a few key accounts and asked me if I could get them on my calendar for a visit. I calmly said to him, "About that, Richard, I have made a very hard decision."

He looked and me and said, "Wait, I have something to say first. Roland, you are a very valuable man to me and my company, and I am happy that you've done great things for us at Sanders Industries, but are you about to tell me you're leaving?"

The normal response would be, in a case like this, is, *How did you know?* And that was pretty much what I said, but perhaps with a little more class. "Yes, Richard, I am leaving."

He immediately said, "Who are you going to go with?" Then he quickly said, "Wait, Roland, I bet you're just going to retire."

I said, "Yes, Richard, that is exactly what I am going to do." I went on to say, "Why would I leave you to go with another company, Richard? You've been way too good to me. This is just something I have to do."

I told him my doctors had been pushing me hard to retire for a long time now. He really did understand, and when we got back to his office, we walked in together, and he closed the door and began to ask me when I was planning on leaving. I answered, "How about in a month? That should give me time to clear up any loose ends with a couple of prospective customers and give you time to find a replacement."

He laughed and said, "A replacement, that isn't going to be easy."

I said, "Damn, Richard, everyone is replaceable."

He said, "Yeah, but you will be hard to replace. You are leaving some large shoes to fill."

That made me laugh, but it also gave me a little bit of a warm feeling in my heart. We parted and it seemed like that month flew by like a jet at full throttle. The next thing I knew, I was sitting back in Richard's office, winding things up with him and was about to leave. It was time to turn everything in, even my company car, so he had a staff member lined up to drive me home to bring the car back to the office. It was a sad few moments, and it was also a moment of what in the hell have I done, thinking to myself.

But it was done now, and the next morning, I was back at the Social Security office, waiting on my number to be called, and luckily, I got the same window and the same lady. She remembered me and said, "Hello, Mr. Beckerman, you're back. Are you ready to proceed with getting this submitted?"

My answer was an astounding yes. "Let's get this ball rolling," I said with a clear mind, knowing everything was going to be all right, not great but all right. I immediately had to look at things to cut from my personal expenses because my income was going to suffer a considerable loss in gross numbers, but it must be done. She took care of the filing process and informed me I would receive confirmation in the mail within a couple of weeks.

So just as she said, within two weeks I received an official notice that my disability had been approved and listed a schedule of when my first payment would arrive and each one thereafter, but I had to go through the six-month period prior to receiving my first payment. I find it odd that you see on TV all the lawyers advertising if you've been turned down by the federal government for disability call them, and they will fight for you. Seems to me if someone is truly disabled, then why do they need a lawyer? Oh well, that isn't for me to decide, so I will leave that alone, just seems odd.

Atticus had been in the loop regarding me resigning and retiring, and since he was very close in on my health and my needs, he informed me he was going to send a life planner to see me at my home. "What in the hell is a life planner?" I asked.

He informed me he was a professional planner that would interview me in the comfort of my home. "And he is going to determine with almost certainty how your life will be affected as you age because of your injury. In reading notes from both of the treating neurologists, they are predicting some skeletal and perhaps even some muscular problems that could easily occur in the coming years because of weight shifts from the way you have to walk, stand, and just in general, your mobility changes all stemming from your injury. So you can expect a call from Jack Rommel, certified life planner, very soon. He travels all over the country but will be nearby in the next few days, so accommodate him as best you can. I really want to get his report because I want to use it when we go to court. And speaking of court, I was just notified that we have a confirmed court date. I will send it to you in writing within the next couple of days, but it looks like we are all set now. Are you ready to go to court?" he asked.

You better believe I was very ready to get this over with. After the conversation was over, I thought it had been a very long time since my injury occurred, and so much has happened that changed my life in a lot of ways, and mostly it has damaged me, and the injury took so much from me, and what it took I will never recover, no matter what the outcome of the lawsuit is because my injury is for keeps. And now I looked at this, and it was hard to say, but it wasn't so much about money, although it would really help me now, but it was more about human decency that seemed to be lacking in the other or, I should say, the opposing fraternity.

I met with Jack Rommel, the guy Atticus wanted me to meet with. We spent the entire afternoon together sitting at my dining room table. He had a recorder set up and made tons of notes. We took a few breaks and went out on the porch and enjoyed the day while sitting in my big porch rockers. It was a very pleasant experience, and he appeared to be very thorough, although I knew nothing about his business, but I learned as we went and seemed like a very legitimate approach to my future, and the pitfalls I would likely have as I aged. I guess it was a shot of reality, although I have had enough of reality for a long time. All I wanted was to just try to relax now that I wasn't working.

As a matter of fact, my first visit to see Dr. Mowji after I retired, he had my blood pressure taken four times while I was at his clinic. The reason was it had dropped, and he couldn't believe it. He said, "See, I told you retirement would be good for you. Just look at this, Roland, this is great. Your blood pressure has dropped, good for you."

But as usual, just before I left, I said to the staff, "Doc says I'm a goner."

We all got a laugh out of it once again. Upon arriving at home, I opened my mail, and there it was, the day I had been waiting on, a court date. There it was in print right before me. I called Atticus and told him I had received the notice and thanked him at least ten times. He made a few comments regarding the date, and then he said, "I have some folks waiting on me in the conference room, but I wanted to take your call." And as usual, he said, "We'll be in touch."

We ended the call.

Chapter 17

Just the thought of having a court date now set seemed to give me some bit of a feeling that accountability and, most importantly, justice would be served. I wondered if I would get that simple apology that I had been hoping to get from the very beginning. Just to hear Dr. Larson say to me, just once, "Roland, I am sorry this happened," just those few words coming from him would have been so welcomed by me, but so far, he had not offered them to me or anything even close. All he had done was deny any wrongdoing whatsoever.

Again I don't think Dr. Larson is a bad doctor, although I am wondering about his humanity and respect for others, ethics, and morals as a person, but a bad doctor, no, I don't believe he is. He just made a mistake. As we all know, everyone runs a stop sign from time to time, maybe didn't mean to, but we do. However, good doctors can do wrong, and in my case, he did something very wrong that could have easily been avoided by simply releasing pressure put on by the retractors that were put in place and not monitored, moved, or adjusted in any way during the entire length of the time I was in surgery. It is even strongly recommended by the designer of the surgical tool to avoid possible nerve damage, as clearly pointed out in his deposition, and is even listed in the literature that comes along with the instruments. Just a simple maneuver would have avoided this from happening to me, but it wasn't to be; therefore, accountability and justice was what I was seeking. I had often thought, more so now than ever, it really wasn't about the money, although I would like to get what I have spent with the various lawyers I worked with, and I wanted Atticus and the law firm of Wentworth & Wentworth to get their large investment back and a profit, of course. Now it had become more about right and wrong and justice. I just wanted someone—Dr. Larson—to be held accountable for what he didn't do and that was give me the normal standard of care that was expected.

Just having the court date on my calendar was a super feeling of accomplishment. As so far this journey was deep into five years of so many ups and downs, highs, and some very low points for me. It had been a financial roller coaster with lots of curves and unexpected severe deep dark plunges. My financial life had taken a terrible beating, and my personal life had been wrecked. My professional life had suffered tremendously and had changed my financial profile in a very negative way. The only spot that continued to shine were my two children and my closest three friends. As you can imagine, they alone had been my savior, emotional support, and what I have held dearest to my inner self.

I expect Atticus would be putting together his court-room strategies, and this was another new experience for me, and these were certainly uncharted waters going to court. I am certain it wasn't uncharted waters for Atticus's legal team and our team of medical experts, as I know they know just how to handle being in a courtroom trying a case. It all seemed unreal to me, and the length of time it took to just get to this point was, to me, staggering. The steps that were required to meet the various levels and the literal feeling of being on a chess board was both mind-blowing and mind-expanding at the same time. I am able to say this from inside experience, and now it seemed I was going to get to experience what a real courtroom trial would consist of.

My good friend Dr. Robin Jensen called me. It was good to hear his voice, asked me to meet him for lunch the next day at our usual spot out in the county for another corn-field conversation. I knew he wanted to discuss something he didn't want anyone to know of the content, hence the name of our meetings. So I was happy to meet him, and we seemed to always just pick up from where we last left our previous conversations, which is what good friends are capable of doing. He went straight into what he wanted to say. He told me that word was passing through the various floors of the hospital that Dr. Larson was having to go to court to defend himself in a medical malpractice lawsuit filed by that guy that he operated on about five years ago that was in the hospital for about a month that had all kinds of problems after the surgery.

My thought was I can't say I was sorry for word to be traveling around, spoken in undertones by various staff members. I will say, I was quite happy it was happening, mainly because of the way he treated me all along, and I think it was partly because of frustration and a guilty conscience that was ever present in him. The fact is, he is human, and we have feelings and emotions, and I just think his treatment of me personally was coming from those two things, frustration and guilt; the guilt was inner guilt because he never once even offered up an apology or anything that would resemble an apology.

Dr. Jensen and I had a really enjoyable lunch, and our cornfield conversation went on as planned. The reason he gave for inviting me to meet for lunch was he was aware of the court date, and he heard it from a nurse on one of the floors at the hospital, so yeah, the word was out. I do wonder how and/or who put the word out, it certainly didn't come from me, and I was sure Atticus or anyone on our team didn't make it knowledgeable to anyone, and why would they do so? But the news for Dr. Larson having to go to court for a medical malpractice lawsuit was not only traveling around the halls and floors of the hospital, it was getting out all over town. That didn't bother me either.

Dr. Jensen and I finished up, and upon leaving, we spent another thirty minutes or so outside, just continuing our cornfield conversation, and he kept telling me he thought Dr. Larson would be held fully accountable for his oversight in my case. He reminded me, Dr. Larson is a good doctor that just overlooked something very important and needs to be held accountable. We exchanged a little more conversation, and each asked about our families, and he also asked about Becky, my ex-wife. I happily told him she had remarried. He smiled and said, "I bet that gave you a bit of relief in some way or another."

My reply was, "Yes, more than you can imagine." And I added, "It gave me some closure to all that had happened."

He was aware of the situation from the beginning, as many people did, because just like word getting out about Dr. Larson, it is not too large of a town, and news will travel quickly from one to another as the local grocery stores seem to be a breeding ground for gossip, and some of the gossip is very likely to have some truth woven into it. I don't think the grocery store method of channeling hot news or topics around town is anything unusual, nor is it unusual anywhere in any city, large or small. It just seems to be the neighborhood meeting place, and while we are here, why not get the items we need at home? Perhaps I have that backward, but you get the meaning and point. So Dr. Jensen and I said goodbye, until the next time. He was one of the most genuine human beings I have ever met. He spoke his mind, and he did so with conviction, truth, and humility. I so enjoy the times we have spent at our cornfield conversations—still haven't seen a cornfield—and we have, on occasion, been socially connected in and around town, as usual, at various events.

I received a call from Atticus, asking me to go to his office in Richmond, at my convenience. He said he needed to go over some points with me regarding the trial. So there I went to Richmond, and upon entering the reception area, I was, as always, greeted with a smile, and the words, "Welcome to Wentworth & Wentworth, Mr. Beckerman." They always make me feel special and treat me with respect. Atticus walked in, and we walked down the hall to the conference room. In the room, already seated was Ben Rosen and Atti Wentworth, and after they greeted, me we all proceeded to listen carefully to Atticus as he was laying out the initial groundwork and explaining to me a lot of rules, simply about just being in court. In other words, he was teaching me some courtroom etiquette. I listened intently and made some notes; as I had mentioned, this was uncharted waters for me once again. We had come a long way, and I certainly didn't want to make an ass out of myself or hurt my team in any way at all in the courtroom. So they all had my full attention.

It was a ten o'clock meeting, and the lunch hour and break were approaching. Atticus excused Ben and Atti and said to me, "Let's go downtown for lunch," and he continued to say, "I can continue to brief you then and finish it up at lunch. I have some folks coming in that I will need to see when we get back, but we can easily finish up.

I thought we were about done anyway with filling me in on what to expect when we go to court, and the lesson on courtroom etiquette was much needed on my part. Atticus again ordered the fried flounder, just as I expected, and I had the sautéed shrimp in lemon sauce. That must be his favorite because that is all he orders when we go there or anywhere that has fried flounder on the menu. Come to think of it, when we sat down, the waiter only gave me a menu, so that pretty much gave it away—it is what he orders' there, plus him greeting Atticus by saying, "Good to see you, Mr. Wentworth." We got back to his offices. I had left my jacket in the conference room, and it was presented to me by a staff member the moment we entered the door. Atticus and I bid our farewell in the reception area, and off I went, and he turned and said, "We'll be in touch."

On my drive home, I felt such a sense of some sort of victory, and we hadn't even entered the courtroom yet, but the level of professionalism from everyone involved, Atticus, his entire firm, our expert medical witnesses, along with our plan of attack, was just almost overwhelming to me. Everyone on my team has treated me with total respect, and I know they all were genuine in wanting to help make this wrong a right. Just look at the mountain of facts we've built. What more could I ask, and again so far, I had only invested ninety-eight dollars into this venture with Wentworth & Wentworth. The money I perhaps gave away frivolously to several other lawyers was something I did, and maybe it was part of the learning curve, I don't really know. But Atticus, I have determined, is the ultimate attorney in his field of expertise. I had mentioned before, I have full trust in him and our team, but my feelings now have been strengthened by watching him work over the years, and how meticulously he had assembled an unmatched team of support for me. I know he does this for his livelihood, but at the same time, he seems to love every minute of it, as if it truly is his passion to help others in need.

He had other cases he was working on besides mine, but he had always made me feel mine was very important to him and seemed he gave me his full attention. Something tells me he treats them all that way, so perhaps I was not as special as he made me feel, but I am going to continue to think otherwise. I keep reminding myself regarding the fact he hasn't asked me for a dime, and I was well aware of the expense he had laid out on my behalf. And in this reminder, I had a very good feeling we would win our case in court.

It really seemed we were going to settle without going to court. I remember it so well during the last of two arbitration meetings held at the conference room of Southern National Bank, when the medical malpractice insurance representative was present and the expectation that a settlement would be offered. That meeting ended abruptly when Dr. Larson clearly and openly said, "I want to go to court because I think the community will bail me out."

The settlement went down in flames under Dr. Larson's wishes. I had all the faith, and I had continued to mount my courage in the fact we would gain what we were all expecting, and that was Dr. Larson would be held accountable, and the amount, to me, at this point, it doesn't matter as long as I get my own money back I invested, and Atticus makes a profit. I just want justice, I just want Dr. Larson to be held accountable, I just want an apology.

We had a couple more meetings prior to our court date and seemed we were ready, and our date was to start the following Monday. It was now Wednesday. On that night, Atticus's brother had a massive heart attack and was in intensive care and wasn't expected to live. It was a grave moment for Atticus, and he needed to handle this dire situation as only he could, in the best interest of all of us regarding the case. Although Ben Rosen could have handled the beginning of what goes on in a trail, meaning selecting the jury, but Atticus and I talked a few times on the phone, and quite honestly, I wanted my quarterback. It wasn't anything negative regarding Ben Rosen, one of his associates, but Atticus's mind was not going to be in the game, so to speak. In the last conversation, I told Atticus I understood his brother was in a very bad situation, and it didn't appear he would pull out of it within any reasonable time frame, if at all.

Atticus suggested we, if he could at this late date, could perhaps ask for a postponement of the trial for a later date. It wasn't reluctance necessarily, but I really didn't want this to occur. A postponement, damn, I just couldn't believe this was happening. *Another low point was just before me once again,* I thought. But I quickly cleared my thought process and thought this was the right thing to do. I learned what I just stated from two men I thought highly of, and one was my father, and he had a friend, a very good friend who happened to be Charles Mitchell's father, Robert Mitchell, but I was told by both of them to always do the right thing. So the right thing to do was to support Atticus in his request to have the trial postponed because of the, as I mentioned, grave situation with his brother.

I had met his brother once during one of my visits to Wentworth & Wentworth in Richmond. Atticus spoke of his brother with very high regard, and I knew they were quite close, just from the various remarks he made of him. So doing the right thing was to give Atticus my full support. This time I felt he needed me as much as I had literally leaned on him for years now. I felt I needed to lighten his load at this time, and as the saying goes, *It is the least I can do,* I thought. I told Atticus to do as he sees necessary, and I wished him and his brother well.

Atticus called me on Thursday afternoon, which was the next day, and informed me not only was he able to secure a postponement from the presiding judge but has also gotten another court date set for ninety days out. It was a little surprising to me it would be set that soon. I was expecting the worst like a damn year out. I had no idea really, but ninety days seemed all right with me. Here we were into this journey that was to be extended even farther out, but it was truly out of our control. Who would have guessed Atticus's brother would become seriously ill right now, of all times. So I thought what's another ninety days added to it, so what?

Atticus did inform me another judge would be assigned to the case, and he really was happy with the judge we had drawn on this case but said not to worry, he was sure we would secure what we would need. I asked Atticus about his brother, and he informed me it really wasn't looking good. As a matter of fact, he seemed to be starting to fail rapidly. I didn't push for anything more regarding that, I was just curious.

The weekend came and lunch with Jeff Greene was, as always, enjoyable, and I informed him of the postponement. He didn't seem to see it the way I did at first, and I think it came from the fact of him knowing how long it took to get to this point. And now it was being postponed because my lawyer's brother was in the hospital, he said rather loudly. I went on to explain just how dire this was, and that my lawyer and his brother are very close, and Jeff calmed down a bit, but again, he just had me in mind and all I had been through up until now. I fully understood him and the way he felt; after all, it was me who had been on this ride.

Sunday night, around ten o'clock, my cell phone rang; it was Atticus. He began to speak, and he didn't have to say another word because just from his tone of voice, I knew the reason he called. His brother had passed away an hour or so ago, and he just wanted me to know. I thanked him, and it was certainly sad news, but it seemed to vindicate everything about the postponement. In as much as I didn't want the postponement of the trial I had waited so long for, I did, however, confirm that we had done the right thing. So the advice I received from two very special and wiser older men of always doing the right thing came into the picture, crystal clear, once again. I strive and will always strive to always do the right thing in every aspect of my life, in any given situation I am faced with, and this was no exception.

We ended the phone call in just a matter of a couple of minutes. After all, what was there to say at that point except I am truly sorry for your loss and that was about it. Prior to the end of the call, he said, "We'll be in touch." It was indeed good to hear what he always said to me upon our parting ways, either on the phone or in person. The call ended, and the reason was very much vindicated as mentioned, but it took on a whole new meaning as Atticus lost his brother, and timing is something none of us can plan out when something like this hits our respective families. One must just do as they see necessary to get on with what is placed in front of them, and Atticus made the right call. I thought now was the time for me to just lay back, and as Atticus said, "We'll be in touch." And I was just going to wait for him to get through all of this and get back on track soon. I didn't know if there would be any reason to prepare again for the upcoming trial that would be here soon, so I would simply wait to hear from Atticus and do whatever he wanted to do in preparation.

Now I felt as if I were a commercial jet circling around the airport in a holding pattern, just waiting for the tower to tell me when I could land. But the reason I was in the holding pattern wasn't anyone's fault. Who would have predicted Atticus's brother would have a massive heart attack and die a few days later, all while the world continued to rotate, with everything happening as normal. So now the only thing any of us could do was wait, but I did get a call from Atticus to thank me for being so understanding. I responded by simply saying we both just did the right thing. I did ask him if getting the postponement was any problem. He paused and didn't really answer the question I posed, but it worked its way back into the conversation, and again, he paused and said it took a judge to push it through because Dr. Larson's team didn't want it postponed.

We didn't know if it was Dr. Larson or his team, but the fact was they didn't want to allow the postponement by showing or giving Atticus any compassion for what he was going through, ultimately to have to accept the death of his brother. So a judge had to make the decision based on the facts. A judge ultimately has to approve something like this anyway, but after he learned the facts of what was going on with a family member of the plaintiff's team, who happened to be the lead attorney, the judge simply took it upon himself to do the right thing and allow the postponement. Seemed we all were doing the right thing, except to Dr. Larson and his team, so there again, that was just giving me more reason to bring him to justice and force him to be held accountable, and maybe he would be moral and enough of a human being to give me that apology.

Chapter 18

There was something very interesting that we had tucked away in our arsenal as part of our offense in the case. A while back, just before we started the long and tedious process of deposing all of the ones involved, or thought to be involved, Atticus learned something about Dr. Larson that we kept to ourselves, to use only if we needed to because it was personal in nature and could be damaging to Dr. Larson. However, as we all know courtroom drama, at times, will pull out all stops to get to the truth. Sometimes it is just a matter of the avenue one has to take to get there, and at times, that avenue can lead down various paths that are not pleasant but necessary to fulfill the canvas of the whole picture.

It was a piece of damaging evidence that truly told more about Dr. Larson than one could imagine about his manner of how he handled his personal life that is relative to his decision-making or lack of while he is in the operating room. This piece of evidence that we decided not to bring up unless we needed, it would only be used in the courtroom as a weapon that would surely push any jury member into making the right decision. It was a real deal maker or breaker, whichever way one would like to look at it, but it is one for the plaintiff, pure and simple. Atticus chose not to use it while Dr. Larson was being deposed that day, when we were all assembled in the conference room in the basement of his clinic. Atticus thought better not to bring this up and not until it was perhaps needed, if it were to go to court.

I don't think Atticus mentioned what he had learned about Dr. Larson's past behavior, having to do with his personal life, to anyone, except for Ben, Atti, and of course, myself. But collectively the decision was made not to use it until we needed it, if we were to need it at all. In my mind, it was truly our secret weapon, only to be used when absolutely necessary. I sort of felt like the cat that ate the canary with a feather hanging out of the corner of his mouth, trying to keep a secret, but keep it a secret I certainly did.

What Atticus learned about Dr. Larson's past to get a feel for him personally during the construction of the case was something very telling about him. We have all made mistakes, perhaps some worse and/or more involved than others, but there are skeletons in many closets, and Dr. Larson had his share of skeletons living in a few of his closets. The question was, do we? And when do we open those doors, and Atticus thought it was absolutely best to only bring it out if we found ourselves needing to use it in court.

Dr. Larson had performed some simple cosmetic surgery—I think it was some kind of facial improvement, let's call it a face-lift—on a local gentleman by the name of R. T.

Jonas. Mr. Jonas was a prominent member of the same community as Dr. Larson, and as a matter of fact, they were good friends. They socialized a lot together, as they were always seen at the annual heart ball and other fundraising events. Ironically he was senior vice president of Southern National Bank, the bank where our two arbitration meetings were held. R. T. Jonas was very well known in the area and was on various boards, and he kept himself busy with many civic-minded duties and events. He was good at raising money, well, he was a banker, you know. He was married and had two children. I knew him fairly well myself, and we were close in age; I think he was just a few years older than me.

The surgery required he be put under general anesthesia for Dr. Larson to perform the surgery, but after the surgery, when he was taken into recovery, all of a sudden, a few alarms sounded, and he was having a cardiac issue that needed immediate attention. The recovery room staff paged Dr. Larson and Dr. Phyllis Meekings, who was the attending anesthesiologist. Neither of them responded. Paging them again, and still no response from either of them; now the recovery room staff was beginning to panic as it was becoming a dire situation. They even checked the staff parking lot, and both of their cars were still there, so it meant they were somewhere in the building. About twenty-five minutes or so later, they were seen coming out of a vacant hospital room together. Just a couple of minutes before they were seen coming out of the vacant room, R. T. Jonas was pronounced dead.

The cause of death was cardiac arrest and it was very likely due to failure of the patient not getting cared for properly. It was quite possible it was due to inappropriate recovery time and premature removal of anesthesia.

The recovery room staff did all they could and knew how to do to try to save him, but he passed away in recovery. If only Dr. Larson and Dr. Meekings could have been located to go assist, perhaps this wouldn't have happened. But they were busy satisfying their personal and inner sexual needs and desires which, to me, tells me of their selfishness during a time they should have been taking care of their patient. There is always time for this, but sexual desires often get in the way at the wrong time, and this was one of those times, and to put it in plain English, it was poor decision-making for two adult professionals at the time.

I mentioned Atticus did some research on Dr. Larson to learn of his profile to get more of an understanding of him personally, and this information was uncovered when he discovered a formal letter written to the state medical board of concern and discipline of Dr. Larson regarding this incident. So again, we decided this would only be used if it were to become necessary in court. We didn't want to use it during the deposition of Dr. Larson because it would give his defense team prewarning of a bombshell that could be of serious consequences to him and his team. Our thoughts were, this would be clear to any jury members that Dr. Larson was not only someone who had sexual activity with someone other than his wife, another doctor in this incident, but also how he—both of them—could allow this kind of activity that could easily compromise his medical responsibilities. They both allowed their desire for a sexual encounter in a vacant room in the hospital for a few short minutes that led to the utmost consequence—death of a patient. Were the few moments of sexual pleasure and excitement worth the life of R. T. Jonas? I don't think so. Not only was he a patient, he was a friend of Dr. Larson. So not using this piece of evidence, although it wasn't evidence directly related to our case, but it was quite directly related to the integrity of his decision-making, was something we were holding tightly to because wouldn't this be a bolt of lightning in the courtroom if and when we unveiled it?

Atticus, in his in-depth research on Dr. Larson, found another damning piece that could be used against him, and this too was filed away for use, only if we had to pull it out in the courtroom. Approximately three years prior to my surgery performed by Dr. Larson, it was widely known that he had quite an open affair with one of his staff members, Katie Zelmyer. Katie was, I guess you could say, his head nurse and operating room assistant. She had been an employee there for several years. Katie was married, and they had three beautiful children, all under the age of twelve. Her husband traveled in his job, very much like I did. He was gone a lot during the week. It was a well-known thing they would work late together, and it was always a given she would accompany him on trips to medical conferences and other events related to his profession. According to the report Atticus uncovered, Katie's husband found out about the affair they had been having all along and was just devastated, as you can imagine. He trusted her, and of course he trusted Dr. Larson and thought it was, well, a professional relationship. Katie was making a very good salary, and he made quite a good living, so between the two of them, they were in really good shape, nice house at the country club, drove expensive cars, and just appeared to be a model family. But model family, I didn't think so; she was literally in bed with Dr. Larson every chance they got. Katie's husband obviously went to a divorce lawyer, and just as my divorce lawyer told me I had a case against Russell, the guy Becky was seeing, for alienation of affection, that was what he was told by his lawyer.

Only he took the advice and filed a suit against Dr. Larson. This being a small town, word was flying about it all over town as it didn't seem to be a secret. Katie and her husband split up, and the relationship with Dr. Larson ceased; as a matter of fact, Katie was asked to resign by Dr. Larson's partners in the clinic. She found employment with another surgical group out of town. Just before the case was going to be heard in court, Dr. Larson paid a substantial undisclosed amount of money to Katie's estranged husband. After he received this payment, the lawsuit was suddenly terminated. It just dropped out of sight, but the one thing that wasn't dropped was word on the street; Dr. Larson's wife rat-

tled her own sword with her husband. I think he was asked
to leave, and he did but for some unknown reasons, he was
allowed back into the house after being out for only a few
weeks. Maybe his wife of many years looked at the big picture and said to herself, thinking she has a beautiful home,
three grown children, tons of freedom, and she is well aware
her husband is a womanizer. But having a great life and all
the money she could spend meant something to her, so they
still go to the heart ball once a year, together, along with a few
other formal events, and they live two lives under the same
roof together.

Just a few days before our trial was about to begin, Dr.
Larson's defense team filed a motion requesting the judge to
not allow either of the incidents involving R. T. Jonas and/
or Katie Zelmyer to be heard in court and kept clear of and
from the jury. Atticus informed me of this motion they filed
with the presiding judge, and I went into a rage of how and
why, can he do this, was my initial reaction to Atticus, and
for the first time, I raised my voice to him in anger. Both of
these pieces of information, we all thought, could be used in
court, only if necessary, but if we needed to use them, they
would be opened up, an entirely open book on Dr. Larson
illustrating how his judgment can be altered under the stress
of performing surgery. By the way, I apologized to Atticus
for raising my voice at him when he informed me the judge
wouldn't allow us to use this in court by way of the motion
filed by Dr. Larson's team. Atticus told me not to worry

about it because it was everything he thought and more, so we're all right.

As much as I disagreed with the judge's decision not to allow this information to be heard in court, I know why Dr. Larson's team pulled that card out of the stack. But I still think the judge should have allowed it because it would have shed a lot more light on the case, all while revealing a lot about Dr. Larson personally and how his medical judging ability could be clouded by his extramarital affairs. This is a measure of his integrity that I think is proof of his mind being altered at the sight or thoughts of various women. It makes me wonder how many other extramarital affairs has he had during his long marriage to his wife. I still feel the jury should have the right to hear this very revealing information, but it wasn't going to happen.

In retrospect, looking back, I still don't understand how or why the judge wouldn't allow us to use these facts about Dr. Larson, just don't understand, and I guess I never will. So off to court we went with a huge arsenal of our expert witnesses, ready to not only tell the truth but explain the truth, backed by scientific fact.

Chapter 19

We were now just inside of starting on year six of this journey. The postponed date was fast approaching now for our day in court. I did make one more visit to the offices of Wentworth & Wentworth prior to our date, just to recap all we prepared for a few short months ago. This meeting was upbeat, and everyone was very positive about our expected outcome of winning the case in court. It seemed, at one time, we were going to get a settlement which would have been great and saved all of us a lot of time and money, but it just didn't happen. Here we were, about to embark on entering the courtroom. I must say, even though we had an extra ninety days to prepare, I was still very anxious about being in a courtroom with a jury and a judge, all new to me.

I got a call from my close friend Charles Mitchell, and he wanted to wish me luck and extended his best wishes. And as always, we asked about each of our children, where they were, how they were doing, etc. I told him or reminded him John was out of college and was doing great and had moved to Boston, and he was spending his first winter there, but I didn't think he was going to last through the winter, just too cold for him, I said. He asked when Gretchen would be graduating, and I informed him she was in her last year. He asked me if I needed anything to help her finish up. Knowing Charles and all he had done for me in the past, I just said, no everything was under control.

The truth was I was trying to figure out a way to pay the balance on her tuition. This was something I didn't discuss much with either of my two children as this was my problem, not theirs. I wanted them to concentrate on school and everything it offered and brought to them, not finances. So I just said, yeah, everything was all right. Perhaps I didn't say it with enough enthusiasm, or perhaps he just knows me that well, but three days later, I received a check for $5,000 with a short note that read, *Pay me back when you get rich*. Of course I called him and thanked him and told him that was the amount I was trying to somehow put together to finish up her last tuition payment. I didn't tell him like I did before, "I can't accept this." Rather I sincerely thanked him. Again he wished me luck on my going to court and asked me to let him know how it turned out and again, wishing me luck. We ended the call, and I had written out a check for $6,100 for the balance that included the $5,000 check from him on the tuition, and that was a load off my mind. Now it seemed my mind was clear of all obstacles as there were not any hurdles in front of me for now, and I was ready to get on with this going to court stuff.

The day had come and I met with my team in a small room just before entering the courtroom. We really didn't huddle up and put a plan together. Our plan had been in place for months, and I had been briefed and educated on the events that were about to unfold in the courtroom. I would like to say we were as ready as we would ever be at that moment. And we entered, and we all rose out of our seats when the judge walked in from a door just behind the bench, his big desk. He was the highest person in the entire room, meaning his bench was the highest point in the room, designating he was in charge, I would guess. But it was quite impressive to witness the respect he received when he stepped into the room and up to his position. Once he sat down, it was announced that court was in order.

The first thing was to go through jury selection, and this was something both sides participated in. Selecting a jury was a tedious process of questions posed to each candidate. Atticus seemed to have a method, and I am sure he used that method every single time he went through the process of jury selection. Even though the process was, as I thought, to be the same, I was certain the line of questions were never quite the same because each case was different, and he would likely be looking for a definite type of candidate to select. Then if he selected a candidate, our opposition could strike that person or could accept that candidate. And this did occur several times, just when I liked one that Atticus approved, it seemed they would get turned down by our opposition. I quickly learned that was going to be the norm, meaning if we liked a candidate, they didn't like them, and if we didn't like a candidate, then they did. So it was a back and forth, and still the chess game was continuing to be played out as usual.

Half of the day was already gone, and we all went to a local deli for lunch break. The conversation was not so much about the case as it was about what was going on in the economy, which was literally tanking. The stock market was headed for some serious losses, interest rates were rising quickly, and businesses seemed to have lost confidence. And when confidence in the economy, as a whole, becomes bleak, then it all seems to fall like dominos in a downward spiral. That was the main topic of conversation during our lunch break. But Atticus did say he wasn't as pleased as he would like with the jury selection so far, but he was feeling positive it would improve. I didn't know exactly what to think of what he said, so I just listened. And the fact was we had only mutually chosen only three jurors, and we had nine more to go. I was sure we wouldn't get this done today, if our morning session was indicative of what was to come, and it held true. The afternoon was equally as slow in choosing candidates both sides could agree on, so it went on into the next day. It seemed like it took three more days just to get our jury of twelve jurors selected.

That part was finally over, and the following day was Friday. Atticus told me not to expect much progress of any kind to begin a trial on a Friday. We would pretty much jockey for positions and make opening comments to introduce what and why we were there, and that would push on into starting again on Monday, with a lot of similar motions being made and introductions. But Monday would be the real beginning. The weekend seemed to last for days, in my anticipation.

I had lunch with my lunch buddy, my good friend Jeff Greene, at our usual spot downtown, and I could feel the tension of various people, and I heard a few words whispered, "Yes, he is the one that is suing Dr. Larson," and on and on. All of a sudden, I felt the wrath of the great doctor being spread all over town that I was the guy. I heard from some I knew that many people couldn't believe I had the audacity to take him to court. I received a few phone calls over the weekend and was told I should drop the case immediately, that all I was going to do was hurt Dr. Larson. *Hurt Dr. Larson?* I thought, *What in the hell are they talking about here, I am the one with a permanent damn injury that he caused.* This infuriated me to no end. What could I do except just let it go.

Atticus had given me his cell phone number a long time ago, and out of respect for his privacy and my decency, I never used it until now. I called him and informed him of what went on during lunch with a very close friend, who happened to be very supportive of me, and I informed him of three phone calls I received on my landline, of people telling me I should drop the case immediately because I was only going to hurt Dr. Larson. This was very upsetting to me, that people were apparently portraying me as the one that was wrong and doing something I shouldn't. What a fucked up place this was, with people like that.

But going back to the fraternities and political groups that are so similar, I just had to consider the sources. He seemed to have a rather large team, but I had the facts and truth on my team. Except for the jury selection, the trial hadn't really started yet with bringing out the facts, and I was already the bad guy here. Atticus just told me as hard as it was, I needed to remain calm and just let it all go, and he also said it was likely to get worse. If things had already started this early in the process, he said just prepare myself for more of the phone calls and the words mumbled behind my back in the presence of various people I might engage in the local grocery store, or he said, "In this case, while eating lunch with your friend Jeff is his name, right?" He went on the say to me, "This is not rare, particularly in a small town. If we were in a large city where the population is much higher, things like this don't usually come into the picture, but in a small town like this, well, it does happen."

He did say this wasn't good for us that these types of things were being said and spread all around town, and the reason was some of it, I was sure, would get to the ears of our jury. Even though they were sworn not to discuss the case at all during the trial, things can and do happen, but not to worry, "We have the truth on our side based on strong facts from some of the most reputable medical expert witnesses I have ever worked with on any case. These guys are just the best and were so willing to assist us with your case, simply because of the principle behind wanting to bring this out so it will never happen again by Dr. Larson." Atticus said, "They want him to understand how critical it is, what he did was so simple to avoid, but due to his negligence, he has harmed a patient—in this case, you—permanently. Every surgeon must be aware of everything going on in the operating room and remain focused on giving the standard of care expected of him every single time he enters the theater of surgery. This time he failed, and that is what we will prove."

The things he said sort of calmed me down as only Atticus could, as he just has a very calm voice, but the things he said all had merit and were all based on facts. But deep down, I must admit, I wanted revenge at some level, and it all came to light over the weekend when these awful things were being said about me for no damn reason. I didn't do anything wrong; I am the one suffering at the hand of Dr. Larson because of his damn negligence.

Monday came, and we were back in the courtroom, and it was a scene I wasn't expecting. It seemed there were a number of people in the courtroom that were all on the left side, seated behind the defendant, Dr. Larson, and believe it or not, I had a few people I knew that took their seat behind us on the right side of the courtroom, the side of the plaintiff, our team. Even though there were lots of people I knew on the opposing side, there were a few that supported me. It felt as if our team was playing the other team on their home field. In other words, we were not welcome and were looked at as vicious rivals. It was a feeling of, *Damn, we are outnumbered.* I didn't even make any mention of this or the way I felt about it to Atticus, but at lunch break, he said, "It appears he brought all of his cheerleaders in for a rally of some sort." He went on to say, "This isn't some kind of show-and-tell of who comes. It rather is a show-and-tell of facts and truth, and we have both on our side."

After all that had been said and particularly what had been done over the years, during my time spent with Atticus Wentworth, I have determined he is truly a seeker of truth. I firmly believe this to be a strong fact. It is a quality I haven't seen in many people, not to say people aren't truthful or even trustworthy of handling the truth, but Atticus is all about uncovering truth. And I believe he had uncovered the truth in my case, along with the help of a team of medical experts that are very well known for their wealth of knowledge and years of experience in their chosen area of expertise and profession, that truly can't be argued. The facts and truth are embedded in their respective records, and they are all on our team. So I was happy knowing Atticus is a seeker of truth; nothing else seemed to matter to him.

The examinations have started, and of course, for every examination, a cross-examination follows. The first round of these witnesses were pretty much character-type witnesses.

Dr. Larson's team brought in and put on the witness stand a long line that resembled a parade of his doctor friends and a few personal friends, all stating how wonderful he was as a human being—I was begging to differ on that—what a great doctor he was, and how many successful surgeries he has performed on so many people in this community. And some spoke of his involvement in his church and how active he was there and all the good he has done. Of course, his civic involvement was none better and was just a pillar of society and on and on. If one didn't know better, he was the savior of all humankind of every race on the entire planet.

Atticus jotted down the word *overkill*, and we just looked at each other and smiled. Atticus did some cross-examinations on several of these character witnesses, but I think all he wanted to do was basically go through the motions and get this part over with and proceed into our character witnesses. I was pretty sure we were not going to have a cheerleading squad placed on the witness stand one by one. Rather he was going to cover the pertinent facts about me and what I might have meant to a few people and to tell the truth of why we were there and what we would prove.

I was right; that was precisely what he wanted to do in this part of the testimonies. My daughter was our first witness to be sworn in. I remember well just how nervous, and perhaps even a bit scared, she was to be put on the witness stand, but she blazed right through it with clarity, confidence, and calmness, a trait she seems to have to this day. She answered all of the questions about what she witnessed regarding my health while the two of us lived together her last two years of high school, prior to her leaving for college.

John had already started college the fall after this surgery occurred. John was in Boston, and Atticus didn't think it would be necessary for him to make the trip down to be a witness. After all, Gretchen and I lived together, and what better person could give a description of what I went through on a daily basis than her during those early years of me trying to figure out how to become more mobile and how to deal with the constant pain that I still endure today. The opposition did cross-examine her, but for some reason, they didn't attack her because all she was doing was tell the truth about her father. She was sworn to tell the truth, and I was very proud of her efforts while on the witness stand and just how she handled herself in general. Perhaps for the first time, I looked at her like an adult, my little girl, but still she handled herself like a responsible adult. It was a very proud moment for me to see her on the stand, talking about all the things she had witnessed me go through, and it was a strong reminder to me just how far I have come physically just to be able to be mobile.

She didn't hold back on explaining the pain she saw me deal with, and so many nights, she said she would be awakened during the night, hearing me walking around in the house because I couldn't sleep. And she also mentioned hearing me making moaning sounds and speaking loudly, using some very unpleasant words during those times, walking around in the middle of the night because of pain. Sadly it was all true. Gretchen must have called her brother, John, in Boston and told him about her experience being on the stand at Dad's trial. He again offered to come and said he would be glad to be a witness. I responded by saying, "I know you would, son, and are willing to do so, but it is a long way—"

He interrupted and said, "If you think getting off work is a problem, don't worry, I have that arranged if needed."

I told him Atticus wasn't even going to use all of our medical experts that were willing to testify because of the strength of just three he wanted to use and thought that should be more than enough. So I thanked him again and just told him if things change, I would let him know. But I knew that as soon as we go through the few character witnesses we had settled on, this part would be over soon, and we would begin the important part of entering our evidence into the trial.

We continued with our character witnesses. My friend Jeff testified on my behalf, just after Gretchen, and he was a good one as he watched as time progressed along and saw just how my mobility was very much compromised. He actually testified he had to go to my house because I had fallen and couldn't get up. Luckily my cell phone was in my shirt pocket, and after about an hour of being on the floor in my kitchen, I called him and said, "Jeff, I really need your help, I have fallen, and I can't get up."

Yeah, just like in the hospital when I said those very same words. I wasn't trying to be a comedian in an attempt to be or say something funny, rather it was just the damn truth—I had fallen, and I couldn't find a damn way to get up. I had forgotten about that night when I called Jeff, but he remembered and told the story on the witness stand. It brought a few smiles to my face as I remembered it so well when he started telling the story of that particular night. It was entertaining, even to me, and I was the subject, but he told it well. Jeff had a way of telling a story, and he had many to tell.

Richard Lancaster, CEO of Sanders Industries, came at the request of Atticus since he was my last employer. Richard gave a full testimony of how he watched my health get worse as time passed. He explained to the court how valuable I was to Sanders Industries and that he and I had become friends, which explained why he allowed me to work at my own pace. He said, "I did see an end was in the near future, but I just couldn't let Roland go, so Roland made it easy for me when he retired on disability. I really hated to see him leave Sanders Industries, but I fully understood. It was the right thing for him to do because of the pain he endured and the limited mobility he suffered from on a daily basis." He closed by saying, "I don't know how he hung in there as long as he did, he is already being missed by all of us at Sanders Industries."

Dr. Mowji even came and testified about how he felt I needed the opiates that he wrote monthly prescriptions for me for years because it was the only thing that helped me with my pain, only after trying various other medications. Even though Dr. Mowji was there, I was certain he didn't feel comfortable being there on my behalf because he worked with Dr. Larson by referring patients to him and, of course, seeing him at the hospital quite often, but still he was there, just telling the truth on my behalf.

Opiates were the only pain therapy medications I took that didn't have the multiple side effects I endured with all of the others that were prescribed by various doctors, except for the fact they are very habit-forming. He went on to say how he had watched me decline physically and, at times, mentally. Dr. Mowji, I know, was generally concerned about my health, and he was the one that pushed me harder than any other doctor, I needed to retire on disability before I hurt myself or someone else.

He was very precise in what he said, and when he was cross-examined by Francis Covington, Dr. Larson's lead attorney, Mr. Covington asked of his neurological and surgical knowledge. And before he could utter a word, Mr. Covington asked him another series of questions—all medical related—but wouldn't allow him to answer before he interrupted and asked yet another series of questions. They sounded like the same questions, just worded differently. I figured it out rather quickly, he was discounting his testimony, and he went right back to the question of his neurological and surgical experience. This time he allowed an answer. Dr. Mowji simply responded to Mr. Covington by saying, "You know I am a general physician, and I have a family practice."

Mr. Covington jumped in and interrupted him again by saying, "That is all I have for this witness."

The judge excused him, and as he was walking toward us on his way out, he just looked at me and smiled, as if to say, *Good luck, I wish you well.* He left and went back to work doing what he does, taking care of his patients. I was appreciative of his testimony, but I also got a good look at the tactic the opposition was going to use. I immediately thought that was their only defense—to belittle the witnesses and confuse the jury with smoke and mirrors.

We had a couple more character witnesses, but Mr. Covington didn't drill them like he did Dr. Mowji. He instead, in his way, belittled them for being a character witness for Mr. Beckerman, referring to me of course. I was actually glad all of the character witnesses were over and done with because I was ready to get serious and start with entering our evidence and to start bringing in our experts to testify and to state what happened to me in the operating room while Dr. Larson was in charge based on cold hard facts. Just from the way Mr. Covington treated Dr. Mowji on the witness stand, I knew he would be doing something very similar to our witnesses, but I was confident they had been through this kind of thing before, and the very important things we had on our side going for us were facts and truth. The truth based on facts and the facts based on truth. That isn't confusing, is it? If so read it and think hard about it, and it will come to light quite easily. It is something I have figured out by listening and watching Atticus work on this case; after all, he is a seeker of truth.

At lunch, this time the conversation had shifted. Instead of small talk and laughter, it was much more serious, and all of the conversation was about the tactics Mr. Covington was obviously going to use against us and how we were going to turn it against him. Here we were, still playing chess. It seemed the more things changed, the more they stayed the same, meaning the heat just got turned up, and I could feel it getting warmer. Atticus and Ben were discussing how they were to handle Dr. Larson's first expert witness, while Atti listened and was taking notes. Atti was learning from two of the best in the business, and I think he knew it, and he was hanging on to every word and comment they made, as if he were still a student. I guess they, and we, all are students in what we do, I guess, that is why we refer to it as a law practice. But Atti was getting schooled in the area of his choice, and so was I, for that matter. I was taking it all in like a sponge and savoring the moments as they passed. I knew I was in good company, and I also knew we were opposed by a shrewd lawyer, but two can play that part of the chess board, and I was very confident in the level shrewdness Atticus possessed. I watched him work during the two arbitration meetings we had, and he sailed through them, spouting facts and sticking to the truth and not wavering away with anything relating to any sort of confusion. He stayed very close to his plan and kept the train on the tracks, so I felt confident, if a battle of who could be more shrewd, I put my money on Mr. Atticus Wentworth, not Mr. Francis Covington.

I pulled into my driveway at home, stopped to get my mail, and I turned to look, and right behind me was Jeff. I pulled into the carport, Jeff right behind me. I had a handful of mail, grabbed my cane, and we went inside. Of course I didn't have to ask, but I offered Jeff a cold beer; after all, it was after five o'clock in the afternoon. We took our seats in the living room, and Jeff started the conversation by telling me he had heard more conversation going around town about me suing the great Dr. Larson, and he kept telling me not to worry about it. In other words, he was simply giving me some support as it seemed the whole damn town was against me and really down on me for shaming Dr. Larson with a lawsuit. The facts were none of the damn people know me or know what I had been through at the hand of Dr. Larson because of a simple mistake that could have easily been avoided, had he paid a little more attention during the surgery, but the truth was he didn't. All the friends of his here in town were simply looking at this whole situation as if they had blinders on to keep them from seeing the truth of the matter.

I was very appreciative of Jeff being so supportive. I was the outsider here, and Jeff was born here and knew everybody. Being a close friend, Jeff knew the facts; therefore, he was my defender, and he defended me openly. While we were sitting there, I was casually going through my mail, and I came across an envelope with my name and address hand-written out. It was rather sloppy handwriting, terrible print. It looked like it was a child's attempt at writing out my name and address. It didn't have a return address. I opened it up, all while showing it to Jeff, and we both joked about what kid wrote this, etc. The note was short, and it simply read, *Drop the lawsuit or else*. I handed it to Jeff, he read it, and we just both looked at each other, as if we, for the first time, were at a loss for words. Jeff spoke first and insisted I call the chief of police as we both knew him personally.

I actually called Atticus on his cell phone. He was likely at his hotel room here in town by now. I read and described the note to him, and he said for me to make a few copies of it and take one to the police department, just for the record, and to bring a copy to court in the morning. He said he would enter it as a piece of evidence, and the defense would surely not be happy with this as it was a very negative thing, and the jury would not be impressed.

The next morning, I handed it to Atticus, and when court was announced it was in session, he asked if he could approach the bench. Of course Mr. Covington joined Atticus at the bench, and this copy was passed to the judge, and Atticus handed another copy to Mr. Covington. The judge announced there would be a fifteen-minute break, and he asked both Mr. Covington and Atticus to meet with him in his chambers. I don't know what was said behind those closed doors, but when the judge came back in, along with both attorneys, the judge announced to the court, for the benefit of the jury, that there seemed to have been some kind of threat made to Mr. Beckerman, and he held up his copy, didn't read it but held it up, and said, "If anyone here knows or has any information on this, please let the court know as this kind of harassment isn't acceptable by me or my court."

Atticus thanked me for the copies and whispered to me, "This isn't good for Dr. Larson."

And the courtroom was still and very quiet. To this day, I have no idea of who wrote that note. It could have been one of Dr. Larson's many cheerleaders acting on his behalf, not thinking how damaging it actually would be.

Court was back in session now, and Mr. Covington called up one of his expert witnesses to testify on Dr. Larson's behalf. I had read his deposition several months ago and wasn't impressed. He pretty much stuck to what seemed like a script written prior to the deposition because it was so close to what I had previously read. But the important points here were, there wasn't any substance in his testimony; it was him pointing to other causes of ongoing pain in various patients he has seen in his career, and they all have causes. He kept referring to diabetics that have neuropathy quite often, and he said, "Maybe Mr. Beckerman is a diabetic and that is what caused his nerve damage."

He went on and mentioned other causes of such problems while never addressing what happened to me or the cause. Finally after his very long testimony of scripted questions from Mr. Covington, along with scripted answers, he was through. Now Atticus took the stage, and he must have listened closely to his testimony because he asked about almost every statement the witness made and made him look like he didn't know what he was talking about, mainly because he didn't. Oh, he knew all right, but he knew he was there to protect his fraternity brother; it seemed that was all that mattered. Atticus doubled down on mentioning I was or insinuating I could be a diabetic and made it clear to the jury that I was, in fact, not a diabetic; therefore, that would have nothing to do with what caused my injury that occurred on the operating table under the watch of Dr. Larson.

It was quite impressive, the way Atticus went over the points the witness attempted to make as he downplayed every one of them tactfully. I don't think the witness had a very good day in court. When he was excused, he quickly left the courtroom. I didn't think his testimony was strong at all. As a matter of fact, I felt it to be quite weak and no help to Dr. Larson at all. *One down and a bunch more to go*, was my thought.

We had to fly our first expert witness in, and he was due to take the stand at two o'clock. Ben Rosen went to the airport to pick up Dr. Durst as his plane was to arrive just before noon, so that should give them plenty of time to arrive for him to testify at two o'clock, when court returned to session. Ben and Dr. Durst met us at lunch, and Dr. Durst and I had some conversation, I guess, since we hadn't met, only spoke on the phone. He wanted to get to know me better and get more of an understanding of me in general. We arrived back in court, and once it was announced court was now in session, Atticus was asked if he was ready to call his first witness. Dr. Durst was sworn in and took his seat on the witness stand.

Court began after lunch; however, just before it came back into session, Ben and Dr. Durst set up a display of the human anatomy to make it easier for the jury to see precisely where the injury occurred. Atticus asked Dr. Durst to demonstrate on the model of the human anatomy, specifically in relation to the abdominal area, where the injury occurred. Dr. Durst went through the area of concern with precision in his explanation as how the injury occurred and why something like this can and did happen. He was quite simplistic in his way of making it easily understood by the twelve jurors; however, one seemed to be asleep during most of the presentation.

One thing I noticed during his demonstration, and also the way Atticus phrased his questions, none of either were confusing. The questions were direct and referenced only the particular areas of concern, and the answers were very precise, and Dr. Durst did a magnificent job of answering each one thoroughly. The point here was not to be confusing;

why be confusing as that would not be in our best interest. He actually brought in a set of retractors he uses himself
that happened to be the same brand and design of the ones
used on me by Dr. Larson, and demonstrated how they work
using the plastic model of the abdominal area he and Ben
Rosen brought in the courtroom. Dr. Durst didn't use any
medical terminology without an explanation that anyone on
any scholastic level wouldn't understand.

I noticed a huge difference in the way testimony was
given by both sides now. The defendant side was out to confuse the jury as their defense, and the plaintiff side, which
was us, stuck only to the facts and held our stance of exactly
how and why it occurred by using strong science to prove our
points. The line of questioning seemed to go on and on from
Atticus, but he was really building what looked to me as an
ironclad case in proving what really did happen that day in
the operating room. It was now approaching five o'clock in
the afternoon, and Dr. Durst hadn't been cross-examined by
Mr. Covington yet. The judge spoke up and said, "Since it
is nearing five o'clock, I think this would be a good time to
adjourn for the day. Court will reconvene at nine o'clock in
the morning." And the gavel sounded.

Another day had ended, and Dr. Durst was very thorough in his testimony. Watching Atticus work through his
line of questioning and to witness Dr. Durst giving his testimony as an expert medical witness was a work of art. I was

quite impressed, but more importantly, I hoped it impressed the jury too.

When morning came, cross-examination came quickly from Mr. Covington, and he seemed to be on the attack, attempting to get Dr. Durst to stumble, and seemed to try to make him contradict himself, over and over asking the same question, only worded a little differently, and that seemed to be a pattern of his. After about an hour and a half of this, I thought to be nonsense, Mr. Covington seemed to change his line of questioning and started making comments about me and my health and said, "Since he is diabetic, don't you think this could have caused this neuropathy in Mr. Beckerman that had nothing to do with Dr. Larson, couldn't this have been the cause?"

Dr. Durst answered slowly, clearly, and with strong conviction, "Mr. Beckerman isn't a diabetic, therefore, everything you just stated isn't relevant to this case at all." He went on to say, "So I would like to make it clear to the court, Mr. Beckerman isn't a diabetic, therefore, that couldn't be the cause of his injury. I have clearly defined what happened and how."

Mr. Covington seemed to walk in a few circles, with his arms crossed and eyes wandering, spoke up and said, "No further questions."

The judge excused Dr. Durst, and shortly thereafter, Ben Rosen and he left, headed back to the airport for him to catch a late-afternoon flight back home. Dr. Larson's team brought in another medical expert, and he was sworn in and put on the witness stand. Mr. Covington started his line of questioning, and once again, it just seemed scripted as it was similar as to the previous line of questioning. It seemed to have the same approach—to try to control and confuse the jurors with medical terminology that much of it I had no idea of the meaning or most of the terms used thinking. I just wondered how much the jurors knew what the meaning of them were.

Atticus slid a note to me, and it read, *Confuse and control.* We were on the same wavelength, without doubt. His witness again said I was a diabetic. Immediately Atticus objected to that statement, and the judge sustained it, and the statement was ordered to be stricken from the record. The only problem was, it was once again planted into the minds of the jurors. It is hard to strike something from memory already heard, and that wasn't the last time it was said during testimony from Dr. Larson's expert witnesses. I am sure they were instructed to say it every time they had an opening during testimony in an effort to further confuse and plant that seed of doubt.

But Atticus would object every single time it was said, and the judge would say the same thing and have it removed from the record, but the damage was done. Before the day was over, one of the expert witnesses for the defendant seemed to turn his answers into a joking and even laughing matter. I didn't think the judge seemed to like it very much as he called him down several times during his testimony. Once the judge even said to him, "This isn't a show, it is a courtroom," and expected him to treat it with more respect. But I didn't think he slowed it down very much as he seemed to continue with the same actions, but perhaps he toned it down a little. But his being smug didn't seem to go over well with the judge, but I don't know about the twelve jurors, especially the one that kept going to sleep. To me he seemed to be a big spoiled kid that always gets his way, and he wanted to push his agenda onto the court in his own childish manner. I just hoped the jurors saw through his tactics as I did, but I was on the other side, and it was easy for me to see it. I was coming from the side of science, and the other side was approaching it from a totally different perspective—confusion and control; what else do they have, nothing.

Days were passing and there had been lots of testimony, and it was our chance again to put another one of our expert witnesses on the stand. Enter Dr. Hyatt, head of neurology, and Mr. Covington started his line of questioning. He started off by making it known to the jury he, Dr. Hyatt, wasn't a surgeon, that he was merely a neurologist. "What is neurology?" he said, and the look of bewilderment seemed to appear on every face of the jurors, except for the guy that slept all the time.

But in a courtroom, when something like that is said, it makes you want to stand up and confront such a belittling statement, like he is merely a neurologist. He is simply attempting to downplay Dr. Hyatt when Dr. Hyatt has a proven record and has achieved greatness and has earned respect as one of the leading neurologists in the country. He has written several books and has spoken all over the world. And for Mr. Covington to belittle him was just a damn disgrace and a personal insult.

It didn't seem to rattle Dr. Hyatt as he continued answering his line of questions but didn't waiver from his position of how this happened. He explained that pressure from not releasing the retractors traumatized the tissue to the degree of cutting off the flow of blood into and through the tissue and starved the femoral nerve. He asked the judge for permission to further explain by using the model of the anatomy that was brought in by Ben Rosen and Dr. Durst. He went further into his explanation of demonstrating how this happened and the tissue that was compromised during Mr. Beckerman's surgery performed by Dr. Larson. He put strong emphasis on the length of time the damaged tissue was held in one spot under extreme pressure, and said that was precisely why this injury occurred and there was no other explanation.

He further stated that Dr. Larson actually pinpointed the problem by ordering several scans on Mr. Beckerman while he was still in the hospital. Mr. Covington asked him what he meant by pinpointing. I was really glad to hear that question because I knew what was coming. Dr. Hyatt said, "By Dr. Larson having all the scans and tests done, it proved what the problem wasn't. On the contrary, it pointed to and proved it was none of the other possible causes, and it left only one conclusion, and that is pressure on the tissue that went unmonitored for hours during the surgery of Roland Beckerman. Dr. Larson caused this injury, there is no doubt about it."

The courtroom erupted, and the judge began pounding his gavel. This part seemed like I was watching a movie, only it wasn't a movie at all. It was real, and it was me in the middle of it. At that point, Mr. Covington said he was through with his questions for Dr. Hyatt. I was very pleased in the manner he handled the questions, and at times, they seemed a little hostile, but Dr. Hyatt held tight to his plan, and he came through it like a champion and a professional.

So now it was Atticus's turn to go to work with Dr. Hyatt, and they performed like a well-tuned piece of machinery with great precision. They didn't leave anything for doubt. Everything was covered from a neurological view. After all, neurology is the branch of medicine that focuses on the nervous system, and we were talking about damaged nerves here, weren't we? I should say yes, we were. I don't think Mr. Covington thought his belittling Dr. Hyatt would have backfired on him the way it did. It was really great to witness Dr. Hyatt explain everything so well, and thinking of the jury, I certainly hope they comprehended how he explained just how this injury occurred. Atticus would literally throw out a question, and Dr. Hyatt would take it and run using facts and speaking only the truth. When you have a team like this that are working toward the truth and happen to have the truth and facts behind them, it seems to flow nicely instead of all the belittling and curveballs thrown in an effort to confuse and control.

It just didn't seem to be working too well for Dr. Larson and his team so far. Instead of being in a conference room at a bank with an insurance representative and a judge presiding, this was the big-time with a judge, jury, and a courtroom full of cheerleaders and well-wishers on one side. And on mine, I had truth, facts, and perhaps three cheerleaders, but they were quite reverent and just there to let me know I did have a few friends in town that believed in me. I was very thankful they were there on my behalf, but my main focus was from where I sat with my counsel and the jury to my right and the judge straight ahead and the home team my opposition was on my left.

Several grueling days have passed since we entered the courtroom, and we had been through several testimonies of Dr. Larson's expert witnesses that were obviously members of the fraternity I have mentioned a few times. Mr. Covington continued his parade of his expert witnesses, all part of the plan to confuse and control the jury as a whole, and between Atticus and Ben, they both tore into their testimony with sharpness and facts by steering toward the truth in the case. Each time Ben Rosen examined a witness, I was more and more impressed with his courtroom professionalism, but

Atticus was the quarterback and was in total charge of the room, except for the judge of course; he is ultimately in charge, that was something I learned pretty quick.

We had what I consider to be our strongest expert witness yet to testify—Dr. Spencer, head of surgery at one of the most prestigious teaching universities in the United States. He happened to be the oldest witness we had, and along with his age came a lifetime of experience and gained knowledge he acquired along the way. He was the one that contacted Atticus after Atticus had told me to seek other counsel and told him he wanted to help Mr. Beckerman define how and why this injury occurred at the hands of Dr. Larson. Dr. Spencer was the reason we were able to get a case filed in the first place and obviously the reason we were all assembled here in the courtroom today. Not only did I have admiration for this old guy, but I appreciated his interest in discovering the truth. Perhaps he was a seeker of truth like Atticus Wentworth is, I don't know, but whatever it is, I am glad he stepped up in my time of need.

Chapter 20

Dr. Spencer was due in court the next day, and for learned reasons, I envisioned his testimony to be long and tedious, and I also knew that Mr. Covington, Dr. Larson's attorney, was going to go after him with everything he had. Dr. Spencer's deposition was likely the strongest of all, and Mr. Covington knew it, so he was going to be on the attack and look for any hole he can expand to discredit him during his testimony and to use every tactic at his disposal. He was also good at theatrics, raising his voice, throwing his hands in the air, speaking out before the witness can finish answering a question, and crossing his arms and pacing the floor.

Dr. Spencer and I had a meeting at his hotel room the night before he was to testify. The meeting was not long, maybe an hour. Atticus was, of course, present, and Dr. Spencer spoke to me with respect and mentioned several times how sorry he was about my injury, and he simply said, "It didn't have to happen. As a matter of fact, it shouldn't have happened, and that is why I am here on your behalf." He went on to say, "I don't think Dr. Larson is a bad person, or even a bad physician, but he made a terrible mistake that will continue to affect you for the rest of your life." He said, "I understand your family was broken apart, and you lost your job."

I stopped him and told him I didn't lose my job, but my general physician, Dr. Mowji, pushed me to retire on disability, and that was what I had done.

He said, "Oh, I remember now, you retired on disability, but did you retire on your own, or did you retire before you employer retired you?" Then he smiled and said, "Do you like retirement?" And he further said, "Maybe I should retire someday soon." And we all laughed.

It was a very pleasant meeting, so I felt it was time for me to excuse myself as Atticus and Dr. Spencer were about to go out to dinner. On my way home, I stopped by the grocery store, and while I was walking around the store slowly, my cane in my right hand while holding on to the shopping cart with my left, not holding the handle as you normally would, I was holding the side as it is just easier to navigate the cart using one hand from the side. I still use this method today, but I was just shopping, minding my own business. I would always see people I knew there as it seemed to be a good place to catch people and chat, but one thing I have noticed over the last few months seemed the people I knew are all, well, mostly, all much colder toward me now, and some just seemed to avoid me altogether, and I have adapted to it by just not paying them any attention. Just making it easier for them as I knew the reason why I was being treated this way, but that's all right; it is what it is.

Two older women I knew were stopped in the middle of an aisle, and as I walked by, I spoke to both of them, and I was verbally attacked by both of them. They told me I should have never taken "our" Dr. Larson to court for something he didn't do. "He is a fine and outstanding man in our church and community, and he shouldn't be put through having to defend himself in court."

I was thinking, *How in the hell am I going to handle this?* I just said quietly to them, "I am sorry you feel that way," and kept on going. I got what I needed and went home. Not just this, but several things had been said to me and about me behind my back, and coupling that with lots of rumors that were simply not true, I was beginning to think I was just not welcome here. I moved my family here when John and Gretchen were small. Becky and I wanted to live and allow our children to grow up in a smaller area, unlike the large city we came from, but looking back, I was thinking maybe that was the wrong thing to do. But I must say, it was a great place for my kids to have grown up in.

Now of course they were both gone. John was in Boston, and Gretchen was in college, and I was doubting they would return, so now I was wondering what my future would be like living here, facing all of the undue static and ridicule I was facing already and thinking after the trial was over, then I really would be a target. And all of this coming from people that have smiled at me for years and seemed to want to be friendly toward me and my family, only to be turned on like I was guilty of personally harming a beloved local doctor. I was just getting sick of this treatment. I was wondering—

Dr. Spencer's testimony was sharp, but Mr. Covington's line of questions literally cut like a knife, but the responses from Dr. Spencer were masterful in every aspect. Covington made every attempt to get him to stumble but wasn't successful at all. I was thinking Dr. Spencer would be our strongest witness, and I wasn't wrong; he indeed controlled the flow with facts, and he stated them in a fashion that even Mr. Covington couldn't refute any of the many facts he laid out for the jury to hear. Once again, it was like watching a movie, only I was in it. Dr. Spencer, without any doubt, placed the burden on Dr. Larson, that it was time for him to admit fault and take responsibility and accountability for what he had done to Mr. Roland Beckerman.

Mr. Covington was once again pacing back and forth, with his arms crossed, and he finally said he was through questioning Dr. Spencer and sat down. Of course Atticus got up to go through some of his questions, but ironically, Dr. Spencer had handled Mr. Covington and his line of questioning and his trying hard to steer it into confusion by barking out medical terms that had no bearing on the case and was constantly being corrected by Dr. Spencer when he used a medical term incorrectly. It was making Atticus's questions much easier. Atticus and Dr. Spencer worked together like a fine watch; they seemed together in every way. Mr. Covington actually laid the groundwork and didn't realize it that he was spinning his wheels by Dr. Spencer pulling on and bringing forth all of his years of knowledge, combined with his expertise, to prove Dr. Larson didn't give Roland Beckerman the standard of care expected from all doctors. It seemed the standard of care is what holds it all together when something is up for grabs.

To put it in simple terms, one either provides a certain level of standard of care, or they don't. That is what it all comes down to, and Dr. Spencer, along with my entire team of highly specialized medical professionals, had proven that I was injured by Dr. Larson by not giving me the standard of care every patient is entitled and expected to receive. So after another long line of questioning from Atticus directed toward Dr. Spencer, we were finally through. Mr. Covington just continued to sit and write notes on his legal pad, but he seemed to have lost his spark after the long and grueling line of questioning, but the testimony of Dr. Spencer was sharp as a knife. Dr. Spencer had shown no sign of fatigue or any sign of weariness from that exchange, but I can't say the same about Mr. Covington as he looked beat.

It was time for Dr. Larson to take the stand. Atticus took the first line of questioning. And just like during the deposition, he literally said nothing of any substance, except at every opportunity, he would say it was impossible for him to have made a mistake or something very close. I think

Atticus sensed that with the strength of the testimony by Dr. Spencer on my behalf, he didn't want to cloud the water or thoughts in the minds of the jury by pushing hard on Dr. Larson, knowing he wasn't going to slip and fall into anything that would point a finger at himself. However, before Atticus ended his line of questioning, he turned back to Dr. Larson and said, "Do you agree you could be wrong, and you could have made a mistake?"

Dr. Larson responded loudly, "No, I could not be wrong, I couldn't have made a mistake."

To me that spoke volumes to the jury. So Atticus just backed off after a short line of questions, and I think that was the best strategy to use on him. Mr. Covington used his time and formed his line of questioning to literally agree with Dr. Larson of it being impossible for him to have made any mistake, and he went on to tell how many surgeries he had performed, and he turned toward the jury when he said, "He has probably helped you or a relative of many in this courtroom."

And it just went on and on from there, about how wonderful he was and how caring and helpful he has been and will continue to be in the community. I had heard enough of that crap by then, but I had to sit quietly. We have had our light shine brightly during our team's testimonies, and I was happy about that, and I must say again, the defense didn't have a fact-based defense, unlike our fact-based scientific offense. They just didn't match up at all; as we were ahead, I was thinking nine to one on the ten-point system.

It was now time for me to take the stand, and I was ready—so ready—to say what I wanted to say on my day in court. Atticus had prepared me for this day, and it had been a long couple of weeks, having to sit in the courtroom and listen to Dr. Larson's team try to belittle and discredit everything our experts said and did everything they could to confuse and rattle the jurors in an effort to control them and their thoughts, but the ultimate bullet that we fired was Dr. Spencer. He was the reason we were able to file the lawsuit in the beginning of which turned into a very long journey. And now thinking back, way back, what my divorce lawyer, James Bogart of Wainwright & Bogart, said to me when I posed the question about what was involved in filing a medical malpractice lawsuit. I immediately got the impression he didn't want to even discuss it because he knew it was a local situation that he wanted no part of, but I remember he told me it would be next to impossible and harder than that to just get it filed and to win, that was when he stopped.

This moment in time resurfaced in my memory; however, after almost six years now and all of the depositions of our expert witnesses and all the hours upon hours of preparation by Atticus and the firm of Wentworth & Wentworth, my thinking was still, *We are up nine to one.* In my mind, I was giving them one point for just showing up, certainly not because of any validity or merit they had shown in the presentation of their case, in defense of attempting to prove Dr. Larson did nothing wrong and didn't cause my injury.

I was asked to take the stand, and I was sworn in. When sitting in the witness box, it is the second-highest spot in the room, except for the judge, and he was seated just a bit higher to my right. It gave me a strange sense of security, being that high above everyone else, except the honorable presiding judge. It felt good just being there, and I was ready for anything Mr. Covington would throw at me because I was confident I was intelligent enough to handle anything he would say and have not just an answer but the right answer to continue to build the strength of our case. He started with a cordial introduction of himself, as if I didn't know, and asked me some very basic questions about me personally—how long I have lived there, asked the ages of my children, and asked how my health was prior to the surgery. He proceeded to announce to the court that without Dr. Larson, I would be dead and that he saved my life. "OBJECTION!" Atticus yelled a little louder than Mr. Covington was speaking when he said the last sentence.

The judge said, "Strike that statement from the record because it is hearsay and not factual."

He then said, "I will reword my statement." Then he said, "Because of your illness, Dr. Larson had to move quickly, is that fair to say?"

I responded by saying, "Yes, that is fair. But prior to the surgery, Dr. Stanton, my gastroenterologist, contacted

Dr. Calabria, who is head of gastroenterology at one of the finest teaching universities, to perform the surgery, and he was making plans to have me airlifted to his facility, but he couldn't work me into his schedule for about two or three days, so that was when Dr. Larson was called in and started talking to me about performing the needed surgery. I don't know if you could say he saved my life, I just don't know about that." He asked me if I appreciated what Dr. Larson did for me. I paused and said, "No, why should I appreciate it? The end result changed my life drastically."

Then the questioning changed course a bit, and he was asking questions about how I felt about bringing a lawsuit against one of the community's finest citizens. Then he asked me how long ago I was diagnosed with diabetes. "OBJECTION!" shouted Atticus.

And I said, "I don't know how many times we have to say I am not a diabetic, and I never have been." The judge again told the recorder to strike that last question. However, the fact was he threw it out there to continue to cloud the minds of the jury, and the jurors heard, it except for the guy that appeared to be asleep again. Referring back to what he asked me about how I felt about bringing a lawsuit against such a fine upstanding citizen and upstanding member of the community, I finally just spoke up and said, "He is no finer than anyone else, including me."

And there was a small bit of noise that came from my three-person cheering section, my support group. I guess they found a little humor in what I said. This kind of questioning seemed to go on and on, and it did literally go on for over almost two hours. Mr. Covington was just pacing back and forth in front of me, as if he was trying to find another question and/or one that would catch me off of my guard and to rattle or confuse me, and after about a full two minutes, I spoke up and said, "Are you going to ask me any more questions or just pace back and forth?"

Once again, my little cheering section made a joyful noise, not too much but still a little noise, and the judge instructed me not to make an outburst like that but to just answer the questions asked of me. I said, "Your Honor, I apologize to you, but he isn't asking me anything."

The judge asked Mr. Covington if he had any more questions, and he answered, "No, Your Honor." And he sat down.

Atticus stood up and proceeded to ask a few very pertinent questions that required very direct and definitive answers. My testimony with him didn't last very long because we had taken this to the edge with precision and professionalism, and it looked like we were approaching the finish line. The next item on the court agenda seemed to be closing arguments. It had been a very tough period of time, a little over two weeks so far, and had been hard for me to endure, all while literally fighting off a couple of threats, and it seemed the entire town was against me, except for my three that were in and out of court during the trial, and it was always good to see them out there, sitting behind me, and my close friend Jeff Greene was one of the three mentioned. A word was never spoken, only physical gestures and a hand up, as if to say, *Hey, buddy, I am here and pulling for you.* Other than that, I had no support, but I didn't feel I needed anything more because I had truth, facts, science supplied by a team of very well-known doctors that have come to my aid to assist me in securing justice.

I was convinced this was all I needed to prove Dr. Larson didn't afford me and/or provide the standard of care that seems to be the written code of ethics in the medical field. I was so appreciative of Atticus and his entire law firm and for all of the expert witnesses that came to my time of need, and unlike Dr. Larson's team that literally paraded six of his "fraternity" brothers to come in and praise him and say how great he is and just how impossible it is for him to have made a mistake that caused my injury and, the whole time, looking at the jury while on the stand. It was their only plan of defense because they had no other plan based on medical facts or any other kind of facts.

So I was feeling pretty good, and I think Atticus was feeling good about what we had been able to do too. It was Friday and the weekend was upon us. Atticus, Ben, and Atti packed up, checked out, of their hotel rooms, and went home to Richmond. But before we said our farewells for the week-end, I invited Atticus, Ben, and Atti to come to my house on Sunday night when they arrived back in town, after they get checked into their hotel, for burgers on the grill, beer, wine, scotch, bourbon, vodka, or whatever they might like, I would be sure to have it. I made it quite clear, this wasn't in any way a celebration of any kind, but I just wanted to show some appreciation to them and offer them a night of just relaxation and enjoyment. "There isn't anything to celebrate yet, but I really would like to have you all at my house."

They all looked at each other, and Atticus spoke up and said, "What time would you like for us to be at your house?"

And I said, "That depends on when you guys get back in town."

He said, "Then how about six o'clock?" Perfect was my answer, and just before we parted, Atticus turned to me and said, "We'll be in touch." They left and I had the whole weekend to think about the entire trial and what transpired and how I thought it all would turn out.

Saturday morning came, and I had a phone call from Charles Mitchell, wanting to know how things were going, and I spoke confidently and told him Monday, we were going to have closing arguments, and the end was finally near. He asked me how long had this been going on now, and I told him we were in the sixth year now, but I did remind him of a three-month delay because of the untimely and sudden death of Atticus Wentworth's brother. Charles said, "Damn, but still six years, that is a long time, Roland, for you to have had to go through this kind of thing. I know it has been hard on you in many ways, my friend."

I didn't disagree as I fully agreed with him and just said, "Yes, it has been pretty damn tough."

We talked on and spoke of both of our children, as we always do. We both have a son and a daughter, in that order, and have so much in common, yet we are as different as night and day. He tells me all the time how weird I am, and my comeback to that is, "You're the weirdest person I know."

That's what close friends do, I guess, is speak their minds to each other without any consequences. I think that is the main rule of being close friends, to be honest with each other and not shy away from saying what we feel. Seemed as soon as I got off the phone from Charles in Florida, my old close friend and ex-employer, Conrad Winchester, called me to check on how things were progressing along. It was a very similar conversation as I had with Charles, and we had a nice chat, and I informed him the trial was winding down, and closing statements were starting on Monday morning. He asked how I was getting around and had my walking improved any, and I simply said, "Yeah, man, I am doing fine."

Conrad wished me all the best and said he was coming to see me soon, and we said goodbye. No surprise, but Jeff called me and said, "Hey, man, it is Saturday. Let's meet for lunch."

I responded by saying, "Are you sure you want to be seen with me out in town?"

He said, "Damn, man, I have been in and out of that damn courtroom off and on for over two weeks now, sitting on your side, so what makes you think I wouldn't want to be seen with you?"

We both laughed, and we picked a place and met for lunch. During lunch, I couldn't help but to thank Jeff for his support, and I told him that Charles and Conrad had both called me just a little while ago, and I said to Jeff, "It sure does feel good, sort of like my troops are rallying around me, not high in numbers, but the level of quality is paramount. It means so much to me to have the three of you so close, and you guys seem to really care about me."

I don't know why I said this, maybe because it was true, but I told him I was tired. Tired of feeling bad, being in pain constantly, and said, "I feel as if I have failed my two children, my marriage went to hell. On top of everything else, I am not able to work and make a living."

I just confided in him and just spilled it all, but the truth was I had spilled it all to Charles about a week ago. I guess that is why he calls me as much as he does, just to check on me to be sure I haven't done anything, like stepping over the line. I had thought about it more than a few times but just haven't because of two people—John and Gretchen. They are really what have kept me from stepping over the line, I mentioned.

While Jeff and I were having lunch, I told him not to tell me anymore about what the latest gossip going around town about me was because I didn't want to hear it. He smiled and said, "You sure?" As if he had something to share with me.

And my answer was, "I'm sure. I just don't want to hear any more of the crap."

He laughed, and actually we both laughed and continued eating our lunch together as usual. Now sitting at home, alone as usual, on Saturday night, in anticipation of what Monday morning would bring, I remembered I had to go the grocery store to prepare for burgers on the grill for Atticus, Ben, and Atti, and that seemed to give me the mental break I needed. Then I looked at what my bar was stocked with, and I was short of my offerings, so I went to the local liquor store and picked up the needed items I had offered because the liquor stores are closed on Sunday, so it was now or I would only have part of my offering available. That just couldn't happen, so I took care of it.

Sunday afternoon came, and I went to the local grocery store to pick up the needed items on the menu for the six o'clock arrival of my legal team to my house for burgers on the grill, and the trimmings of course. I ran into my friend Jeff. He was picking up some items for his aging mother, and I told him I was having some distinguished guests for burgers on the grill later on and invited him to come. He asked who were my guests. I answered, "My lawyers, Atticus Wentworth, Ben Rosen, and Atti Wentworth."

Jeff responded by saying, "Hanging out with a bunch of lawyers, that is pretty rich, man, maybe I will pass on this. I know you guys have a lot to talk about."

I told him, "Actually we don't, the case has been presented, and I am just trying to show some appreciation, respect, and some hospitality."

I asked him again. He thanked me and just said, "No, you just take care of business."

I told him again, "You're welcome to come." And he thanked me again and returned to his shopping mission, and I returned to mine.

They all arrived right on time, and I had already prepared the burgers for the grill, and I picked up some prepared salads and had some cheese and crackers, and the bar was now open. We all fixed our own drinks, and we all just sat, talked, and snacked on cheese and crackers. It was really pretty cool, having these guys here at my house. It almost felt festive for some reason or another, but we were not celebrating anything, nothing at all, not yet anyway.

I put four nice-sized burgers on the grill, and we all just seemed to enjoy being together in this setting and had a very nice dinner of burgers, salads, beer, and drinks of choice, and I had all I had offered. There was very little alcohol consumed, as expected, but we seemed to have a little taste of what was offered, and that was my plan. After our dinner was over, it was time for them to head back to their hotel to rest and prepare for our morning of final arguments.

They left, and there I was, alone again with my thoughts and wishes. My thoughts were plenty, and my wishes were full; however, the main wish was I just wanted Dr. Larson to be brought down to everyone else's level. His arrogance from the very beginning and his way of giving you the impression he is on a higher level than anyone around him just didn't sit well with me because I knew the truth, and it had been proven over and over in the courtroom, and all he and his team had done was belittle our experts, which really didn't work, and push an agenda that truly didn't exist.

I guess you could say it was a long night for me, but getting two late-night phone calls seemed to have had a calming effect on me and appeared to put me at ease with what was about to occur in the morning. Those two calls were from the most important and respected people I know, my son and daughter, John and Gretchen. They both wished me luck and told me they were thinking of me, and as always, we expressed our love for one another, and I made sure they understood my love for them was unconditional.

Chapter 21

Atticus, Ben, Atti, and myself all met at eight thirty that morning at the courthouse just to get our final thoughts together to be ready at nine o'clock to proceed with the beginning of the ending of a long trial that had lasted now, well, over two weeks and pushing hard into the third week. At the end of each day, I would go over in my mind and rate and grade our performance, and I was still holding onto the nine-to-one score. This score was not a biased score at all, if one could believe it, rather it was derived from pure facts that were introduced by our team of medical experts.

Dr. Larson's medical experts not once stated facts, they were only opinions, and most of the opinions they stated were either not relevant or were stated in an effort to confuse the jury while using mixed and irrelevant medical terms. They even confused me at times, so therefore, I knew exactly what their game plan was; there was no other except to use opinions and just try to confuse every one of the twelve jurors and plead on them to have mercy on a local doctor that has treated so many in the community, as if the community owed him immunity.

We were ready, and I was confident Atticus was not going to disappoint me or any of our team members. All along I knew two things, important facts for sure, we all had and have shared all throughout our entire journey—truth and facts. At the end of the day, what else is there in legal matters, and this case was not any different than any others because that is what going to court is for. Seeking truth and justice was why it was established in the beginning, and since I knew we had both of those in our pockets from the start, I felt pretty positive about our outcome. Except for the one juror that pretty much slept through the trial; he should be well rested by now.

I did hope they were able to filter through all of the uncertainty and opinionated statements based on a lot of things that were simply not relevant to my injury. I only hoped and trusted they listened intently to all of the facts that pointed to the same source of my injury, which was pressure that traumatized the blood flow while using surgical tools and, in this case, retractors that were held in place for hours, without monitoring or moving every ten or fifteen minutes to relieve pressure to allow blood flow to feed all of the tissue holding nerves. It is even spelled out in the manual that comes with these particular surgical tools, that they must be monitored, and the pressure is to be released every ten or fifteen minutes to avoid possible nerve damage.

All other reasons were literally ruled out during several scans and various tests Dr. Larson ordered while searching for the reason while I was in the hospital under his care. As mentioned, he didn't realize it, but in doing so, he ruled out all other possibilities which led our team to identifying the source. Dr. Spencer was the first to spot exactly what had happened by simple deduction, and then it became very clear to him and all the others on our team. The answers to problems sometimes just need to be looked at with open and fresh eyes, as the answer is most often quite simple. This was not a complicated case once all the facts were studied, but it took people that knew where to begin to look, and soon after, the answer came quite clear.

It was time for Mr. Covington to begin his closing arguments, and he began by, once again, mentioning various reasons this happened, all pointing to illnesses I never had, and yes, he included diabetes that I have never had and still don't. It was all I could do to sit there and keep quiet when he brought that up again, which was just not true. But he went on and went back through again of how many local people Dr. Larson had helped and how involved he was in the community. He really built him up to be on the highest pedestal there was in town. I knew this was his job, but he went on to say how our team tried to paint a picture of an incompetent surgeon that blundered a surgery, that was just not true. I think Dr. Spencer made comments about him being a good physician, but good doctors can make a mistake, "And he made the mistake of not taking care of Mr. Beckerman and not giving him the standard of care that is expected from all of us in the medical field."

He even pointed to me during his speech and mentioned how healthy-looking I was, all the while I was sitting there and was just awarded 100 percent disability by the federal government without having to go through the legal system to sue to get it. He really did a great job of painting a wonderful picture of how great Dr. Larson was in so many ways, and honestly, I don't really know how much of it to be true, but again, he was doing his job within the system. As he talked on, my mind kept flashing back to the moment I knew something was wrong while I was lying in that hospital bed, but Dr. Larson just kept telling me there wasn't anything wrong, I was just experiencing some numbness, and it would go away in a day or two. That day or two never came.

Looking back, it was now about six years ago, and all of the times I tried to talk to him about how painful my leg was after I was released from the hospital, and he wouldn't even discuss it, and then the door was literally slammed on me, seeing him and so much more. All of this and more just kept racing through my mind during his speech. By now I had heard enough. I don't know how many times he could repeat himself during his time in front of the jury; at least each time, he would change it up a little bit, but it was the same thing over and over while pacing back and forth in front of the twelve jurors. Not once did he offer up any facts or fact-based statements on how the injury occurred. He closed by saying, "We don't know how the injury of Mr. Beckerman happened, but what we do know is Dr. Larson didn't have anything to do with it." He thanked the jury and the court and closed his statements and sat down.

Atticus got up and walked slowly toward the jury and stood there silently for a few moments and started out by thanking them for their service and their attention and reminded them it had been a long drawn-out case with a lot of medical terms being tossed around like a ball from both sides. "But we have only tossed medical terms to you that were pertinent to this case involving my client, Mr. Roland Beckerman, seated right there." And he pointed at me. "We all know why we are here. Mr. Beckerman was injured, not intentionally but still he was injured by an error in judgment by the defendant, Dr. Larson, and we have, without any doubt or room for error, identified how, why, and who caused Mr. Beckerman to suffer from lumbar plexopathy as diagnosed by both of this neurologists. And after the diagnosis, all of us at Wentworth & Wentworth started to work on an avenue of travel to find a way to assist Mr. Beckerman in seeking justice. Studying all of the medical reports and reading the results of the many scans and tests Dr. Larson ordered to be given to Mr. Beckerman truly assisted and gave reasons for Dr. Spencer to contact me and told me he knew what had happened and wanted to help me assist Mr. Beckerman in seeking justice in this case."

Atticus took a few breaths and paused, as if to get his thoughts assembled for another run, then he continued by saying, "Soon after Dr. Spencer joined the team, Dr. Hyatt, the neurologist who had treated Mr. Beckerman, joined in after learning of Dr. Spencer's involvement. The next thing I knew, I was getting calls from other doctors, and a few were well known, and Dr. Durst, head of surgery, came onboard, and then Dr. Rabbinowitz, a very well-known surgeon, expressed his interest in helping to seek justice in the case for Mr. Beckerman. If you notice, we didn't bring Dr. Rabbinowitz in to testify because the three we brought in were enough to prove, without any doubt, they had pinpointed how and why this happened, and they clearly stated Dr. Larson was, unfortunately, at fault, and we just didn't feel the need to have a parade of doctors to come in and waste the time of the court nor your time, so we only used three expert witnesses of several at our disposal."

Atticus paused again and continued, "Mr. Beckerman has suffered in many ways. He is no longer employed and was awarded 100 percent disability that went through the system immediately without any question or delays. His livelihood and financial status has been compromised because of this, and on a personal level, his family has been dismantled, and he will have this injury for the rest of his life, however long or short it may be. So, ladies and gentlemen of the jury, I ask you to put yourself in his shoes, just for a few minutes, and try to imagine waking up from a four-day induced coma after major surgery, only to discover your very large incisions were not the focal point of expected pain when the epidural was removed and the anesthesiologist woke him up. Instead imagine your right leg feeling like it is literally burning as if it were on fire. Even with a morphine drip being administered, the pain wasn't being managed, and after continuing to complain about it and begging for someone to make it stop, but really nothing was being done about it. That, ladies and gentlemen of the jury, is what Mr. Beckerman went through, but it goes on, and he has to take pain medications. He takes prescription opiates just to manage the pain enough to get some rest at night.

"Ladies and gentlemen, just imagine that and put yourself in the position and try to consider the difficulties, along with spending time in a wheelchair, then learning how to use a walker with a locking brace on his right leg to get around, all while going to work, getting on and off jets and in and out of a car, in and out of the offices of his clients, trying to maintain his job. And now, as you have seen, he has to use a cane, and underneath his clothes, on his right leg is a custom-made brace with locking hinges to keep him upright while he walks.

"Ladies and gentlemen this isn't about Dr. Larson being a bad doctor or even a bad person, but it is about right and wrong, and in this case, he was negligent and made a mistake. The cost of the mistake is Mr. Roland Beckerman, sitting right there in front of you, and we are asking you to please hold Dr. Larson accountable for not offering Mr. Beckerman the normal, usual, and expected standard of care that is expected to be given to every patient in every medical situation. I thank you, and our entire team thanks you for your cooperation, and most importantly, we thank you for your consideration to do the right thing today and hold Dr. Larson accountable and responsible for his actions that has cost Mr. Roland Beckerman more than you can imagine. Mr. Beckerman has paid and will continue to pay a very high price, and he will live with his losses every day for the rest of his life. Thank you."

And then he walked back and took his seat beside me and wrote on his legal pad three words and pushed it over so I could see it, and it said, *We will prevail.* We looked each other in the eye and just smiled. For all practical purposes and regarding the legalities involved, the proceedings of the court were over, and I couldn't have felt better about everything we accomplished here. The judge started speaking, making some of his closing statements to officially let the court know now the jury must go deliberate, and he then turned to the jury, and he spoke directly to them and said, "Remember to continue not to discuss this case with anyone outside of the confines of the twelve of you."

And he adjourned court for the day. It was almost five o'clock in the afternoon. He instructed all of us to come back to court the next day at nine o'clock in the morning, in anticipation of a ruling from the jury. We all left the courthouse and talked a bit out in the parking lot about our strengths versus their weaknesses, and I, for the first time, shared my scoring of nine to one out of a ten-point system. They all got a chuckle out of that, and Ben Rosen spoke up and said, "Well, I will give an eight to two."

And I said, "Why?"

And before Ben could answer, Atti spoke up and said, "Ben gave them one point for all of the confusion and for all the irrelevant stuff they threw at the jury in an effort to scramble their thoughts."

Atticus said, "Damn, son, that is pretty good. You were listening, weren't you?"

We all laughed, and Atticus said, "Well, gentlemen, we have done our part, and we did it well. Let's all get some rest, and let's meet back up out in the hall for a few minutes, say, about eight forty-five in the morning, and hopefully the jury will not take too long to come out with the decision we expect and find out what the amount of the reward will be. And hopefully we will all be able to have a celebration, and it will all be over for you, Roland, and you can get on with your life."

Just before we all parted, Atticus looked at me, smiled, and said, "We will prevail." And I envisioned the three words he wrote down before we left the courtroom just a few minutes before we smiled at each other and parted ways.

I went home and had only been there a few minutes, and Jeff stopped by. By me living alone, it was easy for him to just pop in at about any time because after all, it was just me there—oh, and my little dog. He came in, went to the refrigerator, and helped himself to a beer and offered me one out of my own refrigerator—that's what close friends do, you know—and we sat down. We chatted for a couple of minutes, and right in the middle of a sentence, he stopped and asked me, "What does jury tampering mean?"

I said, "What?"

He repeated the question. I gave him my definition of what I thought it meant, and I was pretty sure I was correct, and I asked why ask such a question. He began to tell me he had lunch with a guy we both knew there in town, and he said he had heard that one of the jurors had mentioned he had had conversation with someone close in on the case and had spoken to him about Dr. Larson being not held responsible for the guy that sued him and how much he meant to the community and just stuff like that. I stood up and said, "Come with me."

Jeff said, "Where we going, Roland?"

I said, "We're going to see Atticus Wentworth at his hotel room, and you are going to tell him what you just told me."

Jeff said, "Wait a minute, I don't even know if this is true."

My response was, "Where there is smoke, there is usually at least a spark."

Jeff was a bit reluctant to do this, but away we went. I knocked on Atticus's hotel room door, and I was sure he peeped through the peephole, as if maybe he was thinking it would be either Ben or his son, Atti. He opened the door, and I said, "Hello, Atticus. I want to introduce you to my close friend, Jeff Greene. You may remember seeing him sitting in court on our side."

Atticus said, "Yes, of course I do."

"May we come in? There is something I need to tell—" I stopped and said, "Well, Jeff has something he would like to share with you."

We walked in, and I began to tell him that Jeff stopped by and what he had to say might be of importance, and it sounded to me like there may be some jury tampering going on. Atticus said, "Hold that thought."

He called Ben and Atti and told them to come to his room, I was there with a friend, and we had something we needed to tell them. So just a minute passed, and both were there. The door closed, and I asked Jeff to tell them what he heard earlier today during lunch. After Jeff repeated what he told me just minutes before, Atticus spoke up and said, "I will get to the courthouse a little earlier in the morning before the jury goes in for deliberation in the jury room and request a meeting with the judge and inform him of this." Atticus also said, "It could be true, it could be a rumor, but we must treat it as fact and act on it with the judge." And he added, "I was afraid this might arise because our opposition really don't have a case to defend Dr. Larson, and if it is true, I am not surprised."

I asked Atticus if this had ever happened to him before, just before the close of a case. He sort of laughed and said, "You wouldn't believe some of the crazy stuff that happens, but, Roland, don't worry about it. I will handle it with the judge in the morning."

Atticus asked Jeff the name of the person that told him this. Jeff looked at me, and I nodded, and Jeff told him the name, and he asked Jeff if need be, would he verify what he had said if it became necessary. Jeff said, "To whom?"

And Atticus said, "Well, to the judge in the case."

Jeff and I looked at each other, and Jeff said, "Yes, sir, I sure will."

So we left knowing we had done the right thing, and Jeff knew he had done the right thing first by telling me and secondly by sharing it with Atticus, and if necessary, he agreed he would tell the judge.

The next morning came, and I was anxious to see Atticus and find out what the judge might have to say about this. I was standing in the hall at eight forty-five with Ben and Atti. Just a couple of minutes passed, and here came Atticus, and he didn't say good morning or anything. He went right into what the judge was going to do. He told us the judge took it very seriously, and as soon as the jury gets assembled in the jury room—which would be just a few minutes from now— he was going to meet with them and question each of them, one by one, privately, and see if he senses any merit in what was said. My thoughts on the matter were, *Well, I guess that is all we can do.* I am confident the judge has experienced this before and perhaps has a way of getting to the bottom of it quickly. Atticus said, "We did what we were supposed to do. Let's allow the judge to do his job."

We all went into the courtroom. Dr. Larson's counsel all were assembled in their normal position, and we were gathered in our respective area, and the courtroom began to fill. It seemed I had a few more fans on my side of the courtroom that morning. But I was wondering what the judge was doing, and after about an hour and fifty minutes, a courtroom staff person came out and announced the jury had a slight delay in beginning deliberation; however, it had begun, and the judge would address us in a few minutes. After a few short minutes, the judge came out. We all rose, and he announced again there was a slight delay in the jury getting started, but deliberation had begun, and then he called for Mr. Covington and Mr. Atticus Wentworth to meet with him in his chambers.

I immediately knew what this was about, but I so wanted to be in the room to hear it all myself in real time. But of course, that wasn't to be. Ben or Atti weren't asked to go to his chambers, so I didn't have a chance of getting in. After a good half-hour, they both came back into the courtroom, and we huddled up, and Atticus began to tell us the judge had questioned each juror privately, and none of them admitted or seemed to know anything about what he had been told, nor did he think anyone was contacted, but he can't be certain, and he has allowed all to proceed as normal, as if it never happened.

Atticus did say Dr. Larson's attorney seemed very upset when the judge told him what he had heard, and he demanded to know where the information came from, who said it, and said, "How dare anyone to try to disgrace the case this way."

I just think that was a continuation of the manner they had handled the case from the beginning, nothing new here. So not long after that, lunch came and went, and we were right back in court, spending the entire day, sitting around, waiting on the jury to come back in. Then at four o'clock, the judge announced that it didn't appear the jury was going to have a verdict by five o'clock, so he adjourned for the day and instructed us to be back in the morning. I asked Atticus how long does it usually take for a verdict to be reached.

Atticus said, "Most of the time, the jury is quick to decide, unless there are holdouts, but it appears in this case, it is taking longer. Therefore, the judge must have shook them up regarding the one-on-one questioning, so I think they are just taking a little more time than usual because of that."

I didn't really sense any real concern that he may have had, so I just did what everyone else was doing, and that was wait. What else could any of us do? Dr. Larson didn't seem to be bothered with any of this as he sat in his seat, reading a book that appeared to be a paperback novel that he should be about through with because I noticed him picking it up, reading it off and on during the entire length of the trial. So we all left the courtroom, only to have to return again the next morning.

It was a night of not much rest, mainly because of my pain and not wanting to take enough opiates to rest because I wanted my mind completely clear as this was going to be a big moment in my life, perhaps the largest moment, of hearing a verdict, the amount of the reward, and still I had no thoughts of anything, except the jury would hold him responsible and accountable for his missteps in the operating room that had cost me so much of my life, along with other things too. It was a very long night.

Morning came and off to the courthouse to meet Atticus, Ben, and Atti. We walked into the courtroom together and took our positions, and the opposing team did the same, and the courtroom began to fill up once again. But it was a one-sided fill; the home team had the numbers, but I knew, without any doubt, we had what was important, and that was truth, and the facts to back it up.

After about an hour and twenty minutes, the jury walked in quietly. The entire room was stone-cold quiet, my heart was beating much faster than usual. Even now, while writing this, my heart is racing, damn I am too old for that now. My breathing seemed quick and short and felt extremely nervous; however, all of this was probably normal, I thought.

The judge asked the jury if they had reached a verdict. The foreman stood up and said, "Yes, we have, Your Honor."

He then handed a slip of paper to a court staff member, and he handed it to the judge, and the foreman said, "We do not hold the defendant responsible."

At that moment, I couldn't exactly say how I felt, but for starters, I felt first I heard it wrong, then I felt no, that isn't what I heard. Then I thought, *Wait, this can't be what I heard.* Then it hit me very hard. I just sat, and while I was sitting, the opposition's side of the courtroom all acted like someone had just won the lottery, a very big one. There were screams of joy and congratulations being yelled out across the room, and there I was, just sitting there, trying to think and just trying to get a grip on what, why, how, and just why again, over and over.

I looked at Atticus as he was packing up his briefcase, and Ben was doing the same, and Atti was just standing beside his father quietly, while all of the cheering for Dr. Larson was continuing on, as it seemed it wasn't going to stop. I just continued to sit, and finally, the room started to empty, and the noise calmed down. I was in another world during these moments, but I recall the judge coming over to us, and he said to Atticus, "I am as surprised as you."

And they had a few other things to say; after all, they were two professionals talking, and their job had been completed. Atticus didn't have much to say to me, but he did express sincere appreciation for allowing him to represent me. I didn't think I had much to say either. I was stunned, and I didn't feel anything, as if I had found myself suspended in between two places, and the place I was in was not a good place at all. As a matter of fact, it was the darkest of all the dark places I have visited for over five years now.

Ben sat down beside me and just told me how wrong this was, and he was as surprised as any of us. At that point, all I wanted to do was just get out of the courthouse and just go home. I got up and thanked Atticus and told him I was going home. We just looked at each other, and maybe he sensed now wasn't the time to discuss any of this, and it really wasn't. It all seemed my thoughts and my vision were blurred at this point. At this time, there wasn't anything anyone could do for me. I just needed to go home and let the darkness engulf me, exactly the way it had before; only this time, it was going to be at the bottom of the darkest pit.

Atticus checked out of the hotel and headed home to Richmond, along with Ben and Atti. And when I arrived home, I went straight to my room, closed the door, took off my clothes, and covered up in my bed. What was I doing? It was in the middle of the day, and I was in bed, but that was all I could or knew to do. As I continued to lay there, my mind was in overdrive, and then something hit me pretty hard—humiliation. I don't think I have ever experienced humiliation and certainly not on a level like this.

Later on in the afternoon, I thought perhaps I should notify John and Gretchen before they call me, as I knew they would expect to hear some good news, but that wasn't to be. I called John first and just told him I lost the case, and I really didn't want to talk about it, "So let's talk again soon."

I then called Gretchen, and I gave her the same speech. They both seemed to understand and sensed I was in a bad place and didn't press the issue of talking more. I did get a call the next day, midmorning, from Atticus, and he just said, "I am calling to be sure you are doing all right."

I told him I was in hiding in my bedroom, and I was having a difficult time, and I mentioned the damn strong feeling of humiliation. He then said, "Let's let it rest for a few days, and we'll be in touch."

The call was ended. That night, Charles Mitchell called me, and about all I could say to him, as much as I wanted to talk to him, I just couldn't, so I just told him I fucking lost, and I just don't know what I am going to do about it or anything right now. I told him I would call him back when I dug out of my hole. Since he knew me as well as he did, I think he understood and let me move with it on my terms. Not long after the call from Charles, my doorbell rang. I didn't even consider answering it, then it rang again and again. My cell phone now was ringing. I was still in bed. I answered; it was Jeff Greene, he told me it was him ringing my doorbell. He said, "Word is out in town that Dr. Larson won the lawsuit, and I just wanted to do a buddy check."

I told him I just couldn't see him, but I would call him soon. Then around ten thirty the next morning, after the worst night of my life, Conrad Winchester called. I answered. He said in a very upbeat fashion, "Hey, man, how are you?"

And my answer was quite solemn. I said, "Conrad, I will be brief. I lost my fucking case, and I will have to talk to you later."

He asked if there was anything he could do for me. My answer was, "No, I just need to be alone."

A few days later, I started to come back to life more than the previous days, and Atticus called me, and we talked for several minutes and said we could file an appeal. And of course I asked all about that, he filled me in on the details. All of a sudden, I felt life creeping back into me. "Do you really think—"

He stopped me and said, "Yes, I think we would have a very good shot at an appeal, and the main thing is, we would get to pick a different jury." He continued, saying, "Perhaps someone did get to one or two of our jurors, that is something we will never know, but with your permission, I will look into it."

I immediately said, without any other thought, "Of course you have my permission, please do look into it."

He ended the call as usual by saying, "We'll be in touch." I felt the adrenaline pumping, and I felt so alive. I reached for the phone and called Charles Mitchell. He answered, and I filled him in on the what all had happened because I just didn't feel like talking about it when he called a few days before, and brought him up to date, and then told him

I had just gotten a call from Atticus Wentworth, my attorney, and he was going to look at an appeal. Charles shared in my excitement and told me to keep him in the loop on what happens. And of course, I had to let John and Gretchen know about what Atticus said, so I called them both. They both commented I sounded much better, and they were both concerned about me. I called Conrad Winchester, and then called Jeff Greene; they both were appreciative that I had called them and was keeping them in the loop.

Jeff asked me if I thought what he had shared with me, about hearing about jury tampering, had any truth to it. I answered him by saying that was something none of us would ever know, but I was beginning to think it was highly possible.

Atticus and I talked a few times over the next couple of days, and things appeared to be moving along. Feeling pretty good and just trying put all the pieces together, and Atticus called. I answered, he told me he wanted to read a letter to me, but before he read it, he told me he was sending me a copy for my files. He began to read the letter first, telling me if was from Dr. Larson's attorney, Mr. Covington, and the letter stated, "I understand you are looking into filing an appeal in the case of *Beckerman v. Larson*, and if you do file an appeal, we are going to file a personal lawsuit against Mr. Beckerman for damages to Dr. Larson that would likely be in excess of $500,000."

Just when I thought there was more light at the end of the seemingly never-ending tunnel, here I was, facing another freight train, and this one was headed straight for me at full speed. I was shocked and completely perplexed. I couldn't talk. Atticus asked, "Are you there, Roland?"

I said yes but still couldn't talk. Atticus finally said, "Just call me back in, say, half an hour or so because we must answer this letter."

I told him I would and that was the end of that call, and for some reason, I felt it was just the end of everything all over again. The darkest of dark had come over me when the jury came out and said they would not be holding Dr. Larson responsible for my injury. I just thought that was my darkest moments—not at all. I had now gone even deeper into the darkest abyss, and there wasn't any light showing at all. I called Atticus back in about an hour from when we last talked, and I told him, "I can't take any more of this. Suppose we lose, and if we file the appeal, I will get slapped with a personal lawsuit. What should we do, Atticus?" I said, interjecting again, "I can't take any more of this."

Atticus told me to sleep on it, and I thought, *Sleep, what in the hell is that?* But I agreed, and he said, "We can decide what to do tomorrow. We'll be in touch." And our conversation was over.

I then called Charles and brought him up to date as I just wanted to talk to someone as my mind was so full of doubt and negative thoughts about the case, myself, and just, in general, everything around me. It seemed John and Gretchen continued to be the only meaningful, wholesome, clean, and clear thing I could grasp and hold close for my personal well-being. Charles told me to let it go because, "Just because Mr. Wentworth can file an appeal doesn't mean it is guaranteed that you'll win, plus you're going to be sued, and it sounds like the stakes are pretty high."

Not because he said what he said, but I was right there with him on it, and I thought, *When Atticus and I talk, I am going to tell him not to proceed with the appeal, as long as they agree not to file a lawsuit against me personally.* I guess this would be an exchange of agreements between the two parties. After I gave it my full attention and tossed it back and forth a few times, coming to the same conclusion after talking it over with my closest friend in the world, Charles Mitchell, I called Atticus and told him what I had decided.

He paused and calmly said, "Do you want me to contact them to let them know in exchange for us not filing an appeal in the case, they agree to not proceed with a lawsuit against you?"

I paused, took a breath or two, and said, "Yes, that is exactly what I want." So a couple of days later, I received the copy of the document clearing both sides, as if nothing had happened.

Chapter 22

My journey had come to an abrupt halt after a time span of pushing into six years of constantly pursuing justice. I went through several lawyers in the early stages of this time frame that all expressed and showed promise of being able to win a medical malpractice lawsuit, only to end up at a dead end at my expense. I kept throwing money into what I thought was to be an investment, and I would get it back, perhaps maybe a profit. However, as time passed, the thought of money seemed to start to dwindle, not the monetary value so much as just the sheer thought of winning a lawsuit to secure justice and to hold Dr. Larson accountable for the mistake he clearly made would have been enough for me.

As the days passed, I tried very hard to get on with my life, but so many people in the community made it quite difficult for me to move on because it seemed the talk around town was still about how I did a terrible thing by forcing Dr. Larson to have to go to court and prove he did nothing wrong. It was a bit of a strain for me to even go to my local grocery store without getting "the look" from many that, before this happened, would always talk and exchange pleasantries with me, but not anymore. I was being avoided, and it was easy and quite clear to see.

Jeff Greene continued to defend me, and our friendship never lessened; it actually strengthened. Perhaps he felt some compassion for me, I don't know, but we became a little closer, if that were to be possible. My visits with Dr. Mowji continued, and even he expressed his surprise during our next appointment and opened up to me by saying, "I just knew Dr. Larson would be held accountable and responsible, Roland, for what happened to you. It will affect you the rest of your life, and I am just sorry things didn't go your way." Then he said, "Not just your way but the right way."

It was nice to hear that from my general physician of whom I had become friends with over the years he treated me. I wrote each of my expert witnesses a letter of thanks and for support for me during the depositions and, ultimately, the trial. It wasn't a form letter of one size fits all, not at all. Each were personalized, and I targeted their contribution toward this effort. I felt I must thank them, and I did from the bottom of my heart. I personally thanked each one of my character witnesses for getting on the witness stand and telling the court what a great guy I am. They all did a great job of describing me before the injury and, of course more importantly, after the injury.

My daughter, Gretchen, a young college student found herself perched right up there on the witness stand, telling the truth while watching her father first roll around in a wheelchair, then to move up to a walker with a leg brace, and then to graduate to a cane, still wearing the brace while trying to manage severe pain. I actually learned how to manage being an ostomy patient as a result of my illness, and if that were truly the only result of the first surgery, my life wouldn't have had these severe disruptions that pushed me into becoming disabled. Rather it was the nerve damage and experiencing high levels of chronic pain, along with the loss of mobility and/or limited mobility, that has been the issue that has changed my life in an adverse way. Being an ostomy patient has proven to be something very manageable, in comparison—well, there isn't any comparison to what I have to live with on a daily basis for the rest of my life because of Dr. Larson's negligence.

I don't know where to begin to express my gratitude for all Mr. Atticus Wentworth, of the law firm Wentworth & Wentworth, did for me. He took a hard look at my case for a while early on and, in a professional manner, told me to seek other counsel because of time restraints, only to ask me much later if he could take the case again because he had a strong reason to do so, and that reason was Dr. Spencer, head of surgery at one of the most prestigious teaching universities in the United States. Dr. Spencer was the one that opened the door when he discovered what had happened during my surgery. And he did it by deduction, as was pointed out during his deposition and when he brilliantly answered questions posed by Mr. Covington on the witness stand in the courtroom. And Dr. Hyatt and Dr. Durst both were equally as brilliant in their descriptions on the witness stand, concurring with Dr. Spencer, and of course, the deposition of Dr. Rabbinowitz was so precise, even though we didn't bring him to court as Atticus knew he had all the bases covered.

Our team did their jobs and did it with a level of professionalism, precision, and with medical knowledge that I have never witnessed in any given situation, and very likely never will again. I couldn't have been more pleased and proud. So again, I just don't know how to thank Atticus Wentworth that would be worthy enough of my true feelings. Atticus paid a very high price in this loss, but I have paid the ultimate price in more ways than one. But somehow I am sure he gets it. I sure as hell hope so.

I have concluded from my experiences that I for one do think a medical malpractice suit should be decided by a jury of peers. What is a peer? By definition, it is someone at your own level. I contend, in a medical malpractice lawsuit, there are things that your average cab driver, schoolteacher, electrical engineer, or even a television news anchorman would have a difficult time to grasp the meaning of what lumbar plexopathy would mean, much less how one derives at that diagnosis.

My thought process on this is in my case, yes, the jury were completely confused and, therefore, controlled so much they couldn't make a plausible decision to hold Dr. Larson responsible and accountable for what he did to me by holding my tissue for too long with too much pressure that blocked the blood flow to some very vital areas and, in my case, my femoral nerve.

Did jury tampering actually occur? That is a very big question that will never be answered, and I have to at least consider, perhaps it did. His actions choked the life of blood flow and starved the femoral nerve of life-giving blood. But how many cab drivers, schoolteachers, electrical engineers, or news anchormen or women are schooled on this subject? I would say none. This case wasn't about whether someone ran a stop sign and hit an elderly woman or man and put them in the hospital. This case was much more involved. It was about a surgeon who didn't give me the standard of care that was expected. Aside from the man that slept through the trial while sitting on the jury, I can just imagine the thoughts going through their heads, as if it were, *What in the hell is he talking about? What is the femoral nerve, and where is it? What does it do.* Well, I can tell you exactly where it is, what it is, and what purpose it has. Mine does not work properly nor has it since the day of surgery, and it never will. I just don't believe a jury trial should be held in medical malpractice lawsuits, unless the jury is filled with doctors. Or perhaps have some type of assembly of peers to make these decisions because the average person walking the street just isn't knowledgeable enough to decide the fate of a victim of medical malpractice.

This isn't the fault of the jurors necessarily; this is the fault of the system itself. I hold the system responsible, in large part, for the decision brought down upon me, and I say me because I was the victim. I would love to see the system changed, not that it would help me, but perhaps it might help someone else like me that was wronged by the court system.

Going through this and experiencing all that occurred, something a bit strange happened, and I don't think it would have filtered out the way it did, but Atticus Wentworth and I developed a good friendship, a strong bond that only an unexpected loss could bring. There wasn't any strain between us after the loss. Actually it seemed to bring us closer together. Perhaps thinking back, if things would have turned out differently, I don't think this same type of bond would be present. I do think we would have continued on as friends, but I think more so we would have settled up after the case, if we were to have won, and pretty much gone on our merry ways. But it didn't happen like that at all; however, due to the loss that has baffled many regarding the outcome, this loss is what proved to be the glue that has held us together and has preserved a friendship that has flourished to this day.

If you will go back in this timeline when Dr. Calabria ordered a scan of my abdomen prior to the proctectomy, after he gave me an exam, and he expressed concerns about the way the incision healed up from the complete colectomy Dr. Larson performed and told me it could become a problem. When I asked what he meant by "it could become a problem," he said, "First let's get the proctectomy completed, and then maybe we will talk about it."

So a couple of years after my proctectomy, I began having terrible pain in my abdomen, and I noticed a few spots that were raised up right along the scar from the incision from my sternum all the way down to my pubic bone, as described earlier. I contacted Dr. Calabria's office and requested an appointment. Since being a previous patient and a card-carrying member of that hospital, I was able to get right in. When Dr. Calabria walked into the examination room, he greeted me in a way that convinced me he remembered me quite well. He proceeded to tell me he went back over my records before I arrived, and I didn't even have to tell him why I was there. He asked me to remove my shirt and lie on the table, and he began feeling up and down the area of the very long scar the incision had left from the complete colectomy and said, "I knew you'd be back, it was just a matter of time."

He said the area had several spots where hernias have developed. I asked what would cause them. I went on to ask, was it something I had done? Was it from lifting or what?

He said, "Roland, if you recall, I told you I had concerns about this just before we did the proctectomy." And he continued by telling me when I was put back together by the surgeon that performed the colectomy, and it being such a large incision, my tissue didn't heal properly, leaving spots for hernias to develop. They are called incisional hernias. I asked again, "Is it anything I did?"

And he said, very quietly and spoke directly to me, looking me in the eye, and said, "The surgeon should have done a better job of putting you back together, and if he had, it is very likely this wouldn't have happened." Then he smiled and said, "It is a mess, but don't worry, I can fix you right up." He said, "It would be another extensive major surgery, and you should plan on a staying with us in the hospital for six to eight days."

It was late November, and he said, "Since it is so close to the holidays, would you like to wait until after the first of the year?"

I answered quickly because I wanted to get it over with, and after all, my children were grown, and me recovering during the holidays wouldn't bother me a bit as I didn't have a wife, so the family thing just wasn't the same. So I told him to please schedule it as soon as possible. Dr. Calabria went ahead that day and sent me downstairs to radiology for some abdominal scans and put me on his schedule to open me back up and repair the troubled spots and use a lot of mesh to repair the hernias. After the scans were read, he told me the incision on my left side, which was much smaller than the main one, had some problems that showed up on the scan, so he was going to fix that area too.

So here I go again, thinking this was just adding insult to injury—my own. But maybe after this one, maybe I would be done with having to have surgery. It was again a hard one to recover from, and this time, I was in the hospital for eight days. Dr. Calabria told me to prepare for a six-to-eight-day hospital stay. After a having a hard time trying to recover from this surgery to make the repairs for several days, it was now Christmas Eve. Dr. Calabria came into my room and told me as long as all of my numbers looked good, along with my urine flow, he would make arrangements for me to be released the next day, which was Christmas Day. So I called Gretchen and shared the good news with her and asked if she could come pick me up and take me home.

She said, "Of course, Dad, I will be there."

I didn't see nor did I expect to see Dr. Calabria that day, but he, in fact, made my arrangements, and I was discharged. Being discharged on Christmas Day proved something to me when I was rolled down the halls and taken down to the first-floor lobby. There were not any people hustling and bustling around; it was rather deserted, a very strange and a quite different look indeed. I have never seen it so empty. What it proved to me was only the ones that absolutely can't be released from the hospital have to stay there on Christmas Day. Even the staff was minimal. It was a bit lonely, and especially lonely for the patients that I left behind.

As Gretchen and I pulled away from my home away from home—the hospital—a thought entered my mind. I have spent a little more than eight weeks of my life in hospitals because of what happened during my fist surgery, performed by Dr. Larson. According to all expectations, a complete colectomy should only require a seven or maybe eight-day hospital stay. But because of all that either went wrong or didn't get done properly during the first one, it led to two more major surgeries to finish up what should have been carried out by Dr. Larson the first time. None of that, under normal circumstances or expectations, should have occurred, but sadly for me, it did.

Two weeks later, I was back in Dr. Calabria's clinic for a follow-up. Everything looked good, and he was pleased with how things were healing up. But he did tell me not to lift anything heavier than a knife or fork. I asked, "How about a twelve-ounce beer?"

He laughed and said, "Absolutely you can lift that, no problem." Just as he was leaving, he turned and said, "Roland, you sure are getting around a whole lot better now, and I am happy for you."

That was the last time I saw Dr. Calabria, but I keep up with him to be sure he is still there, just in case.

If we would have won, I had plans of making some donations to some of my favorite charities like St. Jude's Hospital and the local art's council, just to name a couple. St. Jude's has a special place in my heart, as children are so innocent and deserving of a good life that extends at least to becoming an adult. After all, they are our future. On the other hand, if we were to have filed the appeal, that would have immediately placed me in life number 2. After the injury of not only reliving it again through another trial, but also adding the thought, there aren't any guarantees we would win. Plus there I was, slapped with a half-a-million-dollar personal lawsuit. I would be fighting all this during a separate agenda because we filed the appeal.

What I ended up having to do, not by choice, but I had to leave my job and my financial stability and retire on disability. I was literally forced into this arrangement, even though Richard Lancaster of Sanders Industries had worked with me during this period of time. But in truth, how long can a full-time employee that isn't able to do the job sustain his position? I knew what I had to do, and Dr. Mowji knew it was something I must do to improve my quality of life, before it came to a total crash.

It completely changed my psychological and physical profile. That pushed me into the many dark places I visited, along with my physical mobility that is drastically different, requiring my full attention every single step I take, and the continued levels of pain just never going away. The effect it had on my family—still just the three of us, John, Gretchen, and myself, along with their significant others now, no grandchildren yet—but the effect it has had on them and me, it has embedded a feeling I have failed them, and I can't help it, but that sits squarely on my shoulders, and it is heavy.

My financial status has been greatly compromised, and not being able to do things I wanted to do and had planned to do just couldn't happen because of all of this. These are just a few, very few, of the consequences that were forced upon me. And the sad part is, I did not do anything to cause this, and even worse, just knowing it could have easily been avoided by Dr. Larson if he would have just given me the standard of care that was expected of him.

The negative impacts it had on my life is something I am forced to live with, are staggering and ever present, but the financial impact is why I can't fulfill my personal promises and expectations to my family, and that one digs bone-deep in me. It had such a strong impact on just my living there in the town this all occurred in just became a bit much. I was shunned, seemingly by almost everyone, except just a few and, of course, my close friend Jeff Greene. I became known as the guy that tried to ruin Dr. Larson's life, which is very far from the truth. I simply wanted him held responsible for injuring me and causing a series of serious changes in my life. It ultimately led me to packing up and leaving town, never to look back.

I actually visited two of the jurors well after the end of the trial because the verdict continued to eat away at me at an alarming rate. The first juror wasn't very welcoming or warm to the idea of talking to me, but he finally agreed to meet me at a local park. After the greeting was over, I thanked him for meeting with me, and I told him why I wanted to talk to him. I just came out and asked why it ended as it did, thinking and considering the strong experts we had that fully explained what happened. I went on to say they were very clear in their conclusion, based on fact, truth, and science, and Dr. Larson's team never recited a fact related to any of what I just mentioned.

He told me how sorry he was, but he just couldn't go against Dr. Larson. I sharply asked why. He responded by saying he couldn't because he was an experienced doctor that is well known, and that was the end of our very short meeting. But before we parted, he then again told me how sorry he was about the verdict.

The other person that agreed to talk to me was a lady, and she seemed very open to speak with me, and I was invited to her house. I knocked, and her husband answered the door, and I introduced myself, and he invited me in. I sat and he was in the room with his wife, who was one of the jurors, the entire time we talked. I began and asked her what happened in the jury room during deliberation that didn't come back with a verdict in my favor. She was very open about her answer. She said, "There were two jurors that absolutely wouldn't go along with the other ten." Although she didn't say who the two holdouts were, I knew who one was, so I continued to listen, and she said, "Ten of us were voting to hold Dr. Larson responsible." But as she said, "The two holdouts were adamant and nothing anyone could do, it didn't appear to change any of their thoughts, and nothing could convince them otherwise."

I then asked what their reasons were. She quickly offered up the following. She said both of the holdouts had close relatives that Dr. Larson had performed surgery on, and they were not going to go against him for those reasons alone, and she added, "They said one of them was a member of the same church. And he was such a supporter in many ways in the community, and she just couldn't cause him to lose his reputation and maybe ruin his career as a surgeon."

It was very hard to hear all of this because first, it wouldn't have ruined his career, and secondly, I was the one suffering from his mental mistakes. So there I was, right back where I was feeling like everyone was against me, and I hadn't done a damn thing to cause this—nothing. After she told me this, she said to me how sorry she was it ended up the way it did, but she said, "I wasn't one of the holdouts. I just want you to know that it wasn't me." Then she said, "I probably shouldn't say this, but I do think there was someone that spoke to a couple of the jurors and had something to do with them being holdouts. I could be wrong, but I am pretty sure that happened."

I thanked her for her time and told her how much I appreciated her opening up and telling me what actually happened that day. I got up, locked my brace in place, and began to walk to the front door, and her husband opened the door, and she stepped around and gave me a hug and said, "I am sorry."

I thought the meeting went well and was very thankful for her honesty and openness, and just before I walked out, something occurred to me. I asked her if she would sign an affidavit about what she told me. Her husband spoke before she had an opportunity to answer and said, "She will not sign anything."

I looked at her, she looked at her husband, then turned to me and said, "I'm sorry, I can't do that, I am just sorry." It strengthened my feeling that a medical malpractice lawsuit should not be judged by a jury of peers, unless those peers are medical professionals that will look at it based on science and not based on emotion. Emotion is what kept my case from landing in the win column, as was expected, and to me that was just wrong in every way.

Since living there in that little town the same as Dr. Larson just wasn't what it used to be before all of that happened, and people still looked at me as if I were some kind of terrible person, and when passing certain people on the street, I continued to get "the look." And particularly, when I would pass Dr. Larson on the street, I would get a stare with angry eyes. I decided maybe I should just sell my house and leave the area. My two children were both out of college and were out on their own, well, sort of, and I only had one close friend, Jeff Greene, in town, so I thought, yeah, maybe I should just leave and go start off new somewhere else and just leave it all in my rearview mirror.

Incidentally my good friend and cornfield conversation conversationalist, Dr. Robbin Jenson, passed on from a sudden illness. He was truly a great and a wonderfully sincere human being, aside from being a compassionate doctor, that will certainly be missed by many, including me. I called a real estate company, signed some papers, they posted a sign, and listed my house in all of the publications, and before I knew it, I had a buyer. The house was sold, and I made an arrangement with a mover to come pack it all up and load it and take me far away.

I continue to live in a new area, and I haven't been back there, but I still talk to my close friend Jeff Greene that continues to live there. As I mentioned before, he was born and raised there. I have no reason to go back because I do not want to dig up any of the dark memories there, and that is all that seems to be there now. Hey, I am still wondering if I will ever get that "apology" from Dr. Larson. I think not.

About the Author

Roland has lived a life full of various experiences that has awarded him with a lot of knowledge and wisdom. There have been both ups and downs along the way, all of which were learning experiences that have put Roland where he is today. Most of his adult working years were in sales, marketing, and business development; all of them proved to be successful. At times, perhaps his methods were a little unorthodox by definition, but Roland was known as the one who got things done. Going through a period fighting a medical condition also placed him in yet another category that taught him a lot of patience that has stuck and was added to his winning approach and attitude. Life goes on, and the road goes on forever.